TWISTED HONOR

Deep Six Security, Book Two
Slade's Story

Becky McGraw

Acknowledgements

First, I'd like to thank the brave men and women who defend and protect our country at great risk to themselves. A wound is not limited to those that can be seen by the naked eye. The ones that are the deepest sometimes are those that you can't see. The research I did on EMDR (Eye Movement Desensitization and Reprocessing) therapy for this book was fascinating. It is not a new therapy, but has shown such swift and amazing results that it was endorsed and approved by the military two years ago to treat warriors returning home with PTSD.

If you suffer from PTSD or panic attacks, or other unseen wounds or know someone who does, you can check out this amazing therapy here: http://www.emdria.org/?2

Heroes are not just of the human species. Military War Dogs are just as much warriors and veterans as their handlers. Some MWD are trained to do forward observation for military units, others, like Lola in Twisted Honor, are trained in explosives detection and some are specially trained to comfort soldiers while they are deployed and missing home. Some are even trained to be multi-purpose dogs to be used by spec ops teams for a variety of tasks, even parajumping!

When these heroic animals come home, they are often in need of loving forever homes and are adopted out, either by the Department of Defense or several MWD adoption agencies. If you have the facilities and ability to adopt a returning MWD veteran there are several organizations you can contact for more information:

Department of Defense:
http://www.37trw.af.mil/shared/media/document/AFD-120611-035.pdf

Pets for Patriots: http://blog.petsforpatriots.org/about-military-working-dog-adoptions/

Vets Adopt Pets:
http://vetsadoptpets.org/militaryworkingdogadoptions.html

An interesting tidbit about the dog model representing Lola on the cover of TWISTED HONOR:

The dog on the cover is Kelep, a male German Shepherd who was loaned to us for the photo shoot. Kelep's grandmother is an actual canine hero. She participated with first responders as a search and rescue partner after the 9/11 terrorist attacks. More can be found on her and other 9/11 canine heroes in the book *Dog Heroes of September 11th*, which can be found here: http://amzn.to/1LZCEop

Thank you to Eric David Battershell of Eric Battershell Photography/FITography for capturing the perfect image of handsome fitness model Zeke Samples and Kelep for the cover of Twisted Honor. Thank you also to Kelep's owners for allowing him to participate in the shoot. He's a beautiful animal, and my cover is amazing with him on it.

This is a work of fiction. Names, characters, places and incidents are products of the author's imagination or are used fictitiously and are not to be construed as real. Any resemblance to actual events, locales, organizations, or persons, living or dead, is entirely coincidental.

TWISTED HONOR, Copyright © September, 2015 by Becky McGraw.

ISBN-10: 1517262461

ISBN-13: 978-1517262464

Becky McGraw Books

P. O. Box 631

Milton, FL 32570

Ordering Information:
Quantity sales. Special discounts are available on quantity purchases by corporations, associations, and others. For details, contact the publisher at the address above.

Printed in the United States of America

CHAPTER ONE

A red-wrapped box with a big white bow sitting in the center of his desk stopped Slade in his tracks as he flipped on the light in his office at Deep Six Security. Immediately his hackles rose, but he glanced at Lola, who had already taken her position on the pillow behind his desk and relaxed. If there were explosives in the box she'd be up and barking. Lola's training would never go away, even with the additional training she'd received to help him in a different way when they first got home. He didn't like being paranoid, hated it in fact, but had accepted that was part of his makeup since he was medically retired from the Marine Corps.

Walking behind the desk, he sat down and pulled the box to him. Maybe Logan had left him a private gift to thank him for being the best man at his wedding this past weekend. He deserved a fricking medal. One he could pin to the chest of his old uniform above all the others, even the purple heart. Lola deserved one too, since Slade had to put her in a damned kennel most of the weekend.

Playing peacekeeper between all his guys and the politicians, military brass, FBI suits and CIA spooks who showed up to the reception had been absolute hell. Slade would almost have preferred being back in the sandbox with Lola clearing buildings. Pressure built in his head and his muscles tensed. Lola whined and got up to nudge him in the thigh with her nose. Slade blew out a breath then scratched between her ears until the pressure eased.

"Good girl," he praised, and she licked his hand. "I'm fine now—it wasn't anything. You worry too damned much." Lola barked as if she understood. She eyeballed him for a second longer, then seemed satisfied because she walked back over to her pillow to plop down.

Oddly enough, she was the only one who understood him. Since he got home five years ago, Slade just felt like he didn't fit in with most people anymore unless he made them fit. But at least he'd finally found his inner peace again. Between dealing with his head injury and then subsequent heart injury dealt to him by Jeannie, it hadn't been easily found.

He knew now that Lola was the only woman he needed in his life permanently. Lieutenant Lola had been through hell with him in the corps, and she understood him. She'd even dealt with her own injuries too. Somehow they both made it home alive, and he was thankful to still have her. He knew he could always count on her to have his six.

Since he'd come home five years ago, Slade had fought hard to find Zen in his life. The way he'd achieved it was by being in charge of only himself and Lola. He liked it that way, and hoped doing his best friend a favor here didn't upset that Zen. Why Logan thought he was the only one capable of running the company while he was gone, Slade didn't know. If he were Logan, he'd be the last one he chose for that job.

What upset Slade about the whole deal the most is that Logan hadn't mentioned it to him until the last minute at the reception last night. There was a reason for that. Logan knew if Slade had time to think about it or find other options he wouldn't be in this hot seat. Especially since he left him without a single instruction on what the hell was going on at the moment.

This morning he'd tried to call Logan and Susan about ten times each to get a SITREP, but neither of them answered their phone.

With a huffed breath, he fingered the ribbon all the way around the box then leaned down to shake it and listen. Something heavy shifted from side to side in the box. Sliding a nail under the tape holding the ribbon in place, he lifted it then removed the lid on the box. Clouds of white tissue paper covered whatever was inside and he rifled through it until he saw two cell phones at the bottom of the box. One cellphone had an unmistakable sharp-toothed-fish print case on it. *The Barracuda.* That would be Susan's cell phone. The other had a hard tactical case on it and that had to be Logan's.

That answered why they weren't picking up their phones. And it pissed Slade off that they were going off the grid for their honeymoon, and dumping all of this in his lap without a SITREP of any kind. Every problem and decision was his now, without any kind of guidance.

Well, David Logan was going to get what he deserved for doing this to him. If he was in charge, some changes would be made while Logan was away. Changes that he'd been after Dave to make for six months, like hiring more people.

His first hire would be Logan's sister Cecelia, before she signed a new contract with the Army. At the reception, he'd overheard her ask Logan to hire her before she renewed her contract, and his resounding, "Hell no—nothing has changed."

Afterwards Slade struck up a conversation with the pretty blonde to try and find out what was going on between her and her brother. Well, that's what he used for an opening to talk to her. If she hadn't talked for two hours about it, he may have had an opening for his real purpose—asking her out.

He found out from *Captain* Cecelia Logan that she was a com specialist responsible for outfitting spec ops guys at a *very* forward base in Afghanistan during her last deployment, which made him pucker for Dave. Maybe her brother didn't want to know and that's why he didn't talk to her about it. If he heard where her post had been, Logan would have known like Slade that it meant even though she didn't have direct combat experience there, she'd had plenty of combat *exposure,* because the forward bases were always under attack.

If Slade were Logan, he'd have hired her just to keep her from going back. But Logan had just cut her off, and Slade couldn't figure out why.

She had a degree in marketing that could help him get new contracts, relieve some of that stress from him. Her Army background meant she could help Dexter with outfitting them with com for operations. She'd had military training including weapons training.

She would be a good fit for them.

The only reason he could think he wouldn't hire her is that she was family. Maybe he thought there would be family drama in the office. From talking to her, he didn't think that would be the case at all. Or maybe it was because she was a female. But since Susan kicked his ass about not having more women at the company, Slade didn't think that was it either.

Well Slade was in charge now, and he was going to give her the chance to prove herself that Logan denied her. If it didn't work out, Logan could fire her and she could always rejoin the Army, but he didn't think Susan would let that happen.

"Morning," Mac Mackenzie said walking into Slade's office. "Damn, I'm still recovering from that reception, how about you?" He sat down in the chair across from Slade's desk and his gaze locked on the box. "What's in the box?"

"Logan's death warrant," Slade grumbled, picking up the cell phones to put them back inside the box.

"Oh shit…what's in the envelope?" he asked.

Slade's eyes fell to the envelope on his desk,

which he'd forgotten about. "I have no idea. I'm almost afraid to look. It was in the box with Logan and Susan's cell phones."

"That's really odd. Those two *never* go anywhere without their phones. If something happened here that he didn't know about, Logan would have a coronary."

"I don't know what the hell is going on with him." Slade shrugged as he flipped the envelope over to look at the back. "Yeah, he got married, but I think he had a lobotomy or something too. I've never seen the man so goofy as he was at that reception, and he didn't even have a drink except for that sip of champagne during the toast."

"That's what love'll do for you," Mac said, and his eyes darkened. "Hope it works out better for him than it did for me."

"Or me," Slade added.

Jeannie had taught Slade a valuable lesson when he got home from the sandbox. Mac had learned a similar lesson from his ex-wife. Hell, from Logan's experience with his own ex-girlfriend, Slade thought he'd learned too, but against all odds Susan had fixed him.

Susan was a different kind of woman, the kind Logan needed, tough and take-no-shit.

"Love is for fools, but considering who he married, it'll probably work out just fine," Mac said with a laugh. "She'll kick him in the balls if he ever tries to leave her."

"Well, we need to figure out what the status is here." Slade ripped open the envelope, and pulled out the note inside, hoping it had some information for him. "Logan left without even giving me a clue as to what is going on here."

He unfolded the note and scanned it, and it contained nothing more in there than he already knew. Except his boss threatened to kill him if Deep Six wasn't intact when they got back from their honeymoon.

"*We?*" Mac repeated, his eyebrows raised.

Slade's eyes flew up to his. "Yeah, *we*. I'm not about to try and run this place alone. I don't want to run it at all. Y'all are going to step up and help me, and I'm going to help *you* by hiring the people that Dave should have hired long ago to help us."

"Oh, man. You are taking your life in your hands," Mac said, holding his hands up. "I don't want any part of that, buddy. Logan is as tight as Gray's assh—"

"We having a meeting nobody told me about?" Grayson asked shortly, as he walked into Slade's office and took the chair beside Mac. "And my asshole is as tight as your mouth should be, jerkoff. I got a call from the fiancé of the woman you're working for."

Mac's eyebrows shot up. "Jared Calmes?"

Now, Gray looked surprised. "Um, no…this man's name was Fred something…Layton."

"Now, that's interesting, what did he want?" Mac asked, his eyes narrowed.

"Wanted to know why you were talking to his employees about him. Said you should be checking her out not him, because she's the one doing the cheating."

"I'm not stalking him. That's not who I've been following, and yeah, Jared is not cheating." Mac looked thoughtful for a moment. "Layton? I think that's Jared's boss at the plant if I'm not mistaken." He looked at Slade, who had just been listening. "Another prime example of why I don't get involved with women anymore."

"That's a prime example of why you should avoid those kind of cases is what that is. Why do you take those kind of cases?" Gray asked, with a shake of his head.

Mac shot him a look. "To put the beans in the basket so you have something to count, Grayson," he replied smugly.

Slade cleared his throat to break up the argument he saw brewing. "I need you to count those beans and tell me how much leeway we have to hire a few more people and still be comfortable, Gray. Push the envelope, because I want to hire some good people and that isn't going to be cheap. You'll have that bookkeeper if you do things right."

Gray whistled. "Man you like to live dangerously. Logan will have your nuts in a wringer if you do that."

"He left me with them in a wringer, so I'm just returning the favor. Now, get me those numbers and y'all clear out. I'm going to schedule my first interview before she leaves town."

Cee Cee's flight out was scheduled for tomorrow, so Slade needed to talk to her today. Jerking the phone up, he punched in the number she'd scratched on a piece of paper for him at the reception. At the time, he thought he'd catch up with her for a drink before she left town, or *something*, but now he wanted a lot more from her.

"Hello?" she answered, sounding out of breath.

"Cee Cee? This is Slade, we talked at your brother's reception?" When she didn't respond, he charged on. "I'd like you to come by the Deep Six office downtown and talk to me before you fly out."

"Well, my flight out is at zero six hundred, so it'll have to be today. What's up?" she asked, still breathing hard.

"Where are you?" he asked.

"Running by my parent's farm." Slade heard her tennis shoes pounding the pavement. "Gotta keep up the PT if I'm going back."

Well, hopefully she wouldn't be going back. "I have a proposition for you."

"I told you last night I'm not interested," she replied with a sharp laugh.

Blood rushed up to Slade's face. He'd been on his third scotch when he asked for her phone number, and vaguely recalled flirting with her shamelessly to get it. They'd talked so long, he was going in for the close before she left.

What the hell had he been thinking? Logan would fucking kill him.

Slade knew exactly what he'd been thinking, that she looked damned good in that little black dress and come-fuck-me-heels with her blonde spiky hair and tanned skin. At the time he hadn't been too concerned about Logan, because she certainly hadn't looked like anybody's little sister, or a soldier.

Slade cleared his throat. "Not that kind of proposition. But either way, your brother will probably put a bullet in me when he gets back."

Her footfalls slowed then stopped and after several heavy breaths, she asked, "What did you have in mind? You know I'm always up for anything that will aggravate my brother."

Susan was now married to the boss, and had proven herself on their last mission, so Slade knew her days as their secretary were over. Gray needed a bookkeeper so he could do what he did best, slicing and dicing financial records to find bad guys.

"I need a secretary and a bookkeeper. You pick which one you want."

"I can't even balance my own checkbook, so bookkeeper is out." Cee Cee laughed, and after a few more heavy breaths, she said, "Dave won't hire me, so you're wasting your time."

"Dave isn't here, I'm doing the hiring. Our

conversation last night tells me you're more than qualified to work here," he replied.

"While the cat's away?" she asked, with a breathy laugh.

"The *cat* left without giving the mouse any kind of cage or boundaries, so yeah, I'm playing. I'm doing what he should have done himself."

"I want to be an operator, not a desk jockey," Cecelia said flatly.

"Operator will come, but you have to prove yourself first. You'll work for Deep Six, so if we need agents, you'll have your toe in the door."

Slade was determined to convince her and he didn't know why. Yes he did, this woman deserved the chance her brother was denying her. She'd worked hard to develop the skills to work here.

"David will never let that happen, and you know it. I'll be stuck behind that desk for life, if he doesn't fire me when he gets back."

"Better than being stuck in the sandbox, right? There's no telling when that conflict will end. Do you really like it over there that much? Away from your family?" Slade coerced, and she groaned.

"No, I don't *like* it, but I'm doing my duty, and it's the only thing I have."

He heard her weakening, so Slade went in for the kill. "You have your marketing degree, so you could put that to use for Deep Six too. Dave is doing it all right now, so I'm sure he'd appreciate your help there."

11

"He doesn't appreciate anything I do," she replied with disgust and defeat in her tone.

"Give him a chance, and be patient. Susan will have him *whipped* into shape in no time."

Whipped being the operative word in that statement, Slade thought, with a laugh. In his case, that wasn't a bad thing. He needed someone to reel him in sometimes, and Susan was just the woman for the job.

"Yeah, she's the best thing that ever happened to my brother, and I hope he listens to her. He's just so damned stubborn it might take more than one lifetime for her to do that. I like my new sister-in-law."

"I like Snapper too." As unlikely as it was, Susan *was* the best thing that had happened to Dave, and to Deep Six Security. The guys had more comradery now that they'd ever had. That went a long way towards making a cohesive team. "She keeps us all in line around here."

"Okay I'll be your damned secretary, but if he fires me when he gets back you're in big trouble mister, because I'll be unemployed."

"Susan won't let him fire you," Slade said, with slightly more confidence than he felt.

"Okay, let me call command and tell them to get my exit paperwork done, instead of the re-enlistment. I'll still have to go back to the base for a week or so, and then ask for terminal leave, before I can work for you. I think I have enough leave built up to cover the time it will take to process the paperwork, but I'll have to check." Cee Cee took a deep breath and blew it out. "My CO is going to be pissed, because I just told him I was re-upping."

"Try and speed things up, if you can." If it took a few weeks, the odds were Dave would be back then and he *wouldn't* hire her. "Find out your time frame and call me back."

Slade hung up the phone and looked over at Lola, and she lifted her head from her paws to look at him. "Women are more trouble than they're worth, Lt. Lola," he said.

Lola's eyes narrowed, her ears moved forward and she held his gaze for a second, before she barked.

"Not you, baby girl," Slade said, with a laugh. "You're the perfect woman for me. You do what I tell you to do and don't talk back." Looking placated, Lola got up and walked over to him to let him scratch between her ears. "And you help me keep my shit together too."

Slade had a feeling he would need her to do that often during the two weeks he would be tied to this hot seat.

CHAPTER TWO

Somehow he'd survived the first day of his two weeks of hell, so Slade was a little hopeful that it might work out after all, when he sat down behind his desk on day two. He might have more hope though, if Susan and Logan would fucking call him.

He'd just flicked on his computer, when the phone on his desk rang. His heart skipped a beat, then plummeted when he glanced at the display and saw the caller was Jaxson Thomas, not Logan. He wondered what the former Navy SEAL who'd been put in charge of the security detail in Houston needed. There was only one way to find out, so he picked up the phone, connected the call and closed his eyes.

God, please don't let there be a problem.

"What's up, Jax?" Jaxson sighed deeply, and Slade tensed because that was *not* a good sign.

"Logan said you have the con while they're gone and we need you here in Houston ASAP. There's been an incident and the prince is pissed."

"How pissed?" Slade asked, grinding his teeth. "Can I just call him? I have things to do here." He had no idea what those things were, but the last thing he wanted to do was drive all the way to Houston today. No, the last thing he wanted was to be in charge of handling this problem at all. But it had to be handled, and probably with kid gloves. He'd often heard Logan bitching about how hard Prince Ahmed

Khalil could be to deal with sometimes. They had to deal with him though, he was Deep Six's biggest contract right now.

"Pissed enough to order us all out of the hotel," Jax replied, sounding frustrated. "A call isn't going to cut it. His son was kidnapped this morning."

Adrenaline shot through Slade making him dizzy, as he stood. "I'll be there in a few hours." His eyes fell on the box that held Dave's cell phone and he cursed.

"Did you call the police?" Slade asked.

"No, the prince didn't want to involve the police. He didn't really tell me why. He didn't say anything to me other than get out!"

"I'm on my way," Slade said, hanging up the phone to grab his sunglasses and keys off his desk. He stood and looked down at Lola. "Let's go handle this Charlie fucking Foxtrot, Lola. It looks like we are in charge, whether we want to be or not."

An hour later, Slade strode into the coffee shop down the street from the luxury hotel to find his men sitting at small round tables nursing lattes, and looking morose. His eyes landed on Jax, and the former Navy SEAL's lips pinched. "Glad you got here so fast."

Slade sat down in the empty chair beside him. "Okay, what the hell is going on?"

"Sir, I'm sorry, but the manager says you'll have to take your dog outside," a young waitress said, staring at Lola, who plopped down beside his chair.

15

Slade was used to this, but it irritated him every time. "Tell your manager that my *dog* is a *service* animal and under the ADA she *is* allowed to be inside this shop."

Her eyes widened and she glanced back over her shoulder at the man standing behind the pastry counter, who obviously didn't have the balls to deliver the message himself.

Slade waited until the waitress met his eyes again. "Tell your *manager* that unless you'd like to hear from both my attorney and the ADA, he'd better just get back to making his donuts."

When the girl's eyes welled up, Slade blew out a breath. "Just a word of advice? Next time, you might want to ask that question first, sugar."

"I'm sorry." Her lower lip trembled, she bit it. Slade growled as his eyes fixed there, and he watched her mouth move. "Is there something you'd like? It's on the house."

Two of the guys snickered and Slade shot them a look. He wished he'd never mentioned during one of their 'team bonding' nights, which Susan had instituted, that was the one thing a woman could do to drive him crazy. He didn't have time for bonding right now, he needed answers.

"Coffee, black please," he replied, turning in his seat as the girl walked across the shop to the counter. "What happened?"

"Some time after eight o'clock last night someone came up the back stairway to the penthouse level. They walked right past the guard…" Jaxson shot Caleb a glare, which told Slade that Caleb was that guard. "And took Zami from under our noses. I'm not a hundred percent sure of the time, because no one noticed the kid was gone until his nanny went into his room to wake him this morning."

"Anyone check with hotel security to review security video?" Slade asked.

"There is no security video and hotel security has been told not to let us within twenty-five feet of the front door." Jax huffed a breath, looked down at his cup and shook his head. "Even if they had video, I doubt the head of security would cooperate with us."

"Why is that?" Slade asked.

"It's a long story. The HOS is a woman, and the prince being an Arab, doesn't like that fact or acknowledge her. That's why he hired us to work with the guards he brought with him from Saudi." Jaxson looked back up, and his lip pinched again. "Understandably, that didn't put Ms. Kincaid in a very cooperative mood."

"That's a pretty fancy hotel. Why didn't they have security cameras?" Slade asked, giving a distracted smile to the cute little waitress when she delivered his coffee. Any other time, he would've flirted and probably wrangled a date out of her, but he didn't have that luxury at the moment. He needed to fix this cluster and get his ass back to the office.

"Oh they have them, but the prince wouldn't

allow them to be used on the penthouse level. He felt it was an invasion of privacy for his wives and daughters." Jaxson rolled his eyes, and huffed a breath. "You know how that works."

Yeah, after two tours in the middle east, one in Iraq and one in Afghanistan, Slade knew exactly how that worked. He was surprised the prince even allowed his men to be around the women at all since they weren't related.

"Okay, so we have no clue where the kid is or who took him? No ransom notes? Declarations from the kidnappers?" Since a middle eastern prince was involved, this might be a political statement of some kind too. That did not bode well for that boy if that was the case.

"Nothing yet, so for all we know Zami could've just wandered off." Jaxson shot another glare at Caleb.

"I only left for five minutes to go to the damned bathroom at three in the morning!" Caleb shouted, and the three other people at tables in the shop all looked startled. He leaned his forearms on the table, and talked to Jax in a quieter tone. "You said yourself we have no idea when the kid went missing, so stop blaming me. I doubt they had my bathroom schedule, because I don't have one. Unless someone saw me leave and called them, if that was the time he was taken then you better start looking at employees and family."

"You think this could be an inside job?" Slade

asked Jaxson, but he wouldn't meet his eyes. The man's jaw worked plenty though. He knew or suspected something he wasn't telling him. "Talk to me, Jaxson." Speculation at this point was better than nothing.

"I'd rather not say," Jax replied his jaw tight. "There's no proof of anything, so it's better not to muddy the water and put you on the wrong trail."

"Well, this is accomplishing nothing. I guess I'm going to have to go find some proof. That hotel manager and head of security should be able to help me get an employee list," Slade said, pushing back his chair to stand. Pulling out his wallet, he tossed twenty on the table, which should cover all the coffee and a healthy tip for the waitress. He turned toward the door, but looked back.

"I'm telling you they won't let you in," Jax warned. "But if you do get in tread lightly or you may wind up on your ass on the curb out front. The prince is really in a lather. I think he wants everyone's heads to roll."

Slade studied Jaxson's face, and it looked like he'd already made the decision that head would be his, or he was going to offer it up. Not if Slade could help it. He needed the former SEAL's help in finding that kid. Deep Six couldn't afford to lose Jaxson Thomas, even if they lost this contract.

But Slade needed to sort things out at the hotel first. The money the wealthy prince threw at them for this security detail was mind boggling. They really couldn't afford to lose the contract either. Or have an international incident that might damage their reputation so nobody would hire them. This needed to be kept hush-hush and handled quickly.

"Meet me back at the office. We've got a lot of work to do," Slade said, as he walked to the front door.

***

"Mr. Baker, I had no control over what happened on the penthouse level. You know that," Taylor said, folding her hands in her lap.

She wasn't glad the seven-year-old had been abducted, but she was glad for the lesson she hoped it taught the arrogant Saudi prince. Men were not always the better *person* for the job. But that lesson was one a lot of men needed to learn. Especially the old school sheriff in her hometown, who had driven her to Dallas to take this boring job in the first place.

Taylor was damned tired of dealing with men with that perspective. Her present boss, Mr. Baker, seemed different when he hired her for the job, but he sure wasn't that way now.

"You had control over every other level, Ms. Kincaid," he replied, twisting his hands on the desk. "There is no excuse for you not knowing what happened, even if you weren't permitted on the penthouse level. I want you to pull every security tape we have for last night and personally review them."

"I've done that, sir." She'd been doing that

since they discovered the kid missing at seven o'clock that morning. And then she'd interviewed all the staff who'd been on duty. "I told you there was nothing other than two black-clothed men going down the back stairs. They disappeared in the area where I told you six months ago we needed to add security cameras. There's nothing on what kind of car they were driving." Taylor was having a hard time keeping her voice calm and professional.

She didn't want to sound smug, but when she'd brought up installing those additional cameras, this man had treated her like a paranoid woman. She'd proposed them to avoid a situation just like this, where they'd be caught with their pants down.

Who was paranoid now?

Taylor wanted to stand up and shout to this man that whoever took the Khalil boy knew there were no cameras in that area of the parking lot, knew their security protocol, and was aware of the lack of guards and cameras on that level of the hotel. And it was the prince's own damned fault, because he refused to allow her to monitor the floor.

That insider knowledge the kidnappers had meant they had assistance from either someone in the prince's entourage or someone on their hotel staff. The prince would never allow her to interview the family, but maybe she needed to re-interview her staff, ask more questions. Maybe branch out her investigation to staff who weren't on duty.

Mr. Baker let out a long-winded sigh. "If

21

you've looked over the tapes and found nothing, if you've interviewed the staff and found out nothing, I'm afraid I have no choice. I can't go back to the prince without some kind of resolution."

Taylor's eyes flew back to Mr. Baker's. "No choice? No choice in what?" she asked, sitting forward in her chair, her heart pounding in her chest.

"No choice, but to let you go, Ms. Kincaid. At least that might pacify the prince long enough for us to figure out what happened here and find his son."

"You can't *fire* me!" she shouted, vaulting to her feet. "This situation was in no way my fault!" Taylor was not going to let this man make her the sacrificial lamb when the prince had his own personal security, as well as those arrogant men from Deep Six he'd hired because she and her guards weren't good enough for him. *She* wasn't good enough for him.

They are the ones who should be fired, not her!

"I'm afraid it is your fault, Ms. Kincaid, since you are my head of security. Prince Khalil has demanded I get to the bottom of what happened and since you have nothing to help me, I *am* firing you. He is one of this hotel's best customers, and I owe him answers."

"Tell him that this is his own damned fault then!" Taylor walked over to lay her palms on the desk and lean in. "He tied my hands so I *couldn't* help him."

"No, I think you tied your own with your attitude once he refused your assistance and hired the security firm." Mr. Baker's tone was calm, but Taylor heard the tremor in his voice. "If he takes this to our corporate office, I may be fired as well, for keeping you on knowing that. The way you handled yourself in that meeting was just shy of unprofessional."

"He discriminated against me because I'm a woman," Taylor said, standing up to fold her arms under her breasts. "That is what's unprofessional. That's not legal, and you might just be hearing from my attorney." *Once I hit the lottery.* Right now, she was just wondering how she'd keep her house.

"And you acted like one, Ms. Kincaid, by being emotional and taking that as a personal affront to justify removing yourself from anything to do with his security, even though he and his family were still hotel guests."

That meeting two years ago was permanently burned into her brain. Being in a meeting where you are the head of hotel security, but are being talked around as if you are invisible, being excluded from the conversation because you are a *woman*, was just about the biggest slap in the face Taylor could ever imagine. No, the biggest slap had come when the prince came right out and said he didn't want her or her employees providing his security because the guards were under her supervision and she was a woman.

That was the final straw. The camel's back had broken and Taylor felt obligated to let the cocky

Arab know that although his attitude might be accepted in the middle east, it sure wasn't accepted in the United States of America where he happened to be temporarily residing.

Mr. Baker had personally escorted her out of the meeting at that point, but Taylor didn't care. It needed to be said, because it was obvious none of the other *men* in the room were going to clue him in. Especially Dave Logan, the owner of Deep Six Security, who had just been handed a security contract that probably set him up for life.

"I'll have Crawford assist you with clean—" Mr. Baker started, but the knock at his door interrupted him. He glanced at his watch, then at the door. "I have an appointment, Ms. Kincaid. Crawford is waiting in your office to help you gather your things and escort you out of the hotel."

"Watch me gather my things, you mean?" she asked shortly. "I can assure you, Mr. Baker there is *nothing* at this hotel that I want now."

The door opened behind Taylor and she spun to find a man blocking the doorway, his broad shoulders nearly touching each side and his head not far from the top jamb. It was obvious from the way his black t-shirt stretched over his chest displaying his beefy physique that this was one of the Deep Six guys. Not one she'd ever met before, but he definitely fit the profile of the men they hired. His green eyes met hers and held for a moment, before he looked at Mr. Baker, and Taylor walked to the

24

doorway.

"Excuse me," she growled, when he didn't move. "I was just *leaving.*"

"Are you Ms. Kincaid? Head of security for the hotel?" the man asked, and his rich whiskey-laced voice excited every auditory nerve inside her head.

"Not anymore, thanks to the incompetent men you assigned to the prince's security detail." Taylor pushed his arm again, but she may as well have pushed against a brick wall.

"That's what I'm here to discuss, and since you are involved I need you here too," he said calmly looking down at her.

Taylor tossed a thumb over her shoulder. "Talk to the man behind the desk, because I've got to go clear out my office."

He finally turned to the side so she could squeeze past him, but she stopped when she came face to face with a big, beautiful German Shepherd who looked up at her as if assessing her. Reaching out her hand, she let the dog sniff it.

"What's your name pretty boy? You're not supposed to be in here." Because she couldn't help herself, Taylor knelt to caress the dog's face and earned herself a lick on the chin. She needed that lick, and the rub of the animal's soft muzzle against her palm.

"Lola," the big man supplied gruffly. "And she's a service dog, so she *can* be here."

Taylor looked up and met his eyes. "She's a

service dog?" Her eyes soaked up every inch of his very non-disabled-looking body to his toes then streaked back up to meet his green gaze.

His unshaven jaw tightened. "Not all disabilities are apparent to the naked eye, if it's any of your business, *ma'am*."

"And if I'm not mistaken, all service dogs should be on a *leash*, sir." With a final pat to the dog's head, she stood.

"So should some *people*, but that doesn't mean they get one," he growled. "I really would like your input in this meeting so we can figure this situation out, Ms. Kincaid."

"And I'd really love to be in that meeting too," Taylor replied with a tight smile. "But since I was just *fired*, I guess that's not possible, Mr…?"

"Slade," he replied without sticking his hand out to her.

At least that beat the cold-fish handshake she usually got from men. "Well, Mr. Slade, I'll—"

"Just Slade—*no* mister," he corrected shortly. "Don't leave before I talk to you. I won't be long here, so I'll find you in your office."

Who in the hell did this guy think he was?

"I probably won't be there when you finish, *Mr.* Slade. I'm out of here as soon as I can throw my stuff in a box." Taylor turned to walk down the hallway. "You have a nice day now," she said with a finger wave over her shoulder.

"Lola, *pass auf*!" Slade growled, before Taylor

heard the door shut.

She almost laughed, because it sounded like he'd told the dog to *piss off*, but then she felt the dog's hot snorts of breath on her heels as she walked toward her office. The dog followed her inside, and stopped when she did.

"Crawford," Taylor said, as she strode to pick up the box he'd evidently put in the chair across from her desk. "I guess you'll be my replacement, right?"

"I'm sorry about this, Ms. Kincaid," he said and looked damned uncomfortable. "I'll just be out in the hall if you need anything."

Taylor watched him leave, then swallowed down her embarrassment and anger as she sat the box on her desk to start loading it with the pictures of her family from her bookshelves, the awards she'd gotten from the various karate and sharpshooting competitions she'd won, and finally her most precious memento of all—her father's posthumous medal of honor from the Army. Having it in her face now though brought the tears much closer to the surface.

She was almost glad he was dead, so he didn't have to see what a shambles her life had become. He would be so disappointed in her, and Taylor was glad she didn't have to see that look on his handsome face. Not meeting the physical qualifications to be an MP like she'd planned, like he'd helped her prepare for all of her life, seemed to set her life into a downward spiral. Him not being at her college graduation, having that diploma handed to her without him in the seat beside her mother in the audience, had been the most traumatic day of her life.

Taylor needed to recover soon, because the ground was coming at her fast. She needed to figure out what she wanted to be when she grew up, now that her dream was not achievable. It certainly wasn't a hotel security manager whose greatest challenge was filling out a schedule, and supervising former mall cops.

She closed her eyes and took several deep breaths but opened them when something nudged her hip. Lola stood by her side looking up at her with concern in her brown eyes. The dog shouldn't even be in her office, she should be with the man who claimed she was his service dog. Why the dog had followed her in here, she didn't know.

"Go find, Slade," Taylor encouraged, shooing the dog aside so she could get to her desk drawer. But Lola didn't move, she sat down and it looked like it would take a hammer and chisel to move her. With a huffed breath, Taylor sat in her chair and she and Lola had a standoff with their eyes. "Fine, I'll clean out the other side first."

Taylor bent and slid open the bottom drawer, pulled out a couple of empty Tupperware containers and tossed them in the box. She'd just opened the top drawer when she heard a sharp bark and looked up to see Lola sniffing at the hem of Tariq Khalil's pants. She barked again, showing teeth and he backed out of the office.

28

"What can I do for you Tariq?" Taylor asked, standing to walk around the desk. She glanced at the dog whose hair was almost standing on end on her quivering skin. This man made her feel exactly the same way.

"Ahmed asked me to tell you that we received a ransom demand," he said without meeting her eyes in typical middle-eastern male fashion. "The kidnappers want ten million dollars by Friday or they will kill Zami."

Wasn't that interesting how calmly Tariq related that news? His voice almost sounded pleased. "You'll need to give that information to Mr. Baker, but he's in with someone right now. One of the men from Deep Six, I believe."

Tariq's back stiffened, and his eyes flew to hers. "Mr. Baker was told by the prince to have them all leave this hotel and not come back."

And that was even more interesting. Taylor had been tied up interviewing staff and reviewing video tape since the child was discovered missing so she didn't know that. If she was gone, and Deep Six was gone, since the prince also refused to call the police, who would help them *find* Zami? Not her problem now.

"Crawford," Taylor said loudly. "Can you escort Tariq to Mr. Baker's office, please?"

"Yes, ma'am," Crawford replied, appearing behind Tariq. She finally relaxed when he led the richly-suited Arab from her office, and strangely, so did Lola.

A few minutes later, Taylor was just putting the last item in her box, her honors diploma in pre-law from Oklahoma State University, when Slade walked into her office red-faced and looking like he could chew nails. Lola immediately ran over to him to rub her face against his leg. His big body relaxed and he blew out a breath as he reached down to scratch between her ears, and she licked the side of his hand.

"It looks like your meeting went about as well as mine did," Taylor commented with a laugh, as she picked up her box to walk around her desk.

Slade stalked over to her and grabbed the box from her without even asking. "Let's get the hell out of here so we can talk," he growled, turning toward the door.

As she followed behind him, Taylor wondered again who the hell this man thought he was, but she liked his dog, so she followed. Besides she wanted to know what happened in that meeting with Mr. Baker to make him as furious as he obviously was at the moment.

CHAPTER THREE

Taylor often wondered about the corporate offices of Deep Six Security in downtown Dallas. She'd even done a Google Earth search on the address she'd been so curious as to where all the meatheads employed by the security firm were housed. The spacious and sedate neutral-colored lobby that the mysterious Slade led her into wasn't what she envisioned.

There wasn't a weight bench or treadmill in sight, no razor wire fence or bunkhouse-style cots to keep their operatives handy for missions. It didn't smell like a boy's locker room, and there were even a few plants scattered around the office. It actually looked like most any other corporate office she'd been inside.

But the man she followed down a narrow hallway past a conference room with a long cherry-wood table and comfortable looking chairs, as well as a few other offices that she couldn't see inside because the doors were closed, was anything but typical. He was what one would term 'the silent deadly type' at the moment. Anger radiated off of him like a tangible thing, and Lola evidently noticed, because she followed behind him like a shadow seeming to be trying to soothe the big beast.

When the prince insisted on interviewing security companies before he and his family moved into the hotel, Taylor read the qualifications statement

Dave Logan submitted before the prince hired the firm. The copy had been provided to Mr. Baker, but Taylor had no problem whatsoever making herself a copy to study so she was prepared for the meeting with Logan and the prince. Taylor had studied and researched the company until her eyes were crossed to prepare for the meeting. The only thing she hadn't been prepared for was the main reason the prince didn't want her providing his security.

She was a woman.

The one thing she couldn't refute or change.

Just like she hadn't been able to change the fact she was a *petite* woman when trying to join the Army Military Police. At five feet and one-half-inches tall barefooted, she didn't meet the physical requirements. The military seemed to think that scaling a wall in one leap was more important than the fact she could outshoot, and probably outfight, any of the big bulky guys in hand-to-hand combat.

Her father made sure she could take care of herself, teaching her to shoot competitively and enrolling her in martial arts at a young age, in case something happened to him. Which, in the end, was exactly what happened when she was seventeen.

Tom Kincaid, a military policeman himself, died doing his duty in Afghanistan. Since she could walk, Taylor had wanted to follow in his footsteps. But the Army didn't want her for that classification, so she didn't join at all. If she couldn't make it into the military police force, then she had no interest in joining.

It had taken Taylor a while to lick her wounds over that one, but she finally came to the conclusion it was their loss. Just like it had been the prince's that he chose not to utilize her services because she was a woman. Now that his son had been kidnapped under the noses of a big bunch of burly *men*, she hoped he was seeing the error in his judgment.

Slade stopped at one of the doors near the end of the hallway to open the door and walk inside. Taylor followed him inside the small office and the first thing she saw was a crumpled wad of bright wrapping paper and tissue surrounding a box on his desk.

"Is it your birthday?" she asked, shutting the door behind her.

"If it is, it's the worst one I've ever had," he grumbled as he lifted the box and sat it on the floor, before sitting behind his desk.

Taylor took a chair across from the desk. "What did you want to talk to me about?" she asked, crossing her legs. "What happened with Mr. Baker?"

"Mr. Baker is a puss—" he started, but his eyes shot up to hers and his face turned red above his dark, and very sexy beard stubble. "Mr. Baker is a *cake eater*. If you don't know what that means, Ms. Kin—"

"I know what it means," Taylor assured smiling. When he was at home, she heard Tom Kincaid use that term often when describing the local politicians in their small Oklahoma hometown. The description fit both those politicians, including the sheriff, and Mr. Baker. "My father was a military MP."

Cake eater was the term for a soft-bellied politician who never chose a side of the fence to stand on, because he wanted to make sure he came out on the right side of a situation. A politically correct way to say he was a pussy, as Slade almost called him.

His eyebrows raised, and his face relaxed a bit. "Good, we're on the same page then. I need your help to fix this situation, or Deep Six will lose the contract at the hotel. I need to find—"

"I couldn't care less about the hotel or your contract, Mr. Slade." When Taylor walked out of Mr. Baker's office, out of that hotel, their problems ceased to be hers. This was Deep Six Security's problem now. "I have my own issues to deal with that the moment, like finding a new job." One that didn't include a desk, or a cake-eating boss like Mr. Baker.

She expected the big man behind the desk to get upset, to grind his teeth or something to show his frustration, because Taylor had no intention of helping him at all. What Slade actually did surprised her. He smiled, a wide sexy showing of perfectly aligned teeth that had interest sparking in her midsection.

He leaned forward on his elbows to pin her

with amused emerald eyes. "You're very lucky that I like women with attitude, Ms. Kincaid. I happen to be used to dealing with them too, so you don't scare me one damned bit."

Lucky? Like she was fortunate he was so tolerant of her and her attitude? A woman with attitude.

Taylor shoved up her feet and pasted on a smile. "No, you're the lucky one, Mr. Slade. That I agreed to come here at all. I won't waste a minute more of your time with my attitude, or my time giving it to you. Good *luck* with finding Zami."

Taylor turned to grab the doorknob, but his mumbled words piqued her curiosity. She didn't want an argument, but this man was begging for one.

Spinning back, she narrowed her eyes. "What did you say?"

"I said, Susan is going to fucking love you."

Taylor's head rocked back on her shoulders, and her hand fell away from the doorknob. "Who in the world is Susan?" *And what does she have to do with me?* Taylor was starting to think this man had a few screws loose.

"Dave Logan's new wife, and I guess by osmosis, my new boss. Former FBI and about the meanest woman I've ever met. But her *snap* is definitely worse than her bite."

Slade's statement sounded like he was pleased or proud that this Susan person was not only mean, but was also now his boss. It confused and intrigued Taylor enough that she moved back to sit down.

"Deep Six is owned by a woman? I thought Dave Logan was the owner?"

"Oh, Dave is still the owner." Slade's smile broadened, if that was possible. "But I have a feeling Susan is going to be the one in charge when they get back from their honeymoon."

Well, that was probably very good for this company, but had not a thing to do with her. With a huffed breath, Taylor stood again. "I'm sure it will be an improvement here, but I'm afraid it doesn't have a thing to do with me so I'll be going."

"Oh, but it does." His smile faded, his eyes became more intense. "I'm offering you a job, Ms. Kincaid. Dave and Susan left me in charge while they're away, and I need you to help me resolve this situation before they get back."

Shock rolled through Taylor. "You want to hire me? You don't know a damned thing about me or my background." It just didn't make sense to Taylor, and that made her very suspicious. Companies like Deep Six just didn't hire people on the spot without background checks, and multiple interviews. "I have my resume in the car, but it needs to be updated. My handgun license is current, but it's due for renewal soon. I haven't been to the range in a while either."

"I don't need your resume, I need your help. Do you want the job or not, Ms. Kincaid?"

What choice did she have really? She was out of a job and this man, whether he had the authority to do it or not since he was only temporarily in charge, wanted to hire her.

If Dave Logan wanted to fire her when he came back, or if his new wife didn't like her and decided to fire her, Taylor would just have to deal with that then. At least taking this job would buy her some time to find another one.

She sat back in the chair one more time, because there was still one more thing he evidently hadn't considered. "You know the prince will never allow me to be involved in this investigation at all."

Slade laughed. "Well, since Prince Khalil fired us too, I guess he doesn't get to choose who's involved now. We're doing this to salvage our reputation, not because he's paying us. I'm going to find that kid and figure out who and what is behind his abduction, hopefully before Ahmed shells out ten million dollars which will just get the kidnappers richer, and his kid dead anyway."

Taylor sat forward in her chair. "I just found out about the ransom before I left the office, but that's exactly what I think too. And I get the feeling that Tariq is not sad at all that Zami was abducted. Something hinky is going on with him. I've always thought that."

"Well, I haven't been involved in this protection detail at all so I don't know the players, or what's *hinky* and what's not. That is why I need you on this case with me, Ms. Kincaid. Now, do you want the job or not?"

37

"Yes, I'll help you," Taylor replied, with a little seed of excitement blossoming inside her.

This is why she'd chosen the law as her profession. To right wrongs, not sit behind a desk and wither away watching security monitors and babysitting a bunch of washed up mall cops who applied for security jobs at luxury hotels.

"Okay, go home, get some rest and be here tomorrow morning so we can meet with the guys and formulate a game plan." Taylor stood, and Slade's eyes tracked down her body dragging heated blood to her toes, before he met her gaze again. "Lose the suits, okay? Logan hates them. Jeans, tanks, or anything else will work."

This job just sounded better and better. Now, if the pay was even close to what she'd gotten at the hotel, she'd be golden.

"Jeans it is then," Taylor said, with a smile she felt stretch all the way to her ears. "We haven't discussed pay or hours yet."

"The pay is as obscene as the hours you'll be expected to work. We're on call twenty-four-seven, so keep your cell phone on. Give it here, so I can program in the numbers for the team before you leave."

Taylor grabbed her purse off of the chair, found her cell phone and walked to the desk to hand it to him. A dart of fire shot up her arm when his hand brushed hers, standing every hair on end. Why did she think he felt it too, because his body tensed and his eyes met hers as he took it from her?

A knock sounded at the door, before it flew inward. "I need to talk to you." The tall, well-built man with bright blue eyes she knew as Jaxson Thomas, the supervisor of the Deep Six crew at the hotel, filled the doorway, but he didn't come inside. His eyes glanced off of her, then moved back to Slade. "Call me when you finish."

Slade tensed. "I hope this isn't what I think it is, Jaxson. I really don't need more today. Sleep on it, and talk to me tomorrow."

"Nah, I need to talk to you today, man. As soon as possible." The resignation in the man's voice was as firm as his jaw.

"Just wait a minute then." Slade furiously punched numbers into her phone. After a couple of minutes, he handed it back to her. "That's everyone, and I texted myself your phone number. Be here at eight in the morning, unless I call you sooner."

Feeling light inside like she hadn't in a long time, Taylor lifted her hand, bent her elbow and snapped off a salute like her father had taught her. "Zero eight hundred it is, sir."

Slade's eyebrows lifted, but his lips didn't curve. "I'm not a trench monkey or a member of Uncle Sam's Canoe Club like Jaxson here. I'm a Marine, and we don't salute indoors, ma'am. Since you're a civilian, I'll give you a pass, but you need to know none of us are active duty anymore, so saluting is not necessary or acceptable at all. It might also piss

Logan off, so lose the suit *and* the salute."

Trench monkey? Canoe Club? This man was talking a different language. But she understood one thing. Before this was over, the way it sounded, the odds of her pissing off Dave Logan were very high, so she better go with plan A and just consider this job a stop gap measure until she found another job.

"I apologize if I insulted you, Slade." Taylor's cheeks were hot as she turned to the door. "I'll be here at eight in the morning to get started. Call me if you need to go over anything."

Taylor walked to the door and her eyes met Jaxson Thomas's.

"It's not you," he whispered under his breath. "He just knows what I'm about to tell him. Things will be better tomorrow, I promise."

With a nod, she walked past him and he shut the door. Glancing up and down the hallway and seeing it clear, Taylor leaned her ear against the door straining to hear what was being said. The only thing she made out was Slade begging Jaxson Thomas not to quit.

"You know that works better with one of my listening devices," an amused male voice said close to her ear and Taylor almost jumped out of her skin.

Heart pounding in her throat she stepped back to study the stealthy man who'd snuck up on her. Overly long, uncombed dark hair brushed over his forehead and his beard scruff gave him that sexy just-rolled-out-of-bed look. His well-defined chest stretched the red graphic tee with some kind of scientific symbol on the front to its limits, and his almost worn out blue jeans hung on his trim hips. The black half-rim glasses he wore emphasized his piercing blue eyes. The epitome of a hot nerd.

"Come to my office and I'll loan you one. I'm curious what the hell they're talking about too. It can't be good considering how fast Caleb lit out of here a minute ago."

Without waiting for her response, he turned and opened the door across the hallway from Slade's. Because she wanted to know who this man was and what he did at Deep Six to have listening devices in his office, Taylor followed him inside. Boxes and gadgets lined every wall of the man's office, if you could call it that. He had work tables and computers set up everywhere, but not a desk in sight.

"I have a long-range orbiter that would probably do the trick. I just need to remember where I put it." With a laugh, he walked to the right wall and stared up at the stack of boxes. "I told Logan we needed to get a warehouse for this stuff, but he's so damned tight that'll never happen. Caleb barely convinced him to get a gun safe so we could get all the weapons and ammo out of here." He reached for the box on the top of the stack and hefted it down then plunked it on the floor. "We should just move all this stuff out to the compound. I'd be just as happy working out there. Happier, really, because I wouldn't have to dress up for work."

"Dress up?" Taylor repeated with a laugh, taking in his clothes again.

He turned to look at her then his eyes tracked down his body. "Oh, I forgot to wear my t-shirt with the tuxedo on it today." He winked, as he walked over to her and stuck out his hand. "I guess I forgot something else too. I'm Dexter, the spy gadget and electronics guy for Deep Six. Sort of like that guy in the James Bond movies, but on a *much* tighter budget."

"I'm Taylor Kincaid, and I guess I'm a new employee," she said, taking his hand and liking that he actually shook hers with a firm grip.

Dex's eyebrows raised and his eyes took a tour of her body to her toes. "Slade sure works fast, and I like it, but I'm not so sure our fearless leader will when he gets back."

"Our fearless leader can kiss my ass," Slade said gruffly as he walked into the office. "He wants an incommunicado vacation? I'm going to give him one, but I need to hire another operative now, because Jaxson just quit."

"Why did Jax quit?" Dex asked, his brow furrowing.

"Because he's a freaking martyr evidently. He quit the SEAL teams to save his squad embarrassment, now he quit Deep Six for the same reason. He thinks it's his fault the prince's son got kidnapped and believes we'll keep the contract if he's gone."

"Did the prince say that?" Dex asked.

"According to Tariq, the prince's brother, we're out anyway. They don't want us anywhere near that hotel. I planned on speaking to the prince myself, but was told that he was unavailable."

"Tariq likes to run interference—or *interfere*," Taylor interjected, and both men's eyes swung her way. "I don't trust that man as far as I can throw him. He's always coming and going at all hours of the night, or in a corner on his cell phone."

"Do you have his cell phone number?" Slade asked Taylor, but his eyes slid to Dex.

"No, I don't. I was not allowed to be an insider with that family at all. It actually worked out, because I got to observe a lot more since I wasn't directly involved, but your man Jaxson probably has more information than I do."

"Well, Jax is gone, and his mouth was sealed—no pun intended." His chin dropped to his chest as if he were thinking, then he looked back at Dex. "Dave's cell phone is in a box beside my desk. Go through it and see if you can find the prince's number. You know what to do."

Dex nodded, and started for the door.

"He has two or three cell phones," Taylor informed, and Dex stopped in the doorway. She'd seen Ahmed holding conversations on two of them at once one time and was impressed.

"Dex will figure it out. I want to go back to that hotel and run Lola through a search to see exactly where the kid was taken out."

"I watched all the surveillance video. They took Zami out the back stairway and that was the last sighting." Taylor blew out a breath. "I've been after Mr. Baker to put up cameras on the west end of the building for six months, but he refused. Since the last sighting on the video was the stairwell door on the penthouse level, I assume they went west out of the exit door or they'd have been seen on the video."

"Dex, I need a copy of that video footage, and keep a tap into that system so we can keep an eye on things now." Slade thought a minute. "Call Fletch and tell him to get inside the hotel and find that kid's room. I need something with Zami's scent on it. Think you can manage that?"

"Can I manage it?" Dex asked cockily, with an eye roll.

"Forget I asked that, geek boy. Just do it." Slade shook his head as he walked to the door. "As soon as Fletch gets what I need, I'll go back to the hotel to run Lola and see if she picks up on anything."

"*Wait!* I know where you can get something with his scent!" Taylor shouted, following him out of the office into the hallway. She put her hand on his arm, and his muscles flexed. Warmth flowed through her fingers up her arm to ooze through her body.

Slade looked down at her and frowned.

"They send all their clothes out to a local dry cleaner on Tuesday mornings. A batch went this morning. The dry cleaner knows me and will give me the clothes. I'd also like to go with you for the search, since I know the lay of the land at that hotel better than anyone. I know the blind spots, so we can avoid being seen."

Taylor fought a shiver as his eyes slid down her body to her toes. "In that bright blue business suit and heels you're wearing, we're guaranteed to be seen. That's not exactly covert ops attire, ma'am."

"We have a while before dark, so we can stop by my house so I can change too." Taylor was not letting this man go without her. He needed her with him, and it felt damned good to be useful for a change.

Slade studied her for a minute through hooded green eyes, then sighed. "Fine, but you are going to stay in the car and let Lola work."

"Yes, sir." Taylor smiled and her arm itching to snap off another salute at his authoritative attitude, which was actually kind of sexy. But her determination to fit in here kept it firmly at her side. There was a lot she found sexy about her new boss, but Taylor was keeping that firmly where it belonged too.

Out of the picture.

CHAPTER FOUR

Slade followed Taylor Kincaid's directions, as he turned onto a poorly maintained residential street with small, equally unkempt bungalows on either side. Not the best neighborhood for a woman alone to be living for sure. But who was he to judge? He officially lived with his mother when he wasn't out at Logan's compound outside of the city. But that was by choice. He didn't need a place of his own.

"The hotel didn't pay you well did they?" he asked gruffly.

As much money as that luxury hotel raked in on the prince and his entourage, as well as their other high-end guests, that was just sickening to Slade. It's probably why they hired a woman for the position. So they could pay her less.

"Nobody at the hotel is paid well, not even the manager, Mr. Baker," she replied.

Interesting, and it added another notch in favor of the kidnapping being an inside job. The employees there would be ripe for a payoff from whoever was behind the kidnapping.

"Why'd you take that job then? I saw your pre-law diploma." He'd also seen the shooting trophies, and the martial arts awards. This woman had skills that could've landed her a job at most any private investigation firm. That's why he hadn't bothered grilling her about her credentials, or experience. But her silence, and the fact that she was gnawing on her lower lip bothered him for several reasons and in several ways.

There was a story there, one she didn't want to tell him, and if he could get past the distraction of seeing her gnawing her lip he'd find out.

"It's the last house on the left at the dead end," she said, moving to sit on the edge of the seat and look over the dash. "The yellow one. Excuse the yard...I haven't been home much to cut it. The inside isn't much better, because Buddy hates when I'm not home."

Taylor was dodging his question with chatter. Slade would let it go for now, but he would get his answer. Right now, the question burning in his mind was—who in the hell was Buddy? He swung the Humvee into the half-gravel-half-pavement rutted driveway, and stopped. Taylor had the door opened before he took his foot off of the brake and stood outside.

"I won't be long," she said, shutting the door to jog to the front porch in her heels where she hustled up the steps to the door.

Slade had thought about staying in the vehicle, but he knew women and how long it took them to change clothes. He needed to hurry her along, so they could get on the road.

Now that she'd so eloquently outlined the problems he could expect inside the house because of the mysterious Buddy, he also didn't want her going inside alone. If Buddy was an abusive boyfriend,

Slade knew just how to deal with him, and so did Lola.

He opened his door and then let Lola out of the backseat. A loud *woof!* from the porch made him swing his eyes there just in time to see a huge yellow lab launch out of the door to flatten Taylor on the porch. "Buddy, no!" she yelled, answering Slade's question about the identity of Buddy. Slade ran to the porch, and Lola was right behind him. He grabbed the dog's collar, and pulled him away from bathing Taylor's face, while she batted him away with her hands.

Jerking once on his collar, Slade shouted, "*Sitz!*" The dog's big brown eyes watered as he looked up at Slade like he'd clubbed him. Slade pushed gently on his rear. "*Sitz*, Buddy," he repeated in a calm, but firm tone and the dog finally sat. "Good boy."

"Wow, how'd you do that?" Taylor asked sitting up to brush the dirt off of her elbows, before she tried to stand, and stumbled because one heel was broken.

Slade grabbed her arm to help her up, and her skin felt like silk under his fingers. "Buddy is like a spoiled two-year-old. Don't you teach him discipline and manners?"

Taylor slid her shoes off of the tiniest, cutest damned feet Slade had ever seen. She met his eyes and shook her head. "You haven't seen anything yet. It's my fault, because I don't have time to spend with

48

him. This neighborhood is not good to walk him, and he's gotten too big to fit in my car. He is a two-year-old, and needs more exercise, but—"

"But what?" Slade asked gruffly. It pissed him off royally when people bought puppies because they were cute but they didn't think about the time and expense required to raise them. He didn't have kids, had never been around them, but he suspected raising a puppy was about the same as raising a baby. "You committed yourself to that dog and his needs when you got him, so you're right—it is your fault."

It was Taylor's turn to look up at him with guilt-filled moist eyes, and he was the one who felt clubbed this time. "I didn't *get* him, I was *left* with him when I kicked my boyfriend out of my house. I knew I needed to get rid of him too, but I just couldn't make myself do it. And he's a decent watchdog."

She sighed heavily, brushed off her skirt, then bent to pick up her purse, and Slade couldn't stop his eyes from locking on her nicely shaped ass. She stood and pushed the door open wider. "I'll put an ad in the paper tomorrow and try to find—"

"*No*—I'll help you train him." Slade felt sorry for her, but sorrier for the dog. If Buddy went to another home with this lack of training, the odds were he'd end up in the paper again until he finally wound up in a kill shelter. Slade wasn't going to let that happen.

Taylor rolled her eyes, and walked inside.

Glancing back, Slade saw that Buddy was still sitting where he put him, but was squirming, which said once Slade went inside the dog would take off to find more trouble to get into.

"Lola, *pas auf*!" Lola, who was looking at Buddy like he was about the dumbest animal she'd ever encountered, stood and moved up on the porch to sit and block the steps. She'd guard him, while they assessed the damage inside. Slade walked inside, but staggered to a stop.

"Good, *God*!" he wheezed, as he took in the condition of her tiny living room.

Cottony stuffing from something, newspaper and toilet paper shreds and garbage littered the wooden floor. His eyes traveled to the small camelback loveseat against the far wall and he knew where the stuffing had come from. One of the cushions hung off of the seat with a huge hole chewed in the center. It appeared the hole had been covered with duct tape, but that had been ripped off to expose the crater there now. The curtain rod behind the sofa hung lower on one end and he was sure he'd find the bottom of the curtain shredded too.

Blowing out a breath, he walked further inside, and put his arm around Taylor's slumped shoulders. "You have another roll of toilet paper for the mess?" he asked, as his eyes landed on the present Buddy left her on the other side of the sofa.

"I have to get rid of him," she said, her voice breaking.

"No, you need to get me a dust pan and broom, and a roll of toilet paper," he replied, squeezing her shoulders. "Give me thirty days, and Buddy will be the most well-behaved dog you've ever seen." She looked at him with raised brows. "Just trust me."

With a roll of her big blue eyes, Taylor padded off toward the kitchen, which looked to be in equally bad condition. If he wasn't mistaken, Buddy had found the dog food in the pantry, and maybe a loaf of bread and had himself a party in there.

If that dog wasn't sick tonight, which would be another mess, Taylor would be damned lucky. They'd both be lucky, because the dog would have to go with them tonight. Leaving him here alone was not going to work. If he threw up in Slade's Hummer though, he might be the one to deliver him to the pound.

Taylor walked back in the room with the dust pan and broom. She bent and started sweeping up the mess, but Slade took the broom from her. "Just go get changed, and I'll take care of this."

Her brow furrowed and she put her hands on her hips. "This is my problem not yours. I clean this up every day when I get home, so I have a system."

"Well, you're not going to be cleaning it up anymore. Go get changed, and if you have some anti-diahr—" Slade stopped when Lola growled low in her throat from the porch.

Handing Taylor the broom, he reached down

to pull his pistol from his ankle holster. As he crept closer to the door, Lola's growling got louder, and the hair on the back of his neck raised. Stopping behind the door, he rolled past it, glancing out as he flattened his back against the wall by the door. When he saw the problem, he laughed. Lola still sat by the steps blocking them but the big goofy lab was sniffing her up, licking her and bouncing around trying to get her to play.

"I think Buddy likes Lola, but she's just not that into him." Bending, Slade reholstered his pistol, then opened the door wider. "Buddy, *sitz!*" he said firmly.

The lab, who was obviously a fast learner, immediately plopped down to stare up at him. The problem was he plopped right down on Lola's paw. A fierce growl was the only warning Buddy got before Lola nipped his tail.

Slade flinched at Buddy's ear-piercing squeal. He tried to catch him as he shot toward the end of the porch, but only managed to grab his collar just before he went airborne at the edge of the porch. The dog's forward momentum pulled them both right off the end into a big unkempt bush which swallowed them. Buddy squealed, fought and squirmed, making every damned limb of the prickly bush scratch Slade's face and body until he managed to roll out of it.

Slade pointed at Buddy who lay beside him. "No!" he growled, and Buddy whined as he dropped his muzzle onto his big paws. When he heard a throaty giggle from the porch, his eyes swung there to find Taylor standing on the edge of the porch grinning down at him.

"Who's training whom, big guy?" she asked, giggling again. The sound slithered through him, dancing over every nerve. She tossed a purple leash with white dog bones on it over the bush and it landed across his thigh. Crossing her arms over her chest she said, "Don't let him tie you up with it. He's tried that a time or three with me."

Right then Slade would have liked to use it to hang the smug woman grinning down at him. Rolling to his feet, he grabbed the leash and clipped it onto the matching collar on the dog's neck. He slid his hand through the loop and grabbed the leash about halfway down then yanked. Buddy didn't move, he just laid there looking up at Slade. Turning toward the steps, Slade pulled the leash and Buddy stood thank God, so he loosened the tension.

"*Fuss!*," he growled as he took a step, but the dog didn't move. Buddy pulled back on the leash, and Slade spun to pin him with a glare. Maybe the dog wasn't as comfortable in German as Lola. Since they *never* had to worry about Buddy being a guard dog, Slade tried the English command. "*Heel* dammit!"

Big brown eyes wide, the dog whimpered as he circled at the end of the leash which was entirely too long for training a dog. Slade reached for his collar but Buddy sidestepped him and ran around his back then reappeared at his left side.

Lifting his foot, Slade tried to extract himself from the tangled leash, but Lola came around the edge of the porch, and with a loud *woof!* Buddy took off toward her. Slade's feet flew out from under him and he landed hard on his back. The yellow lab lunged toward Lola jerking the leash so hard it felt like he yanked Slade's shoulder out of socket.

Belly laughter erupted on the porch and anger scalded Slade's insides as he scrambled to his feet and wound the leash around his hand until he was at the dog's neck. That turned out to be a mistake. Buddy's back arched twice, he made hollow gagging sounds then dumped his kibble right on the end of Slade's boot.

"Oh, *shit!*" Slade shouted, as he looked down at the mess, fighting back a gag himself. Buddy plopped down on his ass to stare up at Slade, his body still twitching. His eyes widened then with one final heave, he finished emptying the buffet on the leg of Slade's jeans.

Slade closed his eyes and breathed, instead of putting his hands around the dog's neck . Or the owner's neck, because she was howling with laughter now. He even thought he might have heard Lola chuckle. Huffing a breath, Slade gathered his patience.

"Buddy, *Fuss!*" Slade barked, jerking the leash.

To his surprise, the dog stood and when he

took a step Buddy was right at his side. Lola followed on his left side and somehow he managed to get Buddy to the steps where he met Taylor who was still fighting intermittent bouts of laughter.

"Glad to entertain you, *half-pint*, but now I need a shower so you'll have to clean up your house yourself." *Laugh at that*, Slade thought, with an evil inner laugh as he handed her the leash. Turning he walked to his Hummer to get the change of clothes he kept in his go bag.

A *woof!* and loud squeal made him turn to see Buddy lunge to follow Lola who was following him, in the process almost jerking Taylor off of her feet. She managed to get her balance and jerk back on the leash.

"*Sitz!*" she hissed, with another jerk.

It looked like she was learning too, and that was a good thing. How the woman, who probably only weighed ten pounds or so more than the dog, had handled Buddy untrained for as long as she had was astonishing to Slade.

Well, Slade was assuming things.

Her boyfriend could've left last week for all he knew. If she couldn't find the heart to get rid of the wild ass dog who'd torn up everything she owned, he wondered what the boyfriend had done to get kicked to the curb. It had to be bad. Slade had no idea why he cared, but he wanted to find out what he'd done.

With a shake of his head, he opened the hatch on the Humvee and pulled out his bag then shut it.

By the time he got back to the porch, she'd wrangled Buddy into the house, and Lola had followed them inside.

"Where's your bathroom?" he asked, shutting the front door.

"Off the back of the kitchen," she replied, as she swept a pile of paper and stuffing into the dustpan. "Garbage bags are under the sink. You'll probably need one for your clothes, since I don't have a washing machine."

"You don't have a washer?" he repeated incredulously.

She stood and huffed a breath. "Nope—I tried to get Mark to install one for two years when he was home, but finally gave up the last time he was deployed."

It sounded like she'd given up on him the last time he was activated too. The long-ago buried anger at Jeannie tried to resurface, but he tamped it down.

"Deployed? Was he military?" Slade asked, the hard ridge of the handle of his go bag digging into his palm.

"Army Ranger, but newly-pinned as of the time I kicked him out," she replied harshly. "I guess the military doesn't mix very well with commitment, or fidelity. I'm a damned military brat so I should've known that."

"The military in general is tough on relationships," Slade said, trying to keep the anger from his tone. And yeah, if she was a military brat, she should have realized that before getting involved with a military man.

"My mother managed just fine. I was very proud of my father, that's why I thought I could make it work. The man I chose was the problem."

"I'm sorry to hear that." But not sorry at all. At least Taylor Kincaid broke it off with this Mark cleanly, not after she'd made a commitment to him then ditched him when he was at the lowest point of his life.

"I just hope the PTSD he's hiding from the military psychologists doesn't get him killed," she said, her voice trembling as she brushed past Slade to walk to the kitchen.

The tingling started at his scalp, crept down his neck, then zipped to his fingers and they went numb. The go bag dropped on the floor with a thud as his vision narrowed and the electric buzzing started in his ears. Lola whimpered, then barked nudging his thigh with her nose.

God, not now. It had been nearly two years, Slade thought, as he eased down to sit. Lola was in his face then, licking and nudging his cheek with her muzzle. Closing his eyes, Slade gritted his teeth, focused on banishing the buzz before the fireworks started. Lola's wiry fur brushed his cheek, the rasp of her tongue on his jaw soothed him, kept him in the present.

A loud *woof!* preceded something slamming into his crotch causing extreme pain in his balls that sent an electric shock through his body. With a squeal, his eyes flew open and he shoved against the big body in his lap. Buddy moved away, but not before another sharp push of his paw into Slade's crotch. Breathless, Slade fell onto his back, grabbed himself then rolled onto his side to rock.

A giggle floated on the air and echoed inside Slade's skull. Tiny feet appeared beside him and his eyes tracked up very shapely calves to meet Taylor's twinkling blue eyes. "Yeah, he did that to Mark a time or two as well. Buddy thinks he's a lapdog. You okay?"

With a grunt, Slade sat up and shot daggers at Buddy who sat beside Taylor. "I'm fine, but we need to get out of here." He stood, and jerked the trash bag out of her hands then picked up his go bag. "It's going to be dark before we know it, and we've got things to do." And he had things to do tomorrow, like calling his shrink for an emergency appointment.

Taylor's eyes narrowed, her arm jerked and bent at the elbow, but then fell back to her side. He knew she'd stopped herself from saluting him. It was a joke to her, but definitely not to him. Slade never wanted to ever be saluted again in his life. He didn't deserve it, because he'd let down the men who were stupid enough to trust him and give him that honor.

CHAPTER FIVE

Just as night fell, Slade pulled into the large parking lot at the luxury hotel. Following Taylor's direction, he edged along the first row to the corner of the lot then turned toward the west end to avoid being picked up by the security cameras.

Another hot wave of the after effects of Buddy's self-indulgence at Taylor's house wafted to him in the front seat. Eyes watering, Slade lowered his window all the way down and swallowed hard to fight a gag. The Pepto they'd given Buddy before they left her house had settled the dog's stomach but it evidently didn't completely erase the problem. Glancing over at Taylor he saw her cheeks puffed as she held her breath and rolled down her window to stick her head outside.

"Goodness," she said weakly, sticking her head farther outside.

"I think I'm going to have to have my truck steam cleaned and sanitized," Slade said, his voice choked.

"I think I'm going to have to have my nasal passages steam cleaned," Taylor replied with a giggle followed by a gag. "But remember it was your idea to bring him with us. I wanted to leave him at home."

"It would've been worse when you got home and he needed to get out." Slade slowly made his way to the end of the row then stopped. "What now?"

"Edge along the right curb there." Taylor

pointing the way. "Park in that spot in the far corner, or maybe the one beside it, because that's probably where the kidnappers parked."

"Why are you so sure?" Slade turned right and drove along the curb, before parking at the west end of the building beside the first spot.

Taylor turned in the seat to look at him. "Because the more I think about it, the more I know this had to be an inside job. It was too cleanly done. If it wasn't someone who works at the hotel, someone who *resides* at the hotel was involved. I interviewed most of the staff who were on duty, and they are clear."

"*Appear* to be clear," Slade corrected. Just because she'd talked to them one time, did not mean they were clear. "Everyone is still a suspect as far as I'm concerned. I need to get Dex to pull an employee list so you can help me go through it."

"I have the list in my box in the car. I had one in my desk, so I slid it in there before I left," Taylor informed and Slade's eyes flew to hers.

She'd stolen employee records?

Well that wasn't any worse than stealing laundry by telling the Asian man at the dry cleaner they'd accidentally sent in the wrong bundle that morning. The lie had tripped off of her tongue as casually as if she'd been talking about the weather.

In this case that was a very good and resourceful thinking on her part. It would save them a lot of time, but still gave him pause. The only thing

60

he hadn't done was a background check on her to make sure she was clearance-worthy and trustworthy. He'd put Dex on that tomorrow.

"Good, I'll get it from you when I drop you off at your car later," Slade said, as he got out of the Humvee and opened the back door to let Lola out. Buddy lunged toward the door behind her, but Slade pointed a finger. "Buddy, *sitz!*" He was surprised when the dog dropped down on his haunches. "Good boy," he praised, then grabbed the small boy's shirt from the seat before shutting the door.

When he and Lola walked around the front of the vehicle, Taylor leaned out the window. "Stay on the west side of the door. The door is in that camera's range."

Slade followed the finger she pointed with his eyes to the other end of the lot where he saw a camera mounted on the light pole. He had no plans at all to go near the building, and he doubted anyone would be concerned with a stray dog out back sniffing around even if they did see her in the camera.

Bending, he let Lola sniff the shirt, until she looked back up at him. "*Suche*, Lola." Lola jogged off toward the building zigzagging with her nose near the ground and Slade stood.

"What language is that and what did you tell her?" Taylor asked.

"She's trained in German," he replied, watching Lola stop to sniff around cars as she made her way closer to the back door. "I told her to track or find that scent."

"Why German? Because she's a German Shepherd?"

Slade focused on watching for cues from Lola that would tell him she found something, but he couldn't help but laugh. "No, because her breeder was in Germany, so she was used to it when the trainer got her. It's good too because not many people in the middle east speak German."

"She was a military dog?" Taylor asked surprised.

Slade glanced back at her then found Lola again. His heart squeezed, and he sent up a prayer of thanks that she'd survived. "Lieutenant Lola was one of the best multi-purpose explosive sniffing dogs in the service, and I was lucky enough to be her handler."

"Multi-purpose?" she repeated curiously, but Slade zoned in on Lola who stopped, sniffed closer then barked sharply near a sleek black Mercedes parked in the second row back from the rear door of the hotel. The strange thing was with her posture, the high-pitched tone of the single bark, Lola was cueing for a bomb, not telling him she'd found where the kid's scent which she'd been following ended.

Adrenaline pumped through him as Slade jogged across the parking lot, staying out of camera range. He knew he would be seen though when he got to where Lola was standing, so he crouched to duck-walk around the rear of the cars until he stopped beside her. She looked up at him and Slade could practically feel the excitement buzzing from her. Putting her nose at the rear tire she sniffed again, ran her snout along the fender, then along frame of the vehicle all the way to the front tire. With confidence, she stepped back and barked again telling him she was sure.

Sickness curled in his gut, his heart pounded and his ears rang, but Slade made himself inspect inside the tire well. When he found it clear, he finally breathed again, but he knew there was either a bomb or residue from one in or around this car. Lola did not make mistakes, had only ever made one as long as he'd been her handler.

Tension twisted his insides as the buzzing in his ears got louder, but Slade took two deep breaths and fought it. Lying flat, he eased his head under the car to scan the undercarriage. None of the light from the flood lights in the parking lot reached under the car so it was dark, but Slade had excellent night vision. He couldn't be a hundred percent sure until he had a flashlight, but from what he could see it was clean too. Pushing back up he knelt beside Lola and scratched behind her ears.

"Good girl," he praised, and she licked his palm.

Something was fishy with this car and he was going to find out what that was as soon as he could get his flashlight from the Hummer, but he needed Lola back on task to figure out where that kid was taken and if any of these cars was involved.

He pulled Zami's shirt from his back pocket and held it out to her again. She buried her nose in the material and sniffed several places.

"Lola, *arbeit—suche!*"

Lola sniffed the ground and zigzagged through the cars and Slade duck-walked to the rear of the car then turned and bumped into a pair of compact, but shapely legs in tight black yoga pants.

"What did she find?" Taylor asked, putting her hands on her curvy hips to look down at him. "That's the prince's car, but he doesn't drive it. He usually has one of his security guys drive for him."

"I told you to stay in the truck," Slade grated, pushing up to his feet.

"I wanted to tell you it looks like Mr. Baker finally installed those other cameras. Probably to show the prince he was *doing* something." She pointed at the light pole at the west end of the building. "They've seen you, so we probably should get out of here."

At that second, the back door flew open to slam against the brick wall at the same time shouts came from the east end of the hotel as two men ran around the corner. Slade pushed Taylor and she ran for the Humvee.

"Lola, *lass es—heir—schnell!*" he shouted as he ran behind her. *Leave it. Come, and hurry up about it, baby.* Slade didn't speed to a full out run until he saw her dart from behind a car and sprint across the lot toward the Humvee.

Taylor slung open her door and was inside and buckled in by the time he let Lola into the back and got behind the wheel. As he cranked the SUV the two dark-suited men who came out of the back door got into the black Mercedes that Lola had hit on as two other men, hotel guards most likely, ran across the parking lot toward the Humvee.

When Slade threw the Hummer into gear and slammed his foot down on the accelerator, he heard the sirens. Going back through the parking lot wasn't going to work, he thought, as he sped to the west end of the hotel, then gritted his teeth as he hopped the curb to go out across the vacant field behind the hotel.

"What are you doing?!?" Taylor asked gripping the handle above the door.

"Getting out of here before the cops get here and we spend the night in jail for trespassing." Suddenly every hair on his body stood on end as an energy he recognized well filled the cab through the partially open windows, right before the Hummer rocked and his ears rang from the explosion.

Hot air rushed into the windows and debris pinged on the roof and hood of the Humvee. Buddy whined, Lola whimpered, and Slade wasn't sure, but he thought he did too. His chest felt like someone tightened a vise on it, tightening it inch by inch, sweat beads popped out on his forehead and slid across his scalp. He couldn't breathe as his vision curled in on him, but he knew he couldn't stop.

"You're going to have to drive," he said breathlessly, pounding a fist on his chest trying to loosen it. "When we get into that parking lot we'll switch."

Taylor snorted. "That's a first. A man asking—" she said, then stopped to study what he knew must be his paper white face. "Are you okay?" she asked, putting her hand on his shoulder.

"No, I'm not okay," Slade pushed out past his constricted vocal chords.

A bead of sweat streaked down his left temple into his eye to burn as he glanced in the rearview and saw flames lighting up the lot. The two hotel guards picked themselves up from the pavement looking stunned as they staggered back toward the building.

Lola leaned between the seats to lay her head on his shoulder. Her wet tongue washed his neck then his jaw and he tried to focus, but it was getting tough. Somehow he managed to jump the curb and pull the SUV to a stop at the side of the convenience store just as the buzzing occluded every other sound.

Taylor opened his door, Slade slid out, and she helped him stagger around the vehicle to the passenger side. His legs felt like rubber, and he wanted to collapse beside the Hummer and curl into a ball until it was over, but he forced himself inside and she shut the door. Slade bent over, pressed his hands to the sides of his skull and rocked as the fireworks started. He felt the vehicle rock too as she pulled out of the store lot onto the road, but couldn't focus on anything but the repeats of the explosion in his head.

"I've got this. Lean your seat back, and breathe deep, Slade. Try to relax," Taylor instructed, putting her hand on his thigh for a second, but Slade could barely hear her. He fumbled for the seat release and after a few tries it laid back.

"Lola help him," she said and suddenly Lola stood on the console between the seats then moved to lay across his lap and nudge him with her head. He put one forearm over his eyes and dropped his other hand down to her head to rub her fur between her ears.

Slade fought the nausea that rolled in his stomach. "I'm sorry."

"No need to be sorry. I'm used to this," she replied, and Slade figured that was from her former boyfriend who had PTSD. Right then, he realized she probably also recognized his episode at her house. Him falling apart during a tense situation was a scary fucking thing, and could have been deadly to them both.

Yeah, he definitely need a session with his doctor, and maybe a bump in his meds. He just wondered what was triggering all this other than the explosion? The first episode came before the explosion. *Goddamn, he thought he had it beat.*

After a few minutes, the Hummer went up an incline and he figured they were getting onto the interstate. The engine roar came into focus in his mind and Slade realized Taylor Kinkaid was pushing the SUV as hard as she could. A good thing under the circumstances but he had no idea how competent she was behind the wheel.

"Slow down some," he said, weakly. "Don't draw attention to us. We don't know if they got our plate number, or if they're following, but I guarantee they got a description of the vehicle.
Hopefully, the explosion distracted them, but take the next exit so we can use the surface roads just in case."

"I don't know which surface road to take. You haven't told me where we're going. My car is still at your office," she replied with a huffed breath.

"Just hit the GPS and pick home. It's better if you stay out at the compound for a few days anyway. We need to regroup in the morning."

He heard beeps and relaxed a little when the electronic voice gave her the first instruction. Closing his eyes, Slade relaxed and Lola stroked his wrist with her muzzle. The buzzing finally lessened, the fireworks stopped and exhaustion seeped into every muscle in his body making him feel melted into the seat. They drove for a few more minutes, and Slade finally felt the decline as she took the vehicle off the interstate.

"Feeling better?" Taylor asked with concern, and what sounded to be frustration when the GPS said it was recalculating.

"Define better," Slade asked with a dry laugh.

"Buzzing in your head gone? You in the

present with me?" Taylor replied.

"Yeah, it's gone. Sorry, I fell apart on you." Slade huffed a breath, and gritted his teeth. He did not talk about this shit. Ever. But he felt like he owed her an explanation and some kind of reassurance he wasn't a liability. "It hasn't happened in a couple of years. I don't know why it did now but I'll find out tomorrow when I talk to my doctor."

"I don't know what caused it either, but we need to make sure you have a handle on it before you go into action again. That could cause major problems, and you probably should tell your boss about it."

Anger surged through him at her condescending, superior tone. Telling him what he needed to do like she was an expert. Slade could guarantee that she wasn't. She might have had passing exposure to the problem with her ex-boyfriend, but he could guarantee this woman hadn't ever walked a mile in his boots, dealt with the situation firsthand from his up-close-and-personal perspective. So there was no *we* in this equation.

"My boss is on his honeymoon, and can't be reached. I'm in charge of Deep Six right now, and I'll handle this the way I need to." That didn't include discussing it with her, with Logan or anyone other than his doctor. Slade gathered himself, shoved Lola away and jerked the handle to bring the seat upright again. "I'd appreciate you not mentioning this to anyone, including Logan. I assure you it won't happen again."

Slade knew it was an empty assurance, but he didn't need everyone in the company knowing this happened. They'd all either be mothering him, or would be worried that Logan had made a mistake leaving him in charge. Right now Slade needed their confidence in his decisions, and cohesiveness in the team if they had any hope of finding that kid alive. The bomb in that car, probably one wired into the ignition, said these players were serious, and it looked like the kid wasn't the only target.

CHAPTER SIX

"I need to go by my house tomorrow to get some clothes," Taylor commented, as she pulled the Humvee to a stop at the call box by the tall razor-wire topped gate. They'd driven out of town for nearly two hours, and she was damned glad to finally be at their destination according to the GPS. The gate disappeared into climbing vines and scrub, but she could see it was attached to an equally tall razor-wire-edged fence.

Slade had called it a *compound*, but this place looked more like a very secluded prison. Taylor saw lights beyond the fence, but couldn't see buildings because of the black plastic strips that were woven through the holes in the gate.

"Zero six hundred," Slade growled.

Taylor eyes swung to him. "We don't have to go at six in the morning! Just after the meeting some time is—"

"*No*, I'm saying that's the code for the gate," he replied, without looking at her. "Cee Cee probably left some clothes here you can wear. I'll look in Logan's room when we get inside."

"I thought you said his wife was Susan."

Taylor rolled down her window to lean out and punch in the code. The gate swung inward and she let off of the brake. When she drove through the gate, it rattled closed behind her and she stopped to stare in awe at the high-tech military looking buildings scattered around the compound.

"Center one on the right side," he grumbled, and Taylor steered that way.

"This is pretty impressive. What is this place?" she asked, pulling to a stop in the farthest parking spot beside another black Humvee.

"This is mission control. We work out of here more than the office in town," Slade replied, opening his door.

"Do you live here too? The GPS said home?" Taylor got out and let Buddy out of the back door on her side. Slade was on the other side letting Lola out.

"I do most of the time," he replied grumpily as he slammed the door and walked toward the porch with Lola on his heels.

Buddy wasn't nearly so well-disciplined. He sniffed the ground as he lazily followed her to the porch before stopping to sniff the post at the bottom of the steps where he promptly turned, raised his leg and peed.

"*No*, Buddy!" Taylor screeched, reaching for his collar to tug on it.

"It's fine, he's a dog and he's been locked up in that vehicle for hours. Lola probably needs to go too." Slade dropped his hand from the door knob to turn and point toward the yard. "Lola, *geh raus!*"

Buddy looked up at him curiously, but Lola trotted down the steps and headed off toward a long building to the left. Buddy squirmed looking after her, then back to Slade. "Buddy, *geh raus!*" he said, and laughed when the lab sprang into action to follow after Lola.

Taylor watched Buddy catch up to Lola and follow behind her to sniff around for the perfect place to use the bathroom, then looked back to Slade who was standing at the top of the steps watching them too.

"You amaze me," she said with awe. Buddy listened to Slade as if by instinct knowing he was in command. Slade's face relaxed and his white teeth showed in the porch light. Something inside Taylor shifted, and her eyes dropped there. Seeing him relaxed after being in the throes of hell after that explosion was a relief.

"You know there's a new therapy for that other than meds right?" she asked, and his brow puckered as his eyes slid to hers. "For your *problem*. It's called EMDR and the military has even embraced it. Mark went to a therapist in Dallas and got better in just a few treatments. Of course, he did it on his own, so the military didn't find out."

Until he almost choked her one night when he was having an episode and didn't remember it, he refused to admit he had a problem but she wasn't going to tell Slade that.

Taylor was just going to encourage him to get help before his got to that level. She'd done the research for Mark, and found the newly approved treatment. At least Slade knew and admitted he had a problem, and he'd been getting help evidently. Mark had ignored it for several years after he came back from deployment. Several years of hell for her until the final incident.

"They have a fucking acronym for everything," he said with disgust.

"It stands Eye Movement Desensitization and Reprocessing, and it's like biofeedback therapy. Mark really made quick prog—"

His lips curled over his teeth to pinch into a white line. "So, you've known me what eighteen hours and you've got me diagnosed and treated? Did your pre-law degree from Oklahoma State University come with a therapist license too, Ms. Kincaid?" he asked coldly.

Taylor's stomach turned at hearing basically the same words Mark had spoken to her when she tried to point out his problem. "No, it didn't, but trust me when I tell you I understand."

"No, trust *me*—until you've been to war and seen your whole damned squad turned to confetti because you fucked up, you will *never* understand." Slade turned back toward the door. "Lola, *heir*!" he shouted gruffly, and she saw a tremor shake his big body.

Shock and empathy filled her as his words rang in her head like the sound of the explosion had earlier. He was right she would never understand that situation firsthand, and was thankful for that. She could not imagine having to live with that event playing over and over in her head, much less having to witness it with her own eyes.

It had to be horrific, debilitating, and would surely bring even the strongest of men to their knees. But he was still alive, even though his men were dead. Slade needed to forgive himself, and accept that. Like he said though, she was not a therapist. Evidently, he'd been talking to a doctor and that was a good thing. All she could do was causally bring up the new therapy she'd researched again when he wasn't in such a volatile mood.

Lola shot across the yard with Buddy on her tail, and scrambled up the steps just as Slade opened the door and went inside. Taylor followed them inside and shut the door. The first thing that caught her notice was the enormous television mounted to the wall in what had to be the living room. A huge plush sectional sofa cordoned off the area. Slade walked past the area and disappeared into a hallway. She had no idea where he expected her to go, so she went to the sofa and sat down. Buddy came over and hopped up on the sofa beside her, but she shoved him back to the floor.

"Buddy, *sitz!*" she said, trying to mimic the tone she'd heard Slade use.

To her surprise, the lab sat down between the sofa and coffee table, then dropped down to rest his head on her right shoe. Taylor picked up the remote control to turn on the television, but it had so many buttons she had no idea which one turned on the big screen.

The ten o'clock news should be on and she was curious what was being said about the explosion at the hotel, about the two Arab guards who had to be killed in it. After a few failed attempts, she found a larger button on the left side of the control and pressed it. The television came to life, and thank goodness it was already on the local news channel so she tossed the remote on the table and sat back to watch.

Twenty minutes into the program, she sat up straighter when the anchor announced he had late breaking news about an explosion and fire at a downtown hotel. Taylor wanted to bite her nails through the two minutes of commercials she had to watch until the anchor reappeared and cut to a reporter on the scene who was standing in the parking lot.

"ATF agents and FBI are on scene now at an explosion that happened at this hotel earlier tonight. Two men were killed, and one other injured in the explosion. Authorities believe it may have been an attempt on the life of Saudi Prince Ahmed Khalil who is in residency at the hotel. A hotel security guard who managed to escape injury in the blast believes a former employee and a German man may be to blame, but authorities are still investigating."

"They think I'm German?" Slade commented with a harsh laugh.

Taylor jumped, her heart pounding at what she'd just heard. "They recognized *me* and think I tried to *kill* the prince!" Acid pushed up to burn in her throat, so she swallowed hard and turned to look up at him. "We've got to call the authorities and explain what we were doing there!"

His eyebrow lifted. "You want to spend the night in jail? And another week being interrogated by the feds?"

"No, but—" Taylor replied.

"That's what will happen, and we don't have time for it. We need to focus on finding that kid, who I'm sure the authorities weren't told was kidnapped, and figure out who planted that explosive and why." Slade pulled his cell phone out of his pocket and pressed a speed dial number. "I'll call Levi to bring your car out here. The cops will find it in the lot at the office and tie you to Deep Six if we don't."

Taylor groaned as she listened while Slade spouted off instructions. After hanging up with Levi, he called Dex and gave him an update and instructions, including the names of the men he wanted assembled at the compound in the morning. When he hung up, he looked at her.

"We can't go back to your house, until this is over. The feds are probably there turning it upside down right now. Let's just hope the guards or cameras didn't get the plate number on the Hummer."

"My car keys are in my purse," Taylor said, picking it up from the seat beside her.

"Levi is in town and doesn't need keys." Slade cleared his throat. "He'll work it out."

Her heart shot to her throat. She'd just paid the last note on that car, and did not need it damaged. "Work it out? As in hotwire it?" From her experience at the sheriff's office in Oklahoma, Taylor knew what stolen cars that had been hotwired looked like when they were recovered.

"Yeah, he's good at it. Don't worry, he'll fix whatever he breaks." As if that were that on the subject, Slade walked toward the front door, and Lola followed him. "Just get some rest and we'll hit the ground running in the morning."

He actually thought she could sleep? And why was he going back outside?

This man was not leaving her here by herself!

"Where are you going?" Taylor asked pushing up from the sofa. At the door he stopped to look back at her.

"To my apartment at the barracks. The sofa will probably be more comfortable for you than the bunks in the barracks and I know at least two of the guys are out there tonight. I'm sure you don't want to sleep in the bunk below Caleb, hell, even in the same room with him. He snores like a freight train." He gave a chin nod at the sofa. "The right end of the sofa pulls out into a bed. Just move the coffee table. Sheets and blankets are in the closet in the laundry room on the other side of the kitchen."

Taylor was a crack shot, and more than able

to defend herself in an altercation. But she didn't have her pistol with her. That was at her house, probably being confiscated by the FBI at this very moment, and as tired as she was she probably couldn't ball her hand into a fist much less fight anyone.

"I'd rather not be alone over here," she admitted, her voice not hiding her fear or her exhaustion.

Slade blew out a breath and studied her for a moment, before he ran a hand over his beard-shadowed jaw. "Fine, come with me then. I couldn't find extra clothes for you, and I'm too tired to think. I can't sleep in Logan's quarters though, because he'd kill me."

He opened the door and walked out leaving it open. Taylor quickly ran behind him, and shut the door behind her, but heard a whimper and remembered Buddy. She opened it back up and he shot past her to chase after Lola and Slade who were already halfway across the yard. Thank goodness she had on her sneakers, she thought, as she hustled down the steps. With his extremely long legs and ground-eating stride, Taylor had to run to catch up to him too.

It was a long walk to the barracks on the other side of the compound, and Taylor was out of breath by the time she stopped beside Slade at the door while he punched in a security code. Seeing that they had tight security at the compound made her feel a lot more confident that there would be no surprise raids by the feds while they were sleeping. If she was to be arrested and sent to federal prison she would at least see them coming. At the thought, the acid in her stomach turned into a brick and sank down to cramp lower.

Slade opened the door and it was dark inside the building. Reaching inside, he flipped on the lights then pushed the door open and stood aside so she and the dogs could enter. "The sleeping quarters are over there through that door." He pointed to a six-panel wood door on the other side of the office chairs and huge conference room table which must serve as both the dining room and a meeting area. "Let's see who all is here tonight."

The tiredness in his voice was echoed in her body as he walked to door and flung it open to walk inside. Taylor followed behind him, and when she walked through the door to stand beside Slade her eyes landed on three men who sat in hard wooden chairs in front of a small television in their underwear playing a video game.

With muttered curses, they scrambled. One jerked a blanket off a cot and wrapped it around him, while another grabbed a towel. The third ran for his cot to jerk his jeans up to hold them in front of him.

"Think you could knock buddy? Or at least tell us you have a woman with you?" the tallest, leanly muscled guy who picked the blanket to cover himself asked angrily.

"What the hell are *you* doing here?" Caleb asked. She recognized him because he was one of the Deep Six guys who'd worked on the security detail at the hotel.

Taylor gathered up her courage and blew out a breath. "I work for Deep Six now," she announced walking further into the room drawing gasps and groans from all three men. The sofa over at the other building was looking better and better by the moment than bunking with these men who, from their expressions, did not want her in here.

Now, this is exactly how she'd always imagined the offices of Deep Six Security would look, Taylor thought, as she walked down the aisle, her eyes ticking over each of the three sets of bunk beds. She'd just about nailed things all the way down to the razor wire topping the fence that surrounded the compound.

The sleeping quarters reminded her of her dorm in college, only less private and filled with a lot more testosterone. She had survived the quad room at OKU for four years, she could survive this.

"Which bunk is open?" she stopped to ask.

"None of them," Caleb replied shortly, and her eyes flew to his, but he was glaring over her shoulder at Slade who stood behind her by the door. The man's tone, his posture and his attitude told her he didn't want her here, but that was too damned bad.

"Levi, Mac and Dex are coming out here later so they're not late for the meeting in the morning.

Slade should know that since he told Dex to get all of us out here. I don't think it's appropriate for you to be sleeping in here with us anyway."

"Well, I for one don't mind if she sleeps in here," the man wrapped in the blanket announced with a grin as he walked over to her to stick out his hand. "I'm Hawk, the company pilot. And who are you ma'am?"

Taylor forced a tight smile and took his hand. When he shook it firmly, her smile and attitude softened. "Taylor Kincaid," she replied then lifted a brow. "Do all the guys at this company only have one name?"

"Legends only need one name, sweetheart," he replied arrogantly, but his eyes sparked with humor and male interest. "Superman, Flash, Zorro."

"Bullwinkle? Bozo?" Taylor added with a laugh, even though she could almost believe his assertion. Every one of the men who worked for Deep Six were not only muscled out to the max, they were all damned good looking in a rough and capable kind of way.

But she knew they weren't hired for their looks.

Dave Logan wouldn't give a crap if they were good looking. He'd want capable men with exceptional skills. Deep Six Security wouldn't be as well funded as they appeared to be, or as well thought of in the security sector, otherwise. Taylor realized then Hawk hadn't let her hand go, so she pulled it back to wipe it on her thigh.

He winked at her and turned to drop his arm over her shoulders. She heard Slade growl, but Hawk didn't seem to care as he led her down the aisle to his bunk. "I tell you what…since I'm so nice, I'll let you share my bunk tonight." Hawk cut his eyes at Caleb, who glared at them from over by the television. "I'll even loan you my ear plugs so you don't have to hear grumpy over there snore."

"Cut the crap, Hawkins. I'm tired and I don't have time for it." Slade's words sliced through the thick honey in Hawk's words like a knife.

And she did not want to cause trouble here tonight. It was not the way she wanted to start her new job. "As tempting as that offer sounds, *Hawk*," Taylor said with a laugh as she slid out from under his arm. "I don't think that's a good way to start my new job here. I think I will just go back over to the office and sleep on the sofa."

"I'm sure *Slade* has a few other ideas as to where you can bed down, since he brought you over here knowing all the bunks were full," the other guy said as he stepped into his jeans and dragged them up his legs.

"Fletch don't start," Hawk said, the humor in his tone gone.

The man stood back up and pinned Hawk with his eyes while he buttoned and zipped his jeans. "Slade sure is hiring a lot of females, and you know as well as I do, the likely reason he's doing it, Hawkins."

His nasty, insinuating laugh sliced right through Taylor. "Dexter said another one will be here at the end of the week too, so he's probably setting himself up for a twofer."

"Yes, Cee Cee Logan will be here at the end of the week," Slade confirmed with a snarl. "So I'd suggest your change your attitude, Fletcher, and get with the program, show a little respect, or I'll hand your ass to you, along with your pink slip."

Although Taylor would be glad to have another woman to interact with here, she did not like how this man was talking. Like they were token hires, because they were female, and Slade was some kind of degenerate. *A twofer?* This man was not only being nasty to her, he was confusing as well.

"Who is Cee Cee?" she asked, folding her arms over her breasts, where Hawk's eyes appeared to be glued.

"Logan's younger sister," Hawk informed, dragging his eyes up to hers. "She's been trying to get a job with Deep Six forever, and we really need her now. I'm glad Slade hired her."

"The reason Logan didn't want to hire women is because of this exact situation," Fletch said with a short bark of laughter. "We don't need liabilities that will distract us from our job, disrupt our operation, so Slade can get a booty call."

That did it. Taylor had enough. This man wanted a pissing contest with her? Well, he'd just bought himself one, she thought, as her arms floated to her sides and she walked over to Fletch to stare up into his eyes, but Slade suddenly pushed her aside to stand toe to toe with the man. Anger radiated off of him in waves, and was mimicked in the low, throaty growl Lola emitted right behind him.

"I hired her because she's *qualified* and we need her help. Probably more qualified than *you*. I hired Cecelia for the same reason, and if I *ever* hear you say something like that again, I promise I'll be finding a female replacement for *you* on this team. Do you understand?"

Fletch's face turned bright red and his eyes flamed as Slade stepped back. Hawk groaned, and she couldn't be sure, but she thought she heard Caleb cough.

"Yeah, I understand," Fletch said angrily, as he snatched his shirt up from the floor and pulled it over his head. "I'm going to sleep in my fucking truck, so she can take my bed."

"*No*, I'll make other arrangements," Slade said sharply, grabbing her arm. "Get some sleep, Fletcher, because we have a goat fuck on our hands and I need you sharp for tomorrow. Change that attitude by morning though, or you can drive that truck right out of here because I don't need your crap." With that, Slade turned and shoved her toward the door.

CHAPTER SEVEN

Slade couldn't sleep. It was no wonder either, because even as thickly padded and carpeted as the floor was in his bedroom, there was still concrete beneath the padding. The carpet was the rough Berber variety, easily cleaned when mud was tracked over it which happened often, but rough as sandpaper to his skin. Efficient, but certainly not suited for sleeping.

And Buddy still made low mournful sounds from the kennel in the other room, which was what had driven him to the bedroom in the first place. Well, that and the fact his body was too long, his shoulders too wide to get comfortable on the small sofa out there.

Taylor Kincaid was tiny enough to sleep on that sofa, but he just couldn't make himself make her sleep there. His mother had drilled chivalry into his skull since he was a kid, until it was firmly implanted in his psyche, so Taylor was sleeping peacefully a few feet away in his fucking king-sized, memory-foam-padded bed, making soft purring sounds that set his teeth on edge. Rolling over, Slade punched the hard sofa pillow to tenderize it and sighed loudly as he dragged the thin cotton blanket up to his shoulders.

The main reason he couldn't sleep though was his freaking brain wouldn't shut off trying to work out the puzzle that was this kidnapping. That bomb in the prince's car said other factors were in play in the situation. Factors that just didn't make sense. Was the assassination attempt connected to the kidnapping somehow?

The timing was awfully suspect.

With Deep Six gone and the two Arab guards dead, the whole family was vulnerable now to more attempts on their lives unless Prince Khalil hired more security. His mind was probably fucked and that was the last thing he was thinking about though, and maybe that was the goal.

Whatever the reason, Slade needed to try to talk to the prince and convince him the family needed to move out of that hotel. The prince was wealthy, he could afford to rent a secure location somewhere else. That's what needed to happen because they were sitting ducks where they were and he had no idea who was behind all this.

What were the odds the man would listen to him however? Slade had no evidence, the prince blamed Deep Six for allowing the kidnapping, and he was harboring Taylor who was probably wanted for the bombing here. The odds were less than zero that Prince Khalil would listen to anything he had to say, but he was going to try.

He needed Grayson to locate the prince's accounts and keep an eye on them. They needed to know when that ransom money transferred and to whom. That would lead them to the kidnappers and probably the kid. Hopefully, before he was killed, if that was the plan.

The bed covers rustled and a soft moan drew Slade's eyes to the bed. "You can sleep up here you know," Taylor offered in a sexy, sleep-slurred voice, and Slade bit back a groan as temptation clawed at his insides.

God, that's all he needed. To be in that bed with her, feeling her nails raking down his back, hearing her soft moans as he drove into her tight little body. That would solve all of his present problems from the adrenaline crash he was suffering. But it would create so many more.

Slade didn't know much about Taylor Kincaid, but he suspected she was not a fuck buddy type of woman—the only kind he wanted.

Her offer just now was for a slice of the bed, not a slice of her. In the frame of mind he was at the moment, if he crawled up in that bed with her, he knew he'd try to change her mind. There was not a line of her perfectly curved body he hadn't inventoried with his eyes when she changed into those second-skin yoga pants at her house.

The adrenaline crash would pass, but crossing the line with a woman not on the same page as he would not. In the morning, he'd take care of things in the shower and the fire scorching his insides would be gone. Besides, he was not about to give credence to Fletcher's assertion that he'd hired her for a booty call, even if she *was* that kind of woman.

Nope, he was staying right here on the floor where he belonged, even if he didn't get a minute's sleep tonight. He craned his neck to see the green digital display on his alarm clock on the nightstand and saw the night was already half gone.

You've slept in much worse places, man. Close your eyes and clear your head.

Forcing his eyes shut, Slade focused on relaxing his tense muscles from his toes up to his head. When he got to his face, he also mentally clicked off the switch in his brain by focusing intently on the first time he met Lola when she wasn't much more than a puppy. The feel of her soft, but coarse fur as his palm glided over it, the warmth of her wet tongue as it flicked out to lick his chin. His breath left him on a sigh, as he finally found relaxation.

The hum of the ceiling fan lulled Slade deeper into his subconscious. Flashes of the exciting days of working with the trainer and Lola at the center in Yuma floated through his mind. It only took five weeks for them to become a combat explosives detection team, but took two more years in Iraq for them to become best friends and known as the best team in the corps.

Their next deployment was to Afghanistan, and things were okay at first. But then his field commander was promoted, and Slade was put on point for his squad in the field. Put in charge of making decisions for them, deciding on entry strategy and positions, *and* clearing buildings for safe entry.

That changed everything.

It wasn't just a matter of being one of the

guys then, and focusing on what he and Lola did best. Keeping them all safe, by using what seemed to be psychic intuition to identify where tangos would set booby traps and IEDs. No, he'd become so good at that the military wanted more from him. That distraction proved to be fatal for his squad, and almost for him and Lola too.

The tension in his body ratcheted up and his teeth clenched as he fought to keep those images from his dreams, tried to rewind to the training exercises, playing with Lola in that sunny field in Yuma, but there was no going back. He'd crossed that line in his thoughts and images of the mud village in Badakhshan Province gripped him.

Because the intel was supposedly fresh and they were in the area, his squad was sent in at night to find insurgents who were named as responsible for the massacre of a group of aid workers. As it turned out, the intel wasn't fresh as usual. The village appeared to be a ghost town when they arrived, but they had to clear every building to know that for sure.

He and Lola worked through every house and found only a few devices. The entry team gave the explosives wide berth as they cleared the buildings then marked them for detonation crews who would come behind them. Because it would take the longest, they saved the largest mud house in the village for last.

It was nearly sunrise when they finally got to it, and Lola was just as exhausted as the men in the squad, as him. How was she to know there was a second device set up very close to the first one? The scent would've been the same, her alerts would have been the same so he wouldn't have known either. But that didn't make what happened any easier to swallow. It had been his responsibility to keep those men safe and he'd failed them.

Slade gave his men the location of the first device, when he and Lola exited. The squad entered to clear the building and managed to avoid the first device. He set up men to guard the entry team outside, and took up position at the house next door. Close enough to see the stunned expressions on the faces of those men he'd set up directly outside that building to guard the men inside when the second device detonated. Close enough to watch in slow motion as their bodies flew through the air until large chunks of debris fractured his skull, broke bones in his face and slammed him to the ground.

He wouldn't find out until he woke up at the hospital in Germany that the only survivors were him, Lola and the three lucky men he ordered to guard the entrance of the village. Lola was at the vet hospital getting treatment for her injuries, and it was uncertain whether she would have to be euthanized.

Slade wished right then they'd euthanize him. But he was left alive to suffer knowing that he'd killed those men as surely as if he'd set that device himself. To suffer through multiple surgeries to reconstruct his face, shore up his skull and then months of treatments to learn how to function again, to even take a piss on his own. Why that injury couldn't take *those* memories from him like it had his mother's face for a while, he didn't know.

Because you deserve to remember, to live with the hell of seeing those faces imprinted in your mind forever.

"Slade, *wake* up!" an anxious female voice shouted, dragging him from his agony.

As consciousness finally came, the rawness in his throat told him he must've been screaming. A bead of sweat streaked down his neck, and he realized he was drenched. His body shook and his teeth chattered as he heard frantic scratching at his bedroom door that said Lola must've heard him too. He'd locked her out of the bedroom because he knew she'd end up in bed with Taylor Kincaid, where she normally slept with him, if he let her inside.

"Lo-lo-la" he croaked weakly, and tried to get up, but Taylor pushed his shoulder back to the carpet and rose to walk to the door.

"Get in the bed, Slade," she commanded, as she opened the door and Lola dashed inside to run over and bathe his face and neck with kisses. A tremor shook his hand as he raised it to scratch between her ears when she rubbed her face against his shoulder. Inch by inch, his body relaxed, and his breathing slowed.

"I *said* get in the bed!" Taylor repeated, pointing at the bed as she glared down at him like a very sexy little general in her bra and a scrap of lace that posed as underwear.

When she turned toward the bed and climbed up, he saw the cheeks of her perfectly round ass were dissected by a thin scrap of black elastic. He could not climb in that bed in the condition he was in right now, because there wouldn't be much sleeping going on. His heart was fucking racing now, and he had enough adrenaline going to power all of Dallas.

But she leaned over the bed to look down at him. "Put Lola back out in the living room, close that door and get in this bed with me." When he still just stared up at her, Taylor's lips pinched. "*Now*, Slade! I know exactly what you need. This is not my first rodeo, and you are not the first man I've helped through it."

Shock and more than a little excitement launched him up to sit. "Sex would definitely help, but are you sure you want to go there?" Lola sat beside him to look up at Taylor too. Slade was more than onboard with that idea, but he needed to make sure before he climbed up in that bed she knew tomorrow morning there would be no roses or promises. This was not his first rodeo either. "I have to warn you, I don't do anything other than casual sex."

Her brows slammed together. "I wasn't talking about sex, I was talking about a massage." She huffed a breath and rolled her eyes. "I saw some baby oil in the bathroom earlier, so go get it before you get in bed. And take your clothes off."

A delicious shiver zipped down his spine to the end of his now painfully engorged dick. He had never had a woman give him a massage before, and the idea was titillating if it led to sex, but knowing it would only lead to sensual torture in this situation gave him pause.

Maybe it would help though. At the very least he wouldn't be thinking about war zones and explosions for a little while. Pushing up to his feet, Slade pulled his shirt away from his sweaty body.

"I need a shower first." *And I need to knock the edge off of this need clawing in my gut before I let you put those tiny little hands of yours on my body, or we're both going to be in deep trouble since your offer doesn't include sex.*

"You don't need to shower, it's nearly three in the morning," she growled, sitting up on her knees, disappointing him when she dragged the covers up to her chin. She snapped a finger toward the bathroom. "What you need is to relax, so just get the damned oil so we both can get some sleep!"

Slade studied her a minute, then with a huffed breath stripped his shirt over his head and dropped it to the floor. The way her eyes locked on his midsection had his muscles there contracting, his zipper cutting into his cock.

Yeah, relaxation was definitely not going to be on the menu once she touched him, but from the look on her face he knew she wasn't taking no for an answer. And who was he to say no to a woman who wanted to touch him? Especially the sexy Little General sitting in his bed issuing orders. With a heavy breath, he turned to the door, let Lola out then strode toward the bathroom to get the oil.

When Slade returned to the bedroom, Taylor threw the covers back with a whoosh and knelt on the bed. All the blood in his body rushed to his cock, because although the room was dark, the light from the bathroom landed like a spotlight on the creamy skin of her upper body. The cups of her bra, which was as skimpy as the thong underwear he'd noticed earlier, barely covered her nipples and lifted her breasts up like a visual buffet for him.

For a small woman, her full breasts were definitely not proportional and his mouth watered to taste them. His fingers curled around the bottle of oil tightly. Biting back a groan, he quickly handed her the bottle of oil and turned his back to shuck his jeans. He wrapped the towel he'd grabbed around his waist, before removing his underwear, because the last thing he wanted was for her to see how damned hard he was, harder now from the sight of her in that big bed waiting for him.

This was the worst idea in the world, he thought, as he knelt on the bed, laid flat like she instructed. She crawled to the end of the bed as he buried his face in the pillow that smelled like her now. Soft and flowery, clean and womanly. How in the fuck was he going to sleep in this bed again and not think about her sleeping in it? Changing the sheets tomorrow would get rid of her smell, but the vision of her kneeling in the middle of the bed would be with him for a long time.

Slade held his breath when he heard her uncap the oil, then the gurgling of the oil as she poured some in her hands. The warmth of her hands cupped his ankles and his breath came out on a moan which he muffled in the pillow, as a hot wave of lava washed up his body. He gritted his teeth as every muscle in his body went rigid, along with other body parts.

"Relax," she purred softly, as she smoothed her hands up his calves to the backs of his knees spreading the heated oil. She raked her thumbs lightly over the back of his knees and a shiver shook him, as she dragged her palms back down his calves, and his toes curled tightly.

Relax? There wasn't a snowball's chance in hell that was going to happen, Slade thought, as her small but strong fingers dug into the flesh above his ankles. He fisted the pillow, and even bit down on the case to keep from moaning.

"Damn, even your feet are tense. I guess I need to start there." Her rumbly little laugh that rolled through his skull as her weight left the bed. Her thumbs worked along the pad of his feet right below his toes and they straightened.

Her hot breaths heated the back of his heels as her thumbs dug into the fleshy pads on his feet and lazy electrical jolts shot up his legs. Those magical hands of hers worked the tension from every toe, before she moved down the crease between his big toe to his instep, and flattened her thumb to massage a particular place that loosened the tension in his muscles a little.

Gripping the top of his foot, she worked her sharp little fingers through the ridges there while she circled her thumbs at his instep soothingly. Every circle there chipped a little more of the tension away and his focus zoned on the friction she created there, until a shuddering sigh surprised him when it escaped.

"That's better," she said, gliding her hands over his heels to massage on either side of his Achilles, working out the tension there. She pushed the heel of her hand into the back of his legs and slid upward to his knees, before digging her fingers into his calf muscles, working her fingers through every tight string, all the way back down to his heels creating a strange buzzing in them.

Slade wiggled his toes enjoying the tingly sensation. But then the bed dipped and he felt her heat beside him before she threw her leg over him to straddle his lower legs. She settled on her haunches and the heat between her legs scorched him, as she pressed her knees into the sides of his calves, resting her tiny feet across his at his ankles.

His hand flew back to grip her thigh, to tell her this wasn't a good idea, but her small hands landed gently on the area above the bend in his knees and he froze. She leaned over him, glided her hands up the back of his thighs and Slade's hand fell to the bed to fist the sheet as bolts of lightning sizzled up his legs with her hands setting every nerve in his body on fire.

When her hands dipped under the edge of the towel to knead the muscles near his ass, her thumbs dug into his inner thighs near his balls, Slade was unable to stop his loud moan. He gritted his teeth and fought the urge to turn over with everything in him as a tremor rocked him.

"You okay?" she asked with concern.

"No," he grated into the pillow. "You need to get off of me."

"Am I hurting you?" she asked, rolling over to the side to put her hand in the center of his back sending electricity zipping up his neck and over his scalp. He could feel her eyes burning into the back of his head.

"No, but you're not helping either." Slade rolled away to sit on the side of the bed, his dick throbbing in time with his out of control heart. "And I might hurt you if we don't stop this right now. I'm going back to the sofa." He reached back to grab a pillow, but her hand landed at the center of his back again and he tensed.

"What would help you then?" she asked softly, her quick, even breaths heating his shoulder. She leaned in closer, and her warm, wet mouth kissed his shoulder. "Let me finish, and if that doesn't do it, we'll move on to option two."

Option two? Her meaning became clear and he fought back a needy whimper. Just the thought created a craving so intense he likened it to the gnawing in his gut he'd experienced when he battled his addiction to the painkillers they'd gotten him hooked on in the hospital.

"This is not a good idea, Taylor," he said, trying to push up from the bed but she slid off to stand in front of him and shove him back down.

He looked into her soft eyes which sparkled from the light in the bathroom, which was a mistake. The mesmerizing draw of her eyes, her words and her soft, sexy body which was just inches from his, all combined to take the fight right out of him. Her hand drifted to his jaw and Slade fought the urge to lean into her touch, as the light scent of the baby oil on her skin teased him. She studied him for a moment, and he tried to figure out what she was looking for. Whatever it was, she must've found it, because her thumb stroked his cheek.

"It might not be a good idea, but you need some rest. If you're not snoring by the time I finish and we get to option two, I promise when the sun comes up, you'll never hear about it again. Neither will anyone else."

"Women don't work that way," Slade contradicted gruffly, trying to ignore the rise and fall of her gorgeous breasts that were too near his face now. Inches from his tingling lips. Licking distance. Temptation to grab her wrist and roll her onto the bed was strong.

"*This* woman does, trust me on that," she replied with a short, harsh laugh.

"Why is that?" he asked suspiciously. Her lips pinched and Slade began to think she wouldn't answer, but she finally heaved a sigh and looked over his shoulder.

"I'm still pretty raw from breaking up with my boyfriend, so I don't want attachments any more than you do. My boyfriend who was *married*, but failed to tell me that during our three year relationship."

Her words sent shock then outrage coursing through Slade. He wanted to find that sleazy bastard and punch his lights out for her. That rage was quadrupled by his own rage from the ironic similarity to his own circumstance with Jeannie, a woman he planned to ask to marry him when he was back on his feet. A traitorous bitch who claimed to love him for three years, but had taken one glimpse at what a fucked up mess the military had returned to her and ran from his room the day he got back stateside.

Slade hadn't seen it himself, but he imagined his face before the reconstructive surgery was pretty horrific, the shunt in his skull to relieve the swelling in his brain terrifying. Him being gone for twenty-four months of their three year relationship had probably been tough on her too. But in his opinion you didn't run out like she had on someone you claimed to love for three years. The horror on her face, the disgust, was something he would never forget or forgive. The cheating during his deployment that he found out about later just cemented his hatred for her.

The old rage tried to burn brighter, but he held it back by focusing on the vision in front of him. Like his injuries, Jeannie was just a five-year-old distant and unpleasant memory. This woman offering herself to him was the present so he fought to stay focused on her. She made that very easy when she put her hands on her hips to lean in closer and hold his gaze.

"The only thing I need you to tell me is that you're not married or otherwise attached."

Slade swallowed hard then shook his head. His eyes left hers to track over her chin down her chest and along the shadowed cleft between her breasts.

"I'm as unattached as a man can be," he assured, his head gravitating toward the pillowy mounds spilling over the scraps of lace trying to restrain them.

Detached, emotionally unavailable, never getting attached to a woman again. But totally on board with fucking you until neither of us can see straight.

Her scent intoxicated him, her heat singed his lips, but right before his mouth touched her she backed away to point at the bed. "Then lay down on that bed and get ready to meet Mr. Sandman."

Slade's hand shot out, closed around her wrist and she squeaked when he jerked her to him to bury his face in her cleavage and inhale her scent like a

101

crack addict. "Forget, Mr. Sandman. I choose option two," he mumbled against her flesh, as his arms clamped around her waist and he rolled her onto the bed.

CHAPTER EIGHT

"How in the hell could I forget you're a karate expert?" Slade asked with a laugh, as he stared at the ceiling from the floor on the other side of the bed. His head had barely missed whacking the nightstand during his roll over the edge of the bed.

Wouldn't that have just been spectacular?

Taylor leaned over the side of the bed to frown down at him. "We're going to do this my way, so get back up here and let's try this again."

He sat up, then stood to look down at her. "For a tiny woman, you sure are bossy."

"Tiny doesn't mean weak," she replied defensively, lifting her stubborn little chin, sounding as if she'd dealt with that assumption many times in her life.

"Obviously, Little General." Slade laughed as he sat on the bed, then crawled around her to plop down on the pillow.

Her eyes swung to him, and a cute little crease appeared between her brows. "Little General?" she repeated, fishing around under the covers until she found the bottle of oil.

"Yeah, you have a Napoleon complex," Slade explained, then turned over when she tapped his shoulder and circled her hand.

"What the hell does that mean?" Taylor asked, resting her hand at the center of his back, raising goosebumps all over his body.

"You're self-conscious that you're small, so you use a big bark to compensate, hoping people won't notice your size," he mumbled into the pillow, hugging it tighter and gritting his teeth as she skimmed her hand down to the small of his back, over his ass then down the back of his thigh before she straddled him to get into massage position again. Both of her hands landed on the backs of his thighs and her fingers dug in not gently.

"My bite is just as big as my bark and my size has nothing to do with it." The sharp points of her tiny fingers kneaded his muscles from his knees up to his upper thighs and he flexed his ass cheeks against the almost pain she was inflicting.

"I worked hard to develop skills to be an M.P. like my dad, but they didn't want me because I'm *small.*" The more she talked, the deeper her fingers dug into his flesh on the way back down to his knees. "I was a sheriff's deputy in Oklahoma for a while, but the damned sheriff wouldn't let me carry a gun even though I could outshoot him. Because I'm a *small* woman."

Slade was sure she was hitting bone now, her fingers dug so deep. When she punched the back of his thigh twice like she was tenderizing a steak, he moaned.

"He said a normal sized man would overpower me and take it from me, so I carried my personal weapon without telling him. When he found out he put me on desk duty indefinitely, so I left."

Taylor punched his right thigh then, her knuckle dug into the muscle there, and Slade groaned. Her voice wobbled, her motions slowed when she finished with, "I have every reason to be defensive about it." Her motions ceased, she leaned back and a hot, wet drop splashed on his upper thigh then slid quickly down the side.

Was she crying? Slade's heart jerked in his chest at the thought.

With a growl, he twisted to turn over under her, and Taylor sat there staring down at him in the darkness. He wished like hell he could see her face so he could tell, but a second wet drop landed on the front of his thigh, and he knew she was crying. When she swiped her arm across her face, he knew for sure.

"You're tired, and so am I." He grabbed her hips to drag her off of him. "Let's just get some sleep, I'm fine now." Slade pulled her down beside him and closed his arms around her. The feel of her soft flesh pressed against his side reignited the fires inside him, but he ignored it. Hesitantly, her arm crept over his waist and she laid her head on his shoulder.

Silence fell until he could hear the whir of the ceiling fan, and although he was as comfortable now as he'd been in years, he was damned uncomfortable at the same time. His body buzzed with unsatisfied need, but his mind with softer urges he hadn't had in a long time. The need to comfort this woman, protect her, and fix things for her.

How in the hell could that be? He barely

knew Taylor Kincaid. Her problems weren't his. He had enough of his own right now to deal with. Maybe it was because she'd tried to help him.

"Thanks for the massage," he said fighting the urge to kiss her hair when she snuggled her face into his shoulder, tightened her hold on his waist. Tenderness had no place in his life now. He'd tried that route with a woman, and the only thing it had gotten him was gutted. That woman he'd known three years, and this one he'd only known three hours.

"Welcome," Taylor replied sleepily with a deep sigh, and the soft sweep of her eyelashes tickled his chest. "You'd be asleep if you'd have let me finish."

Massage or not, Slade knew sleep was not something he was going to find that night when Taylor pressed her body closer to his, threw her calf over his to rub her foot along his calf. He was in sheer sexual hell as his dick hardened painfully. Her hot, even breaths wafted over his skin, her scent teased him every time he breathed.

"Night," he muttered, as he used his foot to shove her leg off of his.

He turned on his side away from her, and damn if she didn't immediately scoot up behind him and suction her tight little body to his back and snuggle in. She shoved her hand under his arm and pried it up to drape her arm over his waist.

"Slade?" she asked, her voice rumbling over the skin between his shoulder blades.

106

"Yeah?" he replied shortly.

"Will you please let me make an appointment for you with the doctor who helped Mark? I swear EMDR is amazing, and I think it could help you."

Hearing about her two-timing ex-boyfriend again, and the therapy she found for him did not put Slade in a better frame of mind. It made him want to find that bastard and punch him in the face. Give him something to have flashbacks about.

"I *don't* want to talk about it. I told you, I'm calling *my* doctor tomorrow," he growled and his muscles tensed up again.

"It's like bio—" she started, but he cut her off.

"They tried that biofeedback crap on me before I was put on meds and it's a bunch of hokum. Please just mind your own damned business, and let me handle mine."

"I'm just trying to help you," she said softly, her voice sounding a little hurt. "You could at least talk to him, and if you don't think it will help, walk out."

Every muscle in his body was rigid again now, the tension in his gut building. "I don't have time to deal with that shit right now. We have a missing kid and a bomber to find." He lifted up to punch his pillow, then flopped back down on it. "Just get some damned sleep!"

"I have one more thing to say and I will. This is a new therapy, and it wasn't approved five years ago. It's not the same one that they tried on you."

Slade didn't respond. It would just invite more of her unwanted suggestions. He slammed his eyes shut and focused on relaxing again.

"Fair warning..." she murmured sleepily, and her arm tightened around his waist. "I'm not going to give up on convincing you."

Slade finally relaxed when he heard her soft even breaths.

Fair warning to you—you're wasting your breath. I don't deserve help, because I should've died in that blast instead of my men.

***

Taylor was surrounded by delicious heat, wrapped in a comfortable cocoon when she dragged her eyes open. She quickly shut them against the bright light that pierced her brain and offended her senses. That brief glimpse of her surroundings confused her sleep-drugged mind, so she opened one eye a slit to take another look. It landed on a man's broad, muscular back and her heart froze.

Mark? No, Mark was gone from her life, and good riddance.

Her body relaxed, but her mind ran through things, and when the clouds parted in her brain Taylor remembered exactly where she was. At the Deep Six Security compound out in the boonies. Accused of attempting to assassinate Prince Khalil yesterday.

Biting back a groan, both of her eyes popped

opened again to fix on the broad back in front of her. And she was in bed with her new boss whose body was tense even in sleep, so tense her arm, which was draped over his waist, was pinned there.

She didn't want to wake Slade, because he needed the sleep, but Taylor had needs that were pressing. Carefully, she tried to slide her arm from under his, but his heavy forearm pinned it to his side. When she tried again, he grumbled, his hand closed around hers and he tucked it to his muscled chest.

For a minute she laid there, counting the steady beats of his heart against her palm, considering her options. Her need to pee finally won out over worrying about him being asleep though, so she used her free hand to push against his back. The amount of sunlight pouring into the room from the single window in the far corner told her they needed to get up anyway. It was probably well past the time he'd scheduled for the meeting with his men.

"Slade, wake up," she said, rocking her body against his and he moaned. Instead of releasing her though, his body tensed and he gripped her hand tighter almost cutting off the circulation to her fingers.

Taylor shoved him again and with a heavy sigh, his arm finally lifted and she pulled hers free, unglued her body from his and rolled to the other side of the bed. She got up and hurried toward the bathroom, but a flash of red and yellow on the floor beside the bed stopped her.

Curiosity won out over her need to pee, so Taylor bent to pick up a pair of man-sized yellow boxer briefs that sported a big smiley face in the center of the crotch and on the left thigh was printed, "Yes, I'm happy to see you!"

A giggle rumbled in her chest and trickled past her lips as her gaze shot to the bed and she met a pair of sleepy green eyes that were not amused.

Her eyebrow lifted, and he frowned, as a grin stretched her face tight. "Underoos for adults? Someone buy these for you as a gag gift?" she asked, unable to stop another giggle.

Slade sat up dragging the covers with him. His arm reached out to snatch the underwear from her, as a flush crept up his neck to stain his cheeks. "No, camo gets boring, so that was my middle finger to the military. It's the only thing that kept me sane while I was deployed."

The smile slid off of her face, but Taylor couldn't help but ask, "So you have more? You wear them all the time?" The thought of this big beefy man wearing goofy underwear was titillating to her for some reason.

"I have a whole drawer full, if it's any of your damned business," he grumbled as he pulled them on under the covers.

"All with smiley faces?" she pressed, and a growl rumbled in his chest as he stood to glare down at her. Taylor's eyes didn't meet his though, hers fell to the smiley face on his crotch which at the moment was stretched over a long hard ridge that said he was *very* happy. She was mesmerized until his finger tipped up her chin.

"Let's get something straight. I don't want to get to know you, or have you in my business. I don't need a mother, I have one. I hired you to help me find that kid, not as a fuck buddy. You won't be sleeping in my room again, so pick a cot in the bunkhouse today, or get used to sleeping by yourself over in the other building."

His green eyes were hard as granite, his words like bullets that chipped away any soft feelings for him inside of her and Taylor fought the burn in hers. Yesterday had been a nightmare for her, and today wasn't shaping up to be any better. She wished she could just rewind to yesterday morning and have a redo. Then her life wouldn't be upside down, and she definitely would not be here with this hard man.

"I just want to go home," Taylor said, biting her lower lip and Slade's eyes fell there.

She needed to find another job, maybe move somewhere else and start over. That's what she should've done after her breakup with Mark and she wouldn't be in this mess. But she hadn't, and she was in this mess, so she needed this man to help her deal with it so she could start over.

"That's not going to happen until we figure out who planted that bomb unless you want to go to jail."

"I don't have any of my things here, so I'll

have to go by there eventually," Taylor replied with a huffed breath. She didn't even have a toothbrush with her, or clean underwear.

Scratching at the door preceded a sharp bark, and muffled whining. Slade huffed a breath as he walked to the dresser, grabbed his jeans and pulled them on. "I'll send Fletch over there later, so make a list of what you need." He grabbed the doorknob and twisted it. "I'm going to let the dogs out, so you have about ten minutes to shower and get ready. We have a lot to do today and we're late for the meeting."

His brusque attitude this morning evidently didn't extend to his dog, because he opened the door and greeted Lola with soft words and a scratch between her ears, before pulling it shut behind him.

Taylor grabbed her folded clothes from the dresser, then trod to the bathroom on leaden feet wondering what the hell happened to the relatively nice, seemingly easygoing man she'd taken a job from yesterday. The thing that really puzzled her though, was how she could be jealous of a damned dog.

CHAPTER NINE

"Let's get busy." Slade grated, as he strode into the conference room and felt seven sets of eyes glaring at him as he took Dave's chair at the head of the table. His eyes ticked over every face taking roll call in his mind. "Where the fuck is Dexter?"

"Later than you, evidently," Gray shot back, looking up from his laptop. His eyes cut to Taylor, then narrowed as they swung back to Slade. "For a different reason, I'm sure."

Anger scorched through Slade, and he opened his mouth to tell the judgmental pencil-pusher off, and he had plenty of steam to do a good job of it too, but Hawk cut him off.

"I tried to wake him up before I left the barracks, but he's either comatose or dead," Hawk informed with a laugh.

"He didn't get in until four or five this morning," Caleb added, and Slade's anger deflated.

Probably because he'd been working on getting all the information together Slade had requested for this meeting. The geek got a pass this time, but they needed him here, no matter how tired he was.

"Well, somebody needs to go drag his ass up, because we can't proceed without him." Slade eyeballed, Caleb until he finally pushed his chair back.

"Dude, who shit in your Wheaties this morning?" he asked hotly as he stood and held Slade's gaze. He waved his hand at the others. "We're the ones who've been sitting here cooling our heels waiting for you to decide to stroll in."

"Don't push it," Slade warned, lowering his tone a notch. "I'm not in the mood today."

"Drink some coffee then and improve that mood, or we're going to have some serious problems here today," Caleb fired back, not blinking.

"I'll go make some," Taylor offered, pushing up to her feet.

"*No*—sit!" Slade barked, his eyes swinging to her.

"I'm not your damned dog," she ground out, her eyes shooting blue fire at him as she lifted her stubborn little chin.

Slade's eyes fell to her heaving, unbound breasts then ticked down to the waistband of her yoga pants. How in the hell was he supposed to focus on anything today when he knew she wasn't wearing underwear?

He knew this because he found her black thong and bra hanging over the towel bar in *his* bathroom this morning where she'd evidently hung them to dry after washing them in the sink.

But he hadn't needed to see those articles to know.

He'd been treated to a full visual display of swishes and jiggles, while they walked from the barracks to the office a few minutes ago. In the body-hugging top she wore, he also couldn't miss the fact that her large nipples seemed to be in a perma-hard state. Sort of like his fucking cock when he was around her. Every man here had to notice too, and that pissed him off.

Slade might be less agitated at the moment if he could have done something about his frustration in the shower this morning, but she'd only left two damned minutes of hot water.

"Damn, I should've brought my machete to cut through the tension in here this morning," Levi said with a laugh, as he pushed back his chair to stand and stare at Slade. "I'm leaving before it's my turn, so I'll make the coffee." Without waiting, he all but ran for the door. Caleb stalked behind him out of the door.

Knowing he was about to have a rebellion on his hands, Slade dragged his eyes down to the table and took three deep, calming breaths. Lola nudged his hand under the table, and he rubbed her muzzle. Blowing out a breath, he looked back up. "I'm sorry, I'm just damned worried about all of our jobs here. We need to fix this situation fast. Friday will be here before we know it, and that ransom will be paid. Once that happens, we're probably screwed."

"Dex found billing addresses and phone numbers in the hotel database for the prince, so he put me on finding the money," Gray announced, meeting Slade's eyes again. "I found several accounts, but I'm still trying to figure out which is the prince's personal account. I'll work on his brother's when I have that nailed down."

Mackenzie cleared his throat. "I'm doing background checks on the royal family, and the hotel employees he identified from hacking into the hotel database. The list is long, and I'll have to go through Interpol for the family. I'll try to have answers by Friday, but it'll probably take me at least a week to finish."

An involuntary smile curved Slade's lips, as the tension inside of him eased. "What in the hell do you guys need me for?" he asked, and they laughed.

Slade loved when he was reminded just how damned good the Deep Six team was. Dave Logan was either a brilliant strategist when it came to assembling a team, or he had a horseshoe up his ass. Every man here knew his job well, and was the absolute fucking best at it. They might not always get along, but one thing he knew was when it came down to a mission or an investigation they worked together like a well-oiled machine.

His eyes tracked to Taylor, who was sitting again, but still shot hot blue daggers at him from the other end of the table. He hoped his additions to the team so far, Taylor and Cee Cee, didn't mess up their mojo.

"To be the resident grumpy bastard while Dave's out of the position?" Caleb guessed with a derisive snort, as he walked back into the conference room. Dexter stumbled in behind him, his arms loaded down with a laptop and several thick stacks of printouts.

Slade ignored the Deep Six sniper because he deserved that shot, and instead turned his attention to the buttoned-up forensic accountant who was squinting at his laptop screen. "Gray, once you identify the accounts, I need you to watch closely for a ten million dollar transfer."

Grayson's head snapped up again, his eyebrows raised. "Why ten million?" he asked.

"That's the ransom demand and I need to know where it goes, if it's made."

An idea occurred to Slade that would get Taylor Kincaid out of his hair too.

"Mac, I have help for you," he said, meeting the detective's eyes. He waved his hand down to the end of the table. "You haven't met her yet, but this is Taylor Kincaid, the former security head at the hotel. I'll bet she can help you whittle that list down, so you can give me answers sooner." Slade transferred his gaze to Taylor and smiled. "She even has a list of her own that she stole from her former employer so you can compare notes."

Taylor's shocked look and outraged gasp made his smile widen.

"I didn't *steal* it," Taylor hissed, glaring at him. "It was in my drawer, and I had every right to have it. I wasn't *hiding* it from anyone."

"Yeah, it's only taking those hidden things that makes you a thief, right?" Slade asked sarcastically, and rolled his eyes.

"I guess it all depends on the item that's hidden, *Smiley.*"

Taylor's meaning was not lost on him considering the evil smile that punctuated her words. Slade's smile faded and he held his breath as he waited for her to out him on his underwear choices. But she just folded her arms over her chest, thankfully hiding those damned nipples from his view.

"You know I work alone," Mac said gruffly, glancing at Taylor like she had two heads.

Yeah, Slade knew that, but Mac needed to learn to be less of a loner and a control freak, or he was going to burn out. Because it was how he'd always operated during his fifteen years as a veteran detective with the Dallas Police Department, he kept everything too close to his vest until he had all his ducks in a row. Slade also knew, he wasn't overly fond of women since his ex-wife had done a number on him. Yet another reason he needed to work with one to get over it.

Slade leaned back in his chair, proud that he must be as good a strategist as his best friend. Getting into his role as boss, he turned his attention to Fletcher, who appeared to be half-asleep in the chair beside Dexter who *was* slumped down in his chair sleeping.

"Fletch?" he said and the man jumped, then straightened up in his chair. "I need you to *discreetly* get into Taylor's house tonight to retrieve some clothes and things for her. She's going to make a list for you."

"I hope it includes a bra," he said with a rusty laugh, his gaze locking onto Taylor's chest.

Taylor's mouth dropped open, and her cheeks turned bright red.

Anger blew through Slade like a tornado to swirl inside his skull. With every eye in the room on him, even Dexter's who seemed wide awake now, he slowly stood, then strode around the table to tower over Fletcher.

"Stand up, Fletcher," he growled, jerking his chair away from the table.

Fletch pushed up to his feet and took a step back, but Slade stepped forward to grab the front of his shirt and lift the shorter man to his toes. He tried to hide his fear, but Slade saw it in his eyes when leaned down to bring their noses almost tip to tip.

"If I *ever* hear you talk about Taylor that way again, or be disrespectful to *any* woman Deep Six employs for that matter, I will personally throw your ass over that fence outside. Do you understand me?" Fletcher swallowed hard, and nodded, but that wasn't good enough. Slade wanted to hear the words. He twisted his fist and the knot in the shirt tightened. "Answer me, Fletcher, or I swear to God I'll put my fist in your face," he ground out.

"I understand," Fletcher replied, his voice an octave higher than usual.

Slade loosened his grip and lowered the man

back to his feet. "Good, now apologize to her, and make it good," he growled, as he turned and walked back to his chair.

"I'm sorry for being an asshole, Taylor." His gaze darted to Slade as he sat down again. "Really sorry."

The room went dead silent, until Taylor nodded.

"Okay then," Hawk said loudly, as he slapped the table and stood. "I don't think y'all need me anymore, so I'm taking the bird to Houston for some maintenance. Call me if you need me." Before Slade could say a word, he was out of the door. The rest of the room cleared just as fast, but he caught Taylor at the door.

"Taylor, I need to talk to you a minute, please." She stopped, studied him a minute then grabbed a chair, but he caught her before she sat. "*Privately*, so shut the door."

"Am I fired already?" she asked sharply, as she shut the door took the chair to his left.

"No, but you will be if you ever show as little sense about working around men as you did today," Slade replied as calmly as he could manage, because he was seething inside over the whole situation. Mostly at Fletcher, but she had a hand in creating it too.

"What do you mean?" she asked, her brows furrowing in the middle. Slade's eyes fell to her breasts, and she crossed her arms over them.

"These are grown men who work here, mostly single men."

"And?" she replied, her voice a little higher.

Exasperation filled him, because he knew that she knew what he was talking about, she was just playing dumb. Evidently she wanted him to spell it out for her, and he would. "*And* you don't walk around without a bra in front of men like them when you're built like you are."

"Built like I am?" she repeated, sitting a little higher in her chair to lean her forearms on the table. "How exactly am I built?"

"Like a fucking Victoria's Secret model up top," Slade replied gruffly, and her eyes sparked with anger.

"Let me get this straight…" Taylor put a finger to her jaw, looked toward the ceiling as if in thought, then pointed at herself when she met his eyes. "Because I'm a woman with larger breasts, I have to make sure to wear supportive undergarments so the men here don't notice. Is that right?"

"You know what I mean," Slade growled, feeling heat creeping up his throat.

"No, I don't think I do." Her head shake caused her silky dark hair to dance over her shoulders. "Tell me—is there a company policy somewhere that specifies that the more *well-endowed* men here like yourself are required to wear jock straps to hide your packages in case I wanted to stare at them too?" Slade looked away, and she kicked her chair. It rolled to the wall as she stood to lean over the table, putting her breasts very near his arm. "If not, I'd say you and your company could be found to be practicing sexual discrimination in a court of law."

This woman was worse than Susan with that shit. No fucking wonder Logan had waited so long to hire a woman. Fletcher was right, this was a distraction he didn't need. He dragged his eyes back to hers.

"I'm *not* discriminating, Taylor. I'm telling you that teasing them with your um—" His eyes fell to her breasts. "Your *assets* is just asking them to make rude comments."

A throaty growl was his only warning, before her palm stung the side of his face and his head rocked on his shoulders. Lola's secondary growl from under the table had him reaching to put his hand on her head, as his other hand flew up to rub his cheek.

"Your men's lack of *manners*, and your own *shortcomings* in dealing with them are not my fault, Smiley. I *quit*, and I don't need my underwear to give *you* my middle finger." Taylor flipped her finger up under his nose, then spun on her heel to storm to the door. When she flung it open, Slade saw Levi standing there holding a tray filled with coffee cups, and a pot.

"Where the hell did you park my car?" she barked, and the cups on the tray rattled as he took a step back.

"It's over behind the barracks, ma'am. The key I had made is in my pocket, but my hands are kind of full."

"I don't need your key—I just need you to tell me it's operational."

"It's just the way you left it at the office," he assured, and Taylor shouldered her way past him, turned left and disappeared.

Levi blew out a breath as he walked in to set the tray down on the table. "Wow, what in the hell did you do to piss her off?"

"Told her she needed to wear a bra in the office," Slade replied flatly, looking at the empty doorway trying to figure that out himself. He'd tried to be diplomatic, but he'd obviously failed.

"You're lucky you're not dead," Levi said with a laugh.

Slade's eyes flew to his. "Why do you say that? I thought it was a reasonable request since ninety percent of Deep Six employees are men."

"My four sisters would've had the same reaction. So would my mother, except she'd have probably added a frying pan to her lesson."

"You think I was wrong?" That confused the hell out of Slade, who thought he was one of the most forward-thinking men at Deep Six. The only one who appreciated that the right woman could do this job as well as a man.

"I don't know what happened, because I wasn't in here for the fireworks, thank God. But if you said to her what you just said to me, I'd say she had every right to put that handprint on the side of your face."

Maybe he was right, Slade thought, as he pushed his chair back to stand. He needed to go find her and apologize. Brushing past Levi, he walked briskly down the hallway and Lola followed him through the living room to the front door. Just as he opened it, he saw her brake at the front gate. He sprinted to the steps, hustled down them then hit the ground at a full run, but the gate opened and she peeled out before he got there.

Stopping at the gate to catch his breath, Slade watched her speed away as it closed and decided it would probably be best to wait until tomorrow to try and find her so she had time to cool off. Finding her shouldn't be too hard if she was headed to her house, because more than likely the feds would have her in custody for the car bombing.

Not his problem.

He needed to find that kid, and that's what he was going to focus on. Hopefully, when they questioned her, Taylor Kincaid had enough sense not to mention his name. Since she didn't know his full name, he wasn't too worried. Only a few of the local feds would recognize it if it was mentioned to them, and the odds of that happening were slim.

Another thought presented though, that sent a shot of adrenaline through him. All of their cell numbers were programmed into her phone, and he knew that would be the first thing the feds would confiscate to examine.

Now, he was worried.

Turning back toward the office, he ran toward his Humvee. He opened the door and Lola hopped inside, but he stopped feeling his phone vibrate in his pocket.

"Slade," he growled, pinching it between his shoulder and ear as he got inside and leaned his hip up to pull out his keys.

"I think someone is following me," Taylor whispered into the phone.

She couldn't be far from the compound, she'd only been gone a few minutes. Ten at the most, but she had been upset and hauling ass when she left.

"Who's following you and when did you notice?" he asked, shutting the door, before inserting the key into the ignition.

"I'm not sure, for the last five miles or so, maybe. I just turned onto a side road and they did too." The fear in her voice stabbed him in the gut, but he ignored it.

The odds were she was imagining things.

"Describe the vehicle." He put the Hummer into gear, but waited because if he could apologize to her over the phone that's what he would do. This drama and chasing her was not going to get them the intel they needed to figure out this case.

"It's black, and sort of looks like yours, but different. It hasn't gotten close enough for me to get a good look yet."

"Is it a Jeep?" he guessed. The four door model looked a lot like his Humvee from a distance. "Can you see what the driver looks like?"

"No, the windows are blacked out, even the windshield has the tint halfway down," she replied, and an uneasy feeling gripped him.

"Do you have a weapon in your car?" Slade eased his foot off the brake to head toward the gate.

"No, it's at home in a lock box," she replied, then gasped.

"What?" he asked, as he rolled over the trigger to release the gate.

"They're speeding up and getting closer on my bumper. I'm going to speed up and see if they do too."

Slade's throat constricted as he pulled through the gate and onto the road. He had no idea where she was, and if she'd turned off on a side road in this neck of the woods, in all likelihood, she didn't know either.

"Oh wait, it looks like they're trying to pass me," she said, sounding relieved.

Slade's shoulders relaxed then too, and he took one hand off of the wheel to hold the phone. But then another thought struck him, and every muscle in his body tensed. What if they were trying to get parallel with her to take a shot instead of passing her?

"When they try to pass you, as soon as the

nose of their vehicle is even with your rear quarter panel, I want you to slam on the brakes, okay? Turn around and head the other direction as fast as you can."

She blew out a breath. "Okay, they're almost there now."

After a second, he heard tires screech, and held his breath.

"*Oh, God,*" she groaned, and it sounded to him like she dropped the phone, but then he heard a whimper, a pop and her squeal as glass shattered.

"*Taylor*—are you there?!?" he shouted, but there was no reply. Guilt for letting her leave alone, for running her off, when things were so volatile and fluid in this case, pressed down on his shoulders like a lead curtain. He pressed harder on the accelerator, and the buzzing started in his ears. No, not now, not now—not *now*!

Lola whimpered, and stood on the console between the seats to nudge his right shoulder. He had to hold the wheel, so he couldn't scratch her. There was no way in hell he was going to let go of the phone. Holding it in place with his jaw, Slade rolled down his window and the gush of fresh air cooled his skin and woke him up. Lola rubbed her nose on his neck, licked him and he fought the demons trying to take hold of him.

Please Lord, help me so I can help her and I promise I'll try that therapy she wants me to try.

CHAPTER TEN

Stunned, Taylor took a moment to process that someone had just shot out her windshield! Her heart pounded erratically at the base of her throat, but skidded to a stop when she looked down the road and saw the black SUV was stopped too, and trying to turn around on the narrow road. Her compact car was small, so she could turn around easier than they could.

If she could see where she was going, that is.

She scanned the car quickly and saw a fast food bag on the back floorboard. Grabbing it, she stuffed her hand inside, leaned over the wheel and knocked out the shattered safety glass that blocked her view. Without removing the bag, she grabbed the wheel, hit the gas and twisted the wheel hard. Once she was facing the way she'd come, she pressed the accelerator to the floorboard and held on tight as the car launched.

Who in the hell could be trying to kill her? And why? It had to be connected to the hotel, and the kidnapping, but why would they want her dead? The next question was, how had they found her so quickly out at the Deep Six compound? Had they been watching for her to leave alone?

She wished she had her pistol. When she got out of this mess, she was going to carry it at all times, glue it to her side. This would not happen again. Right now, she felt more helpless and afraid than she'd ever been in her life.

And alone.

Taylor sure wished those big beefheads were with her right now. Those killers would take one look at them and back off. That brought her mind back to the fact that she'd been on the phone with Slade when they were shooting at her. He was probably worried about her, and if they could connect somehow he could help her get rid of these guys.

"*Slade!*" she shouted, hoping he was still on the phone and heard her. "I'm fine, but they shot out my windshield!"

Thank goodness, he'd told her to slam on the brakes, or she'd probably be dead right now. Taylor took her eyes off the narrow road for a second to glance in her rearview. The SUV was turned around now and speeding after her.

"I'm headed back toward the main road, but they're chasing me again," she informed loudly, her heart pounding in her ears now.

Taylor hoped like hell he was still on the phone. If not, she didn't know what she would do once she got to the main road.

She'd turn left and head back toward the Deep Six compound. Somewhere she never should've left. She could deal with musclebound Neanderthals, she couldn't deal with these coldblooded killers alone.

Regardless of whether she was talking to herself, Taylor felt better thinking Slade was on the line with her, speeding to help her.

"I'm almost to the main road, but they're catching up with me. The road I turned on was the Farm Road about seven miles from the compound. It's on the right."

Two more miles is what she estimated, before she reached the main road. Glancing in the rearview, she saw the black SUV was still a ways back, but gaining ground on her. Ice flowed through her veins, because she realized their powerful engine had a lot more get-up-and-go than her compact car, so it was a given they would catch up with her before then. Despair and fear tried to take hold of her, but she beat it back, pressed on the gas harder, and prayed.

"Slade, they're catching up. About a mile now, before I get to the main road," she informed, and heard the trembling in her voice. It wasn't worse than the trembling in her arms though. Her whole damned body was shaking from fear and adrenaline.

She caught sight of the intersection with the main road ahead, but it didn't bring her comfort. Her hands were practically melded with the steering wheel as she wondered how she would stop there. As fast as she was going, there was no way she could stop. She would just have to take the turn on two wheels and hope the road was clear.

A big black vehicle turned onto the road, and she squinted. *Please don't let it be more bad guys coming to help the assholes behind me.* If it was, Taylor knew she was done. Her car sped closer to the black SUV coming at her, a tremor shook her, a hysterical giggle bubbled in her throat, as relief became a drug in her veins when she recognized it.

His vehicle zoomed past her, and Slade didn't even look at her. He was focused on the SUV behind her. Glancing in the rearview, she saw him move into the lane behind her, evidently playing a game of Chicken with the bad guys.

"Don't be stupid, Slade!" she shouted, knowing now that he heard her. But Taylor was afraid for him, more than she'd been for herself even. They needed some backup. "I'm going back to the compound to get help!"

Right before the intersection, she took one more glance in the rearview and saw that he'd turned his Hummer sideways in the road to block it. He was alone, facing down those men for her and he could die if she didn't get help.

Her eyes swung back to the road, and she caught a flash of red that was the stop sign at the intersection. She jammed her foot on the brake, her eyes locked on the center line of the main road as she twisted the wheel, but the car didn't turn. It launched into the intersection, her right front tire hit the soft shoulder and instead of blacktop, she saw the crevice of the ditch as her car went over the edge. The car came to a sudden stop, and in slow motion Taylor watched the steering wheel coming at her, gongs went off inside her head and stars danced before her eyes.

***

Slade slammed on the brakes and brought the Humvee to a stop across the road. He already had his pistol drawn and the passenger window down, so he took aim at the driver's side of the windshield and popped off two rounds as the Suburban stopped just before hitting him. Dents appeared where the bullets struck, but the windshield didn't shatter which meant it was bulletproof glass. The vehicle idled there momentarily, before the driver threw it into reverse, the tires burned and he watched it speed backwards down the narrow road. The tail end whipped into a pasture access road then the vehicle charged off in the other direction.

Squinting, Slade tried to make out the license plate, but couldn't. He wasn't giving chase, because he'd accomplished his goal of getting them off of Taylor. And he wasn't in any condition right now for a gunfight. Especially by himself.

Huffing a relieved breath, Slade laid his pistol on the console and did a three-point turn to head back to the main road. When he reached the stop sign, he saw thick black skid marks on the road that led to the ditch and his heart stopped. He turned onto the road and the roof of a light blue compact car came into view, Taylor's car. Fear sliced through him as he stopped the Hummer on the shoulder, told Lola to stay and flew out of the vehicle. He breathed again when he looked over the embankment and didn't see her in the vehicle.

But she was small, so she could be laying on

the seat. Heart in his throat, he slid down the slope and made his way to the car to look inside. His breath came out in a rush, and his body went weak when he didn't find her laying there bleeding to death. He did see her cell phone on the passenger side floorboard. Where the hell was she?

Slade stood back to scan the area and his heart finally beat again when he didn't see her laying anywhere in the area in a crumpled heap. He climbed back up the embankment and shaded his eyes to look down the road. Heat rose off the pavement making her look wavy in the distance, but there she was about two hundred yards ahead weaving as she walked along the shoulder.

"Damned woman," he growled, as he got behind the wheel and put the Hummer in drive. Lola stood on the console and nudged him, but he elbowed her away. "Another example that women are more trouble than they're worth."

But he was thankful this one was still alive. That had been a damned close call. *Two* close calls now, and they were lucky. He wasn't pressing that luck by giving those tangos another shot at her. They needed to get back to the compound and get to work.

Slade quickly caught up to her, and pulled off the road a few feet ahead. He was out of the Hummer and running toward her almost before it stopped. She stopped in her tracks, and slapped her hand over her mouth, as he stopped and grabbed her shoulders. Her eyes were liquid with relief, before he hugged her trembling body to him. Her arms slid around his waist and she squeezed him.

"Thank *God*, you're not *dead*," she sobbed into his shirtfront near his sternum, her teeth chattering. She said it so dramatically, he laughed. He felt a little giddy with relief at the moment anyway.

"I'm bulletproof, little bit," he replied, then shoved her away. Taylor looked up at him, and his eyes focused on the big blue goose egg forming at the center of her forehead. "Are you dizzy? Nauseous?"

"Dizzy with relief." She took a big shuddering breath and a tremor rocked her. "Let's get back to the compound." She turned, took one step toward the vehicle and her knees buckled, but he caught her.

"I don't think you're as okay as you say you are," he growled, bending to sweep his arm under her knees and heft her into his arms. He carried her to the Hummer, opened the door and sat her on the seat. "I'm taking you to the hospital to get checked out."

"No!" she protested, putting her trembling hand to his face. "I just want to lay down for a little while and I'll be fine."

Slade studied her eyes to see that her pupils were even, considered that she seemed coherent. "Fine, but I'm calling in a medic to check you out."

He'd seen a new application in Logan's email from a former Delta Force guy who was also a combat medic, and the man was hired if he could get to the compound in the next hour. The way things were going lately, it looked like Deep Six needed one.

"Slade?"

"Yeah?" he replied.

"I'm sorry for overreacting," she said, putting her hand to his face, her eyes dropping to his mouth making his lips tingle. Her thumb raked over the beard stubble he hadn't been able to shave that morning and the friction caused tingles elsewhere in his body. "In the scheme of things, the least I can do is wear a bra at the office."

His eyes glided down to her pert breasts tipped by still-hard nipples. "I'm okay with you going braless, because I sure don't want to wear a padded jock," he replied with a laugh. "I'm sorry for bringing it up and I apologize for being a hardass this morning."

"I kind of like your hard ass," she said breathily, her eyes catching his.

Heat beat down on his back as he held her gaze, but it nowhere compared to the heat that sizzled through his body at the heat he saw in her eyes. The air between them crackled, the buzz of his lips became electric as he fell into the magnetic pull of her eyes and his head drifted toward hers. Her heated breath brushed his mouth as his lips sealed to hers.

Her hand glided over his neck to his nape to pull him closer, and lightning zipped down his spine when her tongue traced the seam of his mouth. Slade opened his mouth, embraced her tongue and her sweetness engulfed his senses. His hand glided up her side to her breast, and he swallowed her moan when he raked his thumb over her turgid nipple.

Taylor leaned into him, kissed him deeper, and Slade groaned, but Lola's sharp bark jerked him out of the sensual spell. The crunch of tires on pea gravel sent a shock of adrenaline through him and he whacked his head on the doorframe as he pulled away. Heart pounding, he glanced down the road to see the black Suburban parked at the side of the road near her car.

Slade slammed the door then sprinted around the vehicle to get behind the wheel. He cranked the engine and grabbed his pistol from the console, before he eased his foot on the gas, hoping that the men in the SUV hadn't noticed them yet.

"Get my phone off the dash and call Dex. Have him open the gate for us, and tell him to get the guys ready in case those assholes follow us."

With a small whimper, Taylor snatched the phone off the dash and called Dex, while Slade watched the rearview for signs of the black SUV. It was only a few miles to the compound, and safety, but he didn't speed because he didn't want to draw attention to them.

Somehow the perps, whoever they were, knew exactly where to find Taylor's car, so there was either a GPS tracker on her car, or they had tapped into her cellphone. He was going to have Dex find out which it was when they retrieved her car, because if they'd tracked her through her cell phone, the perps now had their team numbers too and could track them as well. It also meant they had a techie like Dex on their side, which was not good news for Deep Six.

Those guys had been following her movements since she left the hotel. They knew she'd stopped over at the Deep Six office in town, and probably took that as a sign she knew something about their operation—whatever that was. Slade knew for sure this thing was about a lot more than a kidnapping now. They wouldn't be trying to kill Taylor otherwise.

"You know what?" Taylor asked, and Slade glanced over to see her brow puckered.

"What?" he asked.

"Lola's bark reminded me of something."

"What's that?" Slade asked, his shoulders relaxing when he saw the gate at the compound was open wide, and Caleb was set up right inside with his rifle. He relaxed more when he glanced in the mirror and didn't see the Suburban.

"The way she barked and acted the night she found that car bomb, was exactly the same way she reacted when she sniffed the hem of Tariq's pants in my office the day I was fired. I just thought she didn't like him, but—"

Slade's muscles tensed as his eyes flew to her again and he swerved. "You think Lola alerted on him?"

Taylor shrugged. "I just know she barked the same and her hair stood up."

"Did she lay down?" Slade asked quickly, as he swung the Humvee into the driveway. If she did that meant, he'd been in contact with the kid too. But then he realized that was before he put her on Zami's scent. And since Tariq was family, he would have had reasonable contact with him anyway.

"No, just hunched and barked."

Taylor gasped, and Slade's body jerked. He wished like hell she would stop doing that! He pulled to a stop near the office, and turned in the seat to glare at her. "What the hell is it now?"

Her eyes were filled with guilt and shame when they met his. "I'm a *terrible* doggie mother!" she admitted, her lower lip trembling. "I left here earlier and forgot all about Buddy being in the kennel in your apartment!"

Slade rolled his eyes, and turned to open the door. "I'm sure he'll forgive you. You were upset and that was my fault. I assure you I'd have taken care of him for you."

By the time he opened the back door and let Lola out, Taylor was halfway to the barracks, running like the hounds of hell were chasing her. And maybe they were, he thought, as he shut the door. But he was damned determined they weren't going to catch up with her.

CHAPTER ELEVEN

Instead of following Taylor to the barracks, Slade went to Logan's office and fired up his computer. He needed to call that medic to come and check her out, then he was going to research that therapy he was now committed to doing.

"What was that all about?" Caleb asked, walking into the office to sit down.

"Someone was following Taylor when she left here. They tried to kill her, and we need to find out why." Slade's stomach clenched at how close they'd come to actually succeeding.

"Well, they didn't follow you back to the compound, so that's a plus."

Caleb sat back in the chair and casually crossed his calf over his knee, like the last thirty minutes had been a cakewalk for him, like standing sniper duty at the front gate in the middle of the morning was all in a day's work. Other than curiosity as to why he was chosen for the duty, he didn't appear to be fazed at all.

They must hand out nerves of steel in the Army along with those sniper pins, Slade thought, because even though he was a former Marine, he felt sick at his stomach and like ants were crawling under his skin right now. That's another reason he was trying to find something mundane to do while he calmed down. Caleb wasn't helping him with that task by sitting here asking questions that reminded him of it.

"Yeah, it's a plus," Slade agreed, clicking the mouse to open Logan's email. "But they know where the compound is now, because we brought her car here, so keep your eyes open."

When the little arrow on the screen wouldn't move to the scroll bar so he could find the damned email, he banged the mouse on the desk as if trying to kill it, until it finally moved.

"How'd they find the compound?" Caleb pressed, and Slade bit back a growl.

"They either have a tracker on her car, or they accessed her cell phone," Slade replied, leaning closer to the screen to focus as he scrolled through the emails.

"Who's *they* and why would they be after her?" Caleb asked like a prosecutor going in the kill in a courtroom.

With a huffed breath, Slade turned to face him, and tried to get a handle on his irritation so it didn't filter into his words. "I have no idea, but her car's in a ditch about two miles toward town. Make yourself useful and go tell Levi to get a tow truck to pull it out. Have Dexter look it over and figure out who *they* is. Her cell phone is on the front floorboard."

"Dex is huddled up with Gray right now, because I think Gray may have a lead on the kidnappers." Caleb laced his fingers over his middle, and the foot resting on his knee began to rock, the only sign he may not be as cool and collected as he wanted to appear.

"What did he find?" Slade snapped, his heart lurching.

"I guess the wire transfers for the ransom have been set up for Friday," he replied with a shrug. "But there's some kind of catch. That's all I heard."

Slade tensed and prepared to stand but plopped back down in the chair. He'd done enough overreacting already today. Although patience was not a virtue he'd been blessed with, he was going to show some, let them work out the details and come to him. His team was good, the best. He knew Dex and Gray would seek him out when they had answers.

"Go tell Levi what I said, okay?"

"I'll do better, I'll go help him to keep him out of trouble." Caleb lowered his foot and stood. "Sounds like he might find some there, and I'm bored. That excitement at the front gate is as much as I've had in three months."

"You could always stay here and mop the barracks," Slade suggested with a tight smile, and Caleb's face paled. "It smells like man funk in there and since we have a couple of women in our ranks now, I'm sure they would appreciate it." With a growl, Caleb spun on his heel and streaked out of there like his tail was on fire.

Slade bit back a laugh, as he turned back to the computer and grabbed the mouse to resume scrolling through the emails to find the word

CLASSIFIED in the subject line. It finally appeared and he double-clicked to open it.

The email had come in nearly a month ago, and from what he'd read when he scanned it yesterday, this guy was not only a combat medic, he was a total badass, which made him wonder why Logan hadn't hired the man himself. Probably because between the wedding plans and practicing for the honeymoon with Susan, he hadn't had time to think about it.

The email opened and Slade skipped over the personal information to go to his qualifications to refresh his memory. With every line he ticked off, Slade got more excited. Honorably discharged Delta Force operator, who was previously an Army combat medic, presently worked for a black ops security firm and had just come off of a mercenary mission in Africa, and finished one in Columbia before that. Weapons and explosives expert, hostage rescue and counterterrorism specialist, spoke three languages including Farsi. By the time Slade reached the bottom of the extensive list to find out that he was also a Texas native he was sold.

The 1st Special Forces Operations Division-Delta did not just sign up anyone who applied, and neither did the black ops companies who hired former soldiers as mercenaries. They required their operators to be eligible for the highest level of security clearance there was next to God. Because of his mad skills, and experience, the only question would be could Deep Six afford him. That could be exactly the reason tight-ass Dave Logan hadn't hired him yet.

Freelance mercenaries got paid a lot of money, because they accepted the missions nobody else wanted. They were hired muscle, and knew every operation could be their last. Most of those guys didn't retire until they were more fucked up than Slade was when he came out of the corps, or dead. Even the government hired those men to handle some of their covert missions when they anticipated a high casualty rate.

Whatever the price though, Deep Six needed more men like Cade Winters on their team.

He located the phone number on the resume, picked up his cell phone and dialed. Winters didn't answer, and his brusque voice in his voice mail message kind of made Slade second guess himself. The thing that made the Deep Six team special was they mostly got along and respected each other. This guy sounded like an arrogant asshole. Short and abrupt. But then most guys who had his kind of credentials were. He'd just have to reserve judgment until he met with the man face-to-face and felt out whether he'd be a good fit for the team.

Slade left a message telling Winters if he was still interested in a job he wanted to talk to him as soon as possible, and not thirty seconds later, his phone rang back. Picking it up he saw it was from the same number he'd just called. He pushed the button to answer, but before he could speak, the man on the other end of the line said, "I got a call from this number."

The hair on the back of Slade's neck stood up as he sat up and cleared his throat. That's the kind of voice and tone the man had. "Yes, I was looking over the resume you emailed to Dave Logan a month ago regarding a job with Deep Six Security."

"You *read* my email?" he growled angrily.

"Logan is on his honeymoon, and he left me in charge of hiring." Not exactly true, but close enough.

"I changed my mind," Winters said roughly. "Logan is a friend, but I don't want to work for a company that is so loose with classified information. It could get me killed. I thought he was better than that."

The line went dead, and anger burned through Slade like wildfire. How dare that cocky bastard speak about Logan or Deep Six like that. *I thought he was better than that.* Like he was some supreme spec ops god who had judged the company and found them not up to his lofty standards. *I don't want to work for a company that is so loose with classified information.*

Well, Slade had a few things to say to him, and he was going to say them if it took him fifteen calls to do it. He hit the recall button on his phone and brought it to his ear, but Dexter walked through the door, and he disconnected. He saw Gray standing in the hall behind him.

"We have a lead, but we may not have enough manpower to follow up on it," Dex said, as he flopped down in the chair across from him, and Gray walked in to sit beside him.

"Why is that?" Slade asked, thinking about Cade Winters again.

"The payment isn't being made in one lump sum," Gray informed. "Half of the ten million is set to deposit into an offshore account in the Cayman Islands. The other half is going to an account in Saudi."

"The Caymans account tracked back to a shell corporation in Houston," Dexter added, then scrubbed a hand over his face. "The other account is owned by a Saudi corporation with ties to radicals."

"Terrorists?" Slade asked, wanting to clarify what Dex meant by radicals.

"Most likely, but we haven't verified that yet," Dex replied. "The only way we can be sure is to send someone over there to investigate, or find someone with knowledge of the terrorist organizations operating over there, because they don't exactly advertise."

"That will take more time than we have," Gray said. "Those transfers will be made first thing Friday morning. I'd hazard a guess that the money will be transferred out immediately and the accounts closed. Tracing it after that will be difficult, because if I were them, I'd send it off in fifty directions."

"Has Mac found anything yet?" Slade asked,

losing hope that anything about this case was going to be easy. "The kid is what I'm most worried about at the moment."

"No, but I did some recon last night on Google Earth, and found a restaurant across the street with cameras pointing directly at the hotel lot. I contacted the owners and their security company is sending me a copy of the footage." Dexter smiled, looking awfully pleased with himself. "There's also a traffic camera at the intersection, and I'm in the process of, um, seeing if it caught anything."

"Good work," Slade said, unable to stop the corner of his mouth from kicking up. The MIT-trained computer geek never ceased to amaze him. "How long before you get the footage?"

"The security company is uploading it to my server as we speak. I asked them for the high resolution version, so probably another hour or so."

Slade opened his mouth, but froze. Those cameras could have also caught whoever planted the bomb on the prince's vehicle. He and Taylor would be off the hook then, and they'd also know who was behind it. Maybe they could determine if there was a connection to the kidnapping.

"Dex can you call them back and get footage for the following day too? If the camera caught the kid being abducted, maybe it caught the bomber too."

"You got it, bossman," he said, shoving up to his feet. He winked, and a wide grin spread over his face. "If you need someone to go to the Caymans,

I'm your man."

No, what Slade needed was someone to get inside that hotel to see what was going on. Someone who knew terrorist organizations, spoke Farsi, and was good at covert ops. Someone who the prince wasn't familiar with, but might trust enough to hire.

The prince needed a new bodyguard and Deep Six needed Cade Winters to be that man. Not as an employee for now, but maybe as a freelance operator. No matter how much Slade thought he was a blowhard, he had to try to hire him.

"Gray, I need you to find me a hundred grand," Slade said, and the accountant's head snapped up from his legal pad and his face went as white as his crisp dress shirt.

"Where the hell do you think I'm going to find a hundred thousand dollars?" he asked incredulously.

"The Deep Six cookie jar?" Slade replied with a laugh, and Gray frowned. "I don't know—sell some of Dexter's toys or something. I need it as soon as possible though, because I have a freelance mercenary to hire."

Gray took a couple of deep breaths and some of his color returned. "Logan is going to kill you when he gets back."

"He can only kill me once," Slade replied, with a laugh. "And the way things are going he'll have to get in line."

A deep sigh was Gray's goodbye as he walked

out of the office.

If this worked out with Winters, they could fast track this investigation but that still didn't put the man here to check out Taylor's health status. That knot on her forehead, any head injury, was nothing to play around with. Slade knew that firsthand.

Worry settled in his gut like a brick as he pushed back his chair to stand. She said she needed to rest, and that was a good plan, but since the injury was so fresh he needed to make sure she didn't go to sleep for a while. That she was still coherent and her brain wasn't swelling.

The thought sent a rush of adrenaline through him as he walked swiftly through the office to the front door. Slade brushed by Levi who was coming up the steps as he went down, but he didn't stop.

"Hey, I need to talk to you!" Levi shouted behind him, but he didn't stop.

He picked up his pace to a jog, then a run as tension ratcheted up at the back of his neck. She could be comatose in his apartment and nobody would know. Having a latent seizure. She could be dying. He flew through the front door of the barracks and ignored Caleb who tried to stop him too.

Slade had one mission on his mind right now and that was taking Taylor Kincaid to the damned hospital whether she liked it or not.

CHAPTER TWELVE

Slade flung open the apartment door and immediately searched the living room for Taylor, but he didn't see her. He slammed the door and heard a whimper from the bedroom. Through the open doorway he saw her in the bed and ran that way. Buddy lay beside her with his head resting on her shoulder.

The dog looked up when Slade stopped by the bed, but Taylor didn't move. Slade's heart stopped, because other than the purple knot on her forehead, her face was as white as the sheet covering her. His hand shook as he strode to the bed and reached out to feel for the pulse at her throat, but Buddy snarled at him and he jerked back.

The starch left his body on a wave of relief when Taylor's hand appeared from under the sheet to pat the Labrador's head. It all congregated in another place when she turned on her side toward him and the sheet slipped to her waist giving him his first full view of her gorgeous, rose-tipped breasts. Dragging his eyes away, he leaned down to snatch the sheet up to cover her, but it was stuck under her forearm.

"Taylor wake up!" Slade growled, tugging on the sheet again. Her eyes fluttered open and she smiled, as her hand drifted up to cup his cheek.

"You should get in bed and take a power nap. It'll make you feel better, I promise," she said groggily, rubbing her hand over his beard stubble, starting fires inside his body. The sleepy, sexy quality to her voice fanned the flames. "You look exhausted."

Slade was exhausted. They hadn't slept more than four hours last night. He would love nothing better than to crawl into that bed with her right now, but he wouldn't be sleeping. She wouldn't either, and probably shouldn't be right now anyway. Her drowsiness could be a sign of a concussion, and she could go to sleep and not wake up.

Something pulled hard inside his chest.

"I'm not sleepy, I'm worried about you. I wasn't able to get the medic here to check you out, so we're going to the hospital." He couldn't stop his eyes from dropping to her breasts again, and a yearning so strong it made his knees weak hit him right in the gut.

Taylor laughed, as she brought her hand up to feel the bump. "I looked at it in the mirror and it's ugly, but I don't even have a headache. It's my own darned fault for not taking the time to take my car in for service when I got the airbag recall last year."

No, her damned no-account cheating boyfriend should have done that for her, Slade thought, as he tried to raise up, but her small hand flew to his shoulder to keep him there. She held his gaze, electricity buzzed between them and she bit her lip. Why the fuck did she have to bite that damned lip?

"Thanks for worrying about me, I'm not used

to that," she said, her voice breaking. "I'm worried about you too. Sleep deprivation can bring on another episode, and so can the stress from this morning. Please just get in bed and take a short nap with me."

Slade dragged his eyes down, and they landed on the pile of clothes by his boot. That told him that, just as he suspected, she was completely naked under that sheet.

"If I get in that bed, there's no way I'll be able to sleep," Slade said, without looking at her.

Her hand glided over his shoulder, up his neck to his face again, and he bit back a groan when she raked her thumb over his lower lip.

"We could explore option two, and maybe that would help you sleep," she offered, and her words rumbled through his body turning his muscles to putty.

The air became heated with his ragged breaths, as Slade fought the urge to take what she offered. But why the hell was he fighting it? She'd said last night it would remain between them, and wouldn't mean anything. Maybe because for some strange reason that bothered him, since he knew she wasn't *that kind* of woman.

"I could definitely go for continuing that kiss in the truck," she purred, stroking his lip again causing a shiver to rock him.

Desire clawed at his insides, and a need as fierce as he'd ever felt engulfed him. With a growl,

Slade's control snapped, he grabbed her wrist to kiss her palm then licked his way up to her elbow and Taylor shivered. He yanked her up to her knees, shoved his hand into her thick hair and slammed his mouth over hers. His other hand found the warm globe of her ass, and her skin was like silk under his fingers as he dug them in to hold her closer.

Liquid heat flowed between them as their tongues met, danced, and her luscious body melted into his. Her hips ground against his fly, her heat scorched him through the denim and he moaned as he tumbled them onto the bed.

A heavy weight landed on top of him, a warm, wet tongue lashed over his ear, and dipped inside leaving behind plenty of slobber. Reaching behind him, Slade shoved Buddy, who must have thought it was playtime, off of his back, before he grabbed the sheet to dry his ear.

Taylor giggled, but Slade wasn't amused as he grabbed the dog's collar and dragged him toward the edge of the bed. Buddy teetered there, pulling back against him, but finally fell off the edge and Slade dragged him to the door to put him out.

He turned back to the bed and lost his breath when he found Taylor laying on her back waiting for him, her knees spread showing him the beautiful pink flesh between her thighs. His tongue tingled to taste her there too, to suck the nipples she was lazily caressing. He wanted to taste every square inch of her, feast on her until this gnawing hunger inside him was gone.

And he would, he thought, as he yanked his shirt over his head then tossed it aside before quickly removing his boots and jeans. Slade stalked to the bed, and Taylor raised up on her elbows, her eyebrows lifted as she smiled at him. He realized her eyes were on his crotch, and looked down.

"Da, dah, da, dah da—*Bat*man!" she sang, with a laugh.

Heat crept up his throat, and Slade decided that maybe it was time for him to buy some regular underwear. Carmen, his last friend with benefits, and the other women he'd slept with in the last five years liked them. But it looked like Taylor Kincaid just wanted to tease him about them.

"I wondered which ones you had on this morning at the meeting," she said, bringing her eyes up to his. "I kind of like the teeny white ones with the red lips."

"You went through my freaking *underwear* drawer?!?" Slade asked incredulously. This woman evidently didn't have any more damned boundaries than her dog!

She shrugged. "I have a curious nature, what can I say?"

With a growl, Slade kneeled on the bed and launched himself at her, eliciting a giggle he felt near his sternum. Pinning her to the bed, he looked down into her sparkling blue eyes.

"You can say you'll never go through my stuff

again, or I'll have to *kill* the curious cat."

"Can you loan me that pistol in your underwear drawer?" she asked, her smile fading. "There's no way we can get mine from my house now, and I'd feel safer."

That was his sidearm from the corps. The pistol he'd been carrying when the explosion happened. The firing pin was broken, and the barrel bent. He'd kept it as a souvenir, but knew it could never be fixed. Sort of like him.

"No, you can't have that one, but I'll get one for you," he said gruffly, as he swooped in to peck her lips.

With a moan, she craned her neck for another peck and he sealed his mouth to hers. She met him stroke for desperate stroke with her tongue, rubbed her calf along his leg and made needy circles with her pelvis that soaked his underwear with her moisture. Things got out hand fast when she wrapped her legs around his waist tightly and her gyrations put her heat in firmer contact with his throbbing cock. His hips moved too, and with each pass, he inched closer to embarrassing himself. He was not going to come until he was inside her body, and she came too.

"I need to get a condom," he said, dragging in breaths as he tried to lift up but her legs tightened around him.

"I have one," she slurred, her eyes as desire-drugged as her voice.

Her legs loosened as she stretched across the

155

bed to shove her hand under the sheet. After a second, her hand emerged and she had a condom between her fingers.

She had a condom ready?

That added to the fact she'd been naked in his bed told him she'd been waiting for him to come to her so they could have sex. She'd probably been laying here fantasizing about it while she waited, not sleeping. That was just about the biggest turn-on he could imagine.

But something else bothered him.

"You went through my shaving kit too?" he asked brusquely.

"No, I found this one in one of the drawers in the bathroom."

She hadn't gone through his shaving kit, but she had gone through the drawers. He wondered what the difference was in her mind.

Slade snatched it from her and rolled to his back to shove off his underwear. His hands shook as he positioned the condom and rolled it on. Before he could get up again, Taylor sat up and pointed to the headboard.

"Lay that way," she said, and he moved vertical on the bed. She straddled him, and placed her hands on his stomach and his muscles contracted.

"You want to be on top?" he asked, surprised.

"No, I want you to relax. Let go and let me drive this time," she said, with a sexy smile as she stretched over him, the ends of her hair tickling his sides as she glided her palms up his chest leaving his muscles quivering behind. She reached down to grab his hands, and her palms met his as she pulled them up over his head.

Slade let her hold them there because that put her incredible breasts right there in his face. He leaned up to nip one, and she giggled, her back arched but her eyes narrowed as she looked down at him.

"You don't get to do that unless I say you get to do it," she said sharply, but her playful eyes took off the edge in her words.

Let go and let me drive. Every muscle in his body tensed as her meaning became clear, and electricity zipped through his body.

Taylor Kincaid wanted him to submit to her.

Slade had tied up women before during sex, because they'd asked him to, been dominant and bossy, but he'd never in his life let a woman do it to him. If she wanted to be in control though, he'd try it. If he didn't like it, it wasn't as if this five-foot-nothing woman could keep him down. It wasn't like she was handcuffing him to the bed or anything. He was afraid he'd have to draw the line there.

"Keep your hands there," she said wrapping his fingers around the narrow square spindles on the inset in the headboard.

She scooted off of him, stuck her hand under the sheet again, then stuck her head under too. When she emerged, a pair of silver handcuffs dangled from her fingers and Slade's butt cheeks tightened. Those had to be the ones he kept in the shoebox in the back of his closet. That meant she probably found the packet of letters from Jeannie he'd saved too.

Slade let go of the spindles and sat up to grab her shoulders.

"Did you read my letters too?!?" he demanded, his fingers digging into her flesh.

"Of course I didn't. That would be an invasion of privacy. I saw them but left them alone," she replied, sounding hurt.

Slade almost wanted to laugh. *An invasion of privacy?* Taylor Kincaid had done nothing but invade his privacy, not to mention his peace of mind, since she'd been at the compound. His fingers loosened and her body slumped.

"I have the key too, but if you don't trust me, we don't have to use the handcuffs if you'd rather not. I just thought since you had them, you'd expect me to…"

He heard the disappointment in her deflated tone, and wanted the excited spark back, the hot momentum they had going a moment ago, but not at the expense of allowing himself to be cuffed. Slade was enjoying her take-charge attitude, and he was okay with trying new things within reason. That did not include allowing her to handcuff him to the bed.

He didn't trust her, because he didn't know her. This was their first time together. He could imagine doing something to piss her off, or her just deciding to leave him there for giggles for the guys to find, or worse.

"Let's skip the handcuffs this time, but I promise to keep my hands where you put them. Does that work?" One corner of her full lips kicked up, and the other followed. Her eyes sparked again as she tossed them over the side of the bed.

She averted her eyes then, and he saw a faint blush stain her cheeks. "Whatever you want is fine. I've just been lying here thinking about doing that to you, and it's been driving me crazy."

She *had* been fantasizing about him and that knowledge made his cock throb. Slade quickly laid back down, stretched his hands over his head and gripped the spindles.

"Have your way with me, Ms. Kincaid," he said, looking down at her where she sat on her knees by his ankles. Anticipation buzzed through him as he wondered what her way would be. She'd had about two hours to come up with a plan, so he'd bet it was going to be good.

But guilt knocked the edge off of his excitement. Slade needed her to hurry too. He had a lot to do at the office, and the guys were working their asses off to help him. He needed to be there when the video finished downloading. He needed to get with Levi and Dex about her cell phone and car. He needed to find out if Gray had the money together so he could call Winters.

He needed…a groan rolled from his throat when her small hand closed around him. What he *needed*, he thought grinding his teeth, was to feel her tight pussy wrapped around his dick.

"Wow, my fingers don't even touch," she said with a now agitating giggle, as she squeezed her hand tighter and his balls tightened more. He shoved his hips upward needing to feel the friction of her hand moving on him, but she released him and raised up.

"I said relax—that's *not* relaxed." At her dark, abrasive tone, Slade's eyes flew open to glare at her.

"How in the hell can I relax when you've got my cock in your hand? When I want to be inside you so bad I can taste it?" he fired back.

"If you're a good boy, we'll get to the tasting part," she said slyly, as she grabbed his ankles and nudged them apart. "Open your legs, and relax."

If he was a good boy? It sounded to him like she thought she was training a dog.

With a frustrated breath, he let her spread his ankles wide and relaxed back on the pillow but his fingers gripped the spindles so tightly, he was afraid they would snap. He was even more afraid of that when her tongue licked a circle around his ankle and fire shot up his leg to his balls.

Slade looked down his body at her but couldn't see what she was doing because her hair covered her face. He felt it though when she suctioned her mouth to the indentation on the inside of his ankle beside his Achilles and pulled hard. His body jerked rattling the headboard as tingles danced up the inside of his thigh, his cock swelled and he threw his head back to moan.

Who the hell knew that was an erogenous zone?

Holding the pressure of the suction, she slid her mouth up to his knee and found another hidden spot there when she flicked her tongue behind his knee. A tremor shook him and he groaned at the sensual torture she was putting him through with each tiny kiss and nip she made on her path up to his inner thigh. Her hot breaths scorched his already sizzling skin, his nerves were electric and his balls were so tight they hurt, as he waited to see what she would do next.

The witch let him wonder, stew in the sexual hell where she held him hostage for a full minute, before the wet heat of her mouth touched his skin again and he groaned. She slid her mouth lower then sucked hard on the artery there drawing blood to his balls and come to the end of his dick. Slade held his body rigid as the condom became a tourniquet on his cock, and he fought to keep from coming taking shallow breaths that sounded almost like whimpers.

Every muscle in his body was taut with frustration as he leaned up to glare down at her. And then her teeth clamped down on his skin, pain shot through his groin to zap his brain, and he screamed, as he let go of the bars to launch up and grab for her with his throbbing fingers. When she moved away, he rubbed the welt on his inner thigh.

"You promised not to let go of the slats," she

said angrily, narrowing her eyes.

"You bit me—and I'm *not* into pain—*at all*," he growled hoarsely, his cock throbbing in time with the welt that was now forming a distinct ridge around the edges. "And this has gone on long enough, I need you to stop messing around and *fuck* me!"

"That's not the way to ask when you want something is it?" she asked, her brows pinched into a scowl. "Ask nicely."

"Nicely for what?" he asked with frustration.

"For what you *do* want...I don't know what you like, and I—I don't want to do anything else to upset you," Taylor folded her arms over her breasts. Was that fear in her eyes?

"I want to have *normal* sex with you right now—*please*!" Slade ground out.

"This is *normal* sex, isn't it?" she asked, her voice and lower lip wobbling, as she unfolded her arms. Her surprised look and the confusion in her eyes, told him she wasn't kidding, and his instincts told him something was *very* off here.

"No, ma'am this is kink, and I'd love to explore it with you if that's what you like and it doesn't involve pain—when we have more time. That's not something you can rush or take lightly without talking about it first, or someone could get hurt."

Namely him in this case. His fingers rubbed the ridge on the welt, and fear shot through him as he realized exactly how close she'd come to his balls.

Taylor stared at him a moment more as if trying to determine if he was telling the truth. Suddenly, he heard her gag and a shiver shook her as she bent down to grab her clothes. When she stood again, her face was a horrified mask.

"Oh my, *God*. I'm so sorry...so embarrassed," she muttered, as she turned and dashed for the bathroom with the clothes clutched to her chest.

It looked like he wasn't the only one with some issues that a little therapy would help, Slade thought, as he crawled out of the bed to go find her. What he'd really like to do is find that bastard who'd fucked her head up so badly about sex, handcuff him to the bed and give him more than a little pain.

Taylor wasn't a kid though, he'd guess she was in her late twenties, and she was obviously *very* experienced at sex, so what puzzled him more is why she believed whatever she'd been told.

Hadn't she ever had normal sex before?

It just didn't make sense to him.

CHAPTER THIRTEEN

Taylor was mortified, as she leaned against the vanity in the bathroom, refusing to look at herself in the mirror. How could she have been so stupid?

Just because Mark, and his best friend Matt before him, told her that the strange things they asked her to do to them, the odder things they'd done to her in bed, were what good sex was all about, she'd believed them. Just like she'd believed Mark loved her until the night he tried to kill her with his crazy games and blamed it on a PTSD episode.

Now that she'd seen a real episode firsthand with Slade, she knew Mark had been faking it to cover his abuse—the spankings he said would relieve his stress, the domination he said would help him get control of his demons, which lasted even when they weren't having sex.

The days when she was off work and he was *visiting* her, as Taylor called it that now because she knew he had a wife, a home and a child, when he demanded she walk around naked all day for him to fuck at will in whatever orifice pleased him. The *toys,* which were pretty close to torture devices that he used on her to get his jollies, the same toys he demanded she use on him when she cuffed him to the bed and beat his ass.

Toward the end, that was the only time she *really* enjoyed sex with him, because she got a little payback for what he dealt to her. Dealing him pain had definitely been her pleasure then.

Taylor hadn't questioned it—and they'd pushed the limits because they knew she wouldn't. Matt had found a naïve virgin and trained her gently to accept, even like sometimes, what he did to her, so she didn't know any better. He pretended to care about her to convince her that they had a normal relationship. That what he did to her, what he had her to do to him in the bedroom was normal. When he got tired of her, he passed her off to Mark, a much more depraved man, and probably gave him a playbook which he expanded.

Her chin dropped lower to her chest, and she groaned. "How in the hell could I have been so stupid?"

And because she was so stupid, and evidently a degenerate herself, she'd believed Slade would like the same things they had when she found the handcuffs in his closet. From the look on his face and his anger, that definitely was not the case. He'd enjoyed some of it, but thought she was a freak. Sickness boiled in her stomach, as she wondered how in the hell she'd ever face him again.

The door knob rattled, and she gasped as it flew inward and he filled it with his naked body. His green eyes met hers, and they were full of confusion, sympathy and hot anger as he shut the door, and leaned on it.

"I think we need to talk, little bit," he said gruffly. "Tell me what that bastard did to you."

Taylor swung her eyes back down to the vanity. "I can't," she replied, her voice barely above a whisper. "You'd think I was an idiot."

Slade pushed off of the door, and she saw his muscular calves as he stopped beside her. His big hands dropped on her shoulders and he turned her to face him, then tipped her chin up so she had to look at him. "No, I'd think that you are a beautiful, but naïve, woman who was conned and probably abused by a slick sonofabitch with no morals or respect for women."

"Slick sonofabitch*es*," she corrected, her lower lip trembling and her eyes burning as shame washed through her.

God, if her father was alive and knew he'd probably kill Mark. Slade looked like he might be considering that at the moment too. He'd have to get in line, because Taylor wanted the first shot at him, and she didn't miss.

"Who were they?" Slade demanded, his fingers tightening on her shoulder. Taylor tried to drop her chin to get away from the intensity in his eyes, but he held it firm. When she didn't reply, his face darkened, and he pinched her chin. "*Who*, Taylor?!"

"My ex-boyfriend Mark and his best friend Matt," she admitted, pinching her lips shut.

"How did you meet them?" Slade's eyes narrowed, and he stared into her eyes as if he'd find every answer there.

166

"I met Matt first at the recruiting office in Oklahoma when I went there the day after I graduated from college. The recruiter said because of my size, I wouldn't qualify for MP training and I was pretty upset. Matt was there renewing his contract and convinced me he could help me because he was an MP training officer." Taylor stopped as emotion clogged her throat.

"*More*, I want every fucking detail, Taylor," Slade growled, a white line appearing around his mouth.

"I took a job with the sheriff's office, worked my ass off with him at night, and started staying over at his apartment when we finished with PT. One thing led to another, and even though I never got accepted as an MP, we became a…couple."

Taylor blew out a breath to fight through the sickness that burned in her throat. A growl rumbled in Slade's chest and she knew he was going to make her finish.

"Things were good, Matt got a permanent station at Fort Sill, but then his best friend Mark was transferred there and he introduced us. Mark hit on me constantly, and there was no way that Matt didn't notice because he did it in front of him too. Matt just didn't seem to care, even seemed to kind of like it. I took that as a sign it was time for me to move on, my blowup with the sheriff sealed that, so I started looking for a job out of town."

"Okay, so you found the hotel job, moved to

Dallas—how did Mark get back into your life? Didn't you think he was an asshole for hitting on you when you were his best friend's girlfriend?" Slade demanded, his brow puckered.

Taylor shivered, not wanting to continue, because she knew Slade would really think she was a degenerate. She *was* one, because at the time she'd *liked* it. What they'd done that night was a stretch, but not too far from normal for the sex life she and Matt shared. But she couldn't let Slade think she was a cheater.

"Oh, I thought he was an asshole at first and avoided him, but when Matt decided he was done with me and all but threw me to him."

"So you had sex with Mark, before you moved and he followed you to Dallas?" he asked, and blood scalded Taylor's face.

"Sort of," she said, averting her eyes, even though he still had her chin in his grasp.

"You don't *sort of* have sex, Taylor. What made Mark follow you to Dallas?" A tremor rocked her, and Slade's body tensed. "Tell me!" he shouted.

"Mark showed up one night and said he locked himself out of his apartment. Matt was finally showing interest in me again, so I was frustrated when he told Mark he could stay. It was an efficiency apartment and the sofa was small so he got in bed with us and…" *I was already tied to the bed and blindfolded. They both took turns fucking me for hours and making me guess which one of them was up to bat, as Mark called it. They*

168

gave me an orgasm if I got it right. Before they untied me, they fucked me at the same time and it hurt some, but not bad enough that I didn't like that too. Yes, I'm a freak, and so ashamed for not being smart enough to realize they were turning me into one.

Slade's hands fell away, and Taylor's eyes flew up to see his face was ashen. He looked disgusted, and she had to get away from that look. "If my car's not trashed, I'll be out of here in a few minutes," she said, her body shaking violently as she scooped up her clothes from the counter. "If it is, I'll walk to town and call a cab."

"So after *that* you invited the bastard to move in with you in Dallas?" he asked incredulously.

"*No*—that's *not* what happened! I didn't invite him anywhere. He just showed up one day at my house saying he was in town for a training," she shouted back, turning to face him. "He took me out to dinner, and we just talked that first time. The next time he came back was the same..."

"But the third time was a charm, eh?" Slade guessed, his breathing shallow, his nostrils flared and his fists clenched at his sides, as the dark flush on his face nearly covered his shoulders.

"Yeah, he came back every time he was on leave, left clothes there and even got mail at the house. He called me every night, came home—um, *visited* my house—every two or three weeks for a few days. Longer when he got vacations. He said he was living with me."

"For how long?" Slade asked, his voice a smidge calmer.

"Three years."

"What happened to make you finally break up with him?" he asked, the anger in his tone escalating again.

Hysterical laughter bubbled in her chest as the thought hit her that she was standing here buck naked telling this man, her new boss at her shiny new job, who was standing before her naked too, things she'd never told another soul. She'd told him everything else, so why not finish it? He certainly couldn't think any worse of her.

"He almost choked me to death one night during sex, and it scared me. Told me it was a PTSD episode afterwards, like he'd done for a while when he got too rough. I researched EMDR trying to help him and myself, because I really did care about him. But then his wife had divorce papers delivered to my house six months ago, and I kicked him out." When Taylor finished, it felt like a huge weight had been lifted from her shoulders.

"I want to know who these motherfuckers are because I have connections with the Army. They were both Army right?" he demanded, and her blood froze.

All she needed was Slade to create drama by confronting them or calling their superiors. That would mean she would be dragged in the middle of an investigation to testify, then have to repeat the process in court. Taylor was embarrassed enough without recounting the depths of their sordid sex games in public, and she wasn't sure there was anything that could be done about it anyway.

What happened was entirely her fault. Mark and Matt had *duped* her, but they hadn't forced her to do anything. Everything she'd done with them had been consensual.

Because she was a naïve idiot.

"I'm not telling you," Taylor replied, lifting her chin. It's over and done with and they are out of my life." She put her hand on his chest. "Just let sleeping dogs lie."

With a growl, he pulled her to him and hugged her tightly, which surprised her. His angry words rumbled under the ear pressed to his chest. "Those *dogs* used a military uniform, an honorable uniform your father wore, to convince you they *had* honor so they could use and abuse you. The twisted bastards need to be shown what honor is and be punished so they don't have a chance to do this to anyone else."

Taylor shivered in his arms, and her eyes burned again. Was that why she'd been so susceptible to Matt and Mark's games? Because they wore an Army uniform and that made her trust them? The misery in her gut boiled into anger, and she pushed back from him.

"They did didn't they?" Taylor said, looking up at him, her voice stronger as her anger burned brighter.

"Damn straight they did," Slade agreed, his eyes like granite as he looked down at her. "And I'm pretty good at figuring things out on my own. You don't have to tell me where to find them, I'll find them." His hand shot out and he grabbed her wrist, and the clothes in her arms tumbled to the floor. "But what I want to do right now, is show you how a real man makes love to a woman."

Taylor pulled back, and he stopped to turn and hold her shoulders. "If you don't feel like it anymore, I understand. I should've asked, because that was a *major* emotional dump you just had. I'm sure you're pretty raw."

"I'm sorry for dumping on you," she said, looking down. She really was sorry, but he'd pressed and pressed until she spilled it all to him.

Slade tipped her chin up. "Tell me what you want, little bit," he said gruffly.

Her throat worked, and her eyes focused on his lips, as a need for intimacy and emotional contact tugged at her insides. "If making love with a real man includes kissing, then I want you to show me what normal sex is like, please."

Slade's eyes were green fire as he studied her for a minute before he dropped a light, sweet kiss on her mouth and took her hand.

CHAPTER FOURTEEN

Leading her to the bed, Slade stopped to cup her face in his palm, and his eyes fixed on her mouth as he stroked his thumb over her bottom lip.

"Do you like it when I kiss you, Taylor?"

Taylor remembered the delicious kiss Slade laid on her in the truck and a thrill raced through her. That kiss is why she'd been waiting for him in bed, hoping he'd come to her to finish what he started. That single touching of mouths had created a burning need in her body greater than any she'd ever experienced in her life.

There was no fear, no pain in that act—just tenderness and incredible need.

Neither Matt nor Mark thought kissing was a part of having sex, so Taylor had never experienced the intimacy of mouths touching, the silent communication that happened between souls through an exchanging of breath. Slade's kiss had shown her why she'd never felt really connected with either man during sex, or any other time.

"Yes, I *need* you to kiss me," she whispered against his thumb, and he smiled as his head drifted toward hers.

His mouth met hers with a moan, their breath mingled and sweet need sprouted in her chest. Taylor's mouth opened on a sigh and Slade kissed her deeper, held her closer and the delicious tension in her belly grew. His hand skimmed over her waist, to her hip, leaving goosebumps behind on her skin, but when the warmth of his palm settled on her ass, Taylor clenched her cheeks and he jerked his hand back.

"Did I hurt you?" he asked, his eyes dark with concern.

"No, just habit," she replied, sliding her hand down his arm to take his hand and put it back there. No sex ever started with Mark unless he spanked her until her butt felt raw first. Sometimes it was delivered with his hand, sometimes with a hard wooden paddle that she hid from him, which earned her more licks with it when he found it.

Taylor got very good at hiding it.

Slade's eyes sparked with anger, but cleared as his head bent toward her again, his mouth covered hers and he moaned. He kissed her deeply, feasted on her mouth as his left hand found her other cheek She clenched again, but his fingers dug into her flesh and he lifted her up to her toes. His groan mixed with her whimper as her sensitive, hardened nipples raked up his chest.

He shifted her weight and suddenly the tip of his rigid cock pressed against the swollen nub at the top of her thighs. He held her there, gyrated his hips against her as he deepened the kiss until she felt like he was inside of her, lifting her spirit up like he had her body. Her breath came in snatches, her head swam, and need clawed at her insides. Throwing her legs around him she pressed down on him, rotated her body with his and a violent tremor rocked through him.

"We need to get in the bed," he groaned, sliding his mouth from hers. "I need to be inside of you now." Breathing hard, he sat on the bed with her on his lap.

Wanting that badly herself, Taylor scrambled off of his lap and crawled toward the head of the bed. Laying down in the middle of the bed she brought her knees under her to lift her ass high in the air and felt her insides open. She lifted higher by arching her back as she stretched her hands toward the headboard.

Her inner muscles and anus pulsed in time with her out-of-control heart as she imagined the incredible friction and burning stretch when his huge cock drove into her.

The question was which would he choose.

She whimpered and her ass muscles clenched thinking about him choosing her anus. As big as he was that could hurt badly without lube of some kind. It hurt bad enough when Mark did it and he wasn't nearly as big. The bed dipped, and she felt Slade crawl up behind her.

"Please get the baby oil if you want anal," she begged, flinching when he touched her.

She heard a choked sound behind her, his hand shook then suddenly she was flipped on the bed and he glared down at her.

"I'm sorry," she said, her lip trembling as fear

shot through her.

Taylor didn't know this man, and right now, he looked mad enough to kill her. She tensed and ticked off possible moves in her mind she could use to get him off of her if necessary. The same way she had when Mark pushed her too far.

"Sorry for *what?*" he growled, pulling her to him as he lay down beside her. "I'm going to kill that fucking bastard for doing this to you."

"Doing what?" she asked.

"For doing a complete mind fuck on you where sex is concerned." His arms loosened, and eased her back onto the mattress. "I want you to close your eyes and relax."

Taylor shut her eyes, and huffed out a breath but she still wasn't relaxed. The thing she hated worst was being blindfolded and not knowing what was coming at her next.

"I'd rather keep my eyes—*oh*," she said, on an indrawn breath as his warm, slightly callused palm glided down her body leaving a trail of fire. His other hand slid under her neck and he drew her closer to his side, before throwing his calf over hers to nudge her knees apart.

"You have the most incredible breasts," he murmured, and his voice rumbled through her body, relaxing her a bit. His hot breaths got closer and brushed her skin. "Your nipples are always hard, and that is sexy as hell. Seeing them makes *me* rock hard."

"There's a reason for that," she said, her ass

cheeks tightening.

"You're turned on? Genetically gifted?" He smiled against her breast, before he raked the flat of his tongue over the hypersensitive tip. He sucked her into his mouth and pulled, his moan vibrated through her nipple setting her nerves on fire.

Taylor slammed her eyes shut, curled her fingernails into her palms, and a long, low moan vibrated in her throat, as her body trembled and she fought to endure the almost electric connection between her breast and her clit. Moisture gushed to her folds, tension built in her head, and her body shook hard, but she fought harder, because she did not want to come yet.

Slade finally released her with a wet pop and her breath came out in a rush, and her body jerked as latent jolts zipped through her. Heaving a deep breath she blew it out.

"No, it was the suction cups and cream," she replied, breathlessly. "They're oversensitive now too, so I come quickly if you suck them." In two point three seconds, Mark had timed it and laughed. It became a game, a challenge to him, to see how fast he could get her there. She'd almost just beat the record.

Taylor heard Slade's indrawn breath, felt his thick, long cock jerk against her thigh but he didn't suck her again to test the claim. She wished like hell he would, almost wanted to beg him to put her out of her misery. Her body was so agitated right now, it wouldn't take much to push her over the edge.

"Suction cups and cream?" he repeated, lifting his head from her breast.

Taylor opened her eyes and heat scalded her face as she met his eyes. "Matt made me wear nipple suction cups to make them larger, and use cream to make them permanently hard. He liked to see them through my clothes, because he wanted to think I was turned on by him twenty-four hours a day."

"He *made* you wear them?" Slade asked, his voice disbelieving.

"I didn't like the consequences if he caught me not wearing them," she explained, and a shiver rocked through her. The weighted clamps hurt too badly. When he tied her hands behind her back and put them on, it was excruciating. Enduring twelve hours of that would convince anyone to just wear the suction cups.

Slade sat up and shoved a shaking hand through his hair, his back muscles flexing with his agitated breaths. "What a sadistic, misogynistic piece of *shit!*"

Taylor decided right then it was best if she kept the rest to herself. This man did not need any more pressure, stress, or worry than he had on his plate right now and neither did she. What was done, was done. She was fine now, they were out of her life and she wanted him to show her how it was *supposed* to be so she wouldn't look like a fool with the next man she slept with.

She got up to her knees and put her hand on

his back to lean in and kiss the side of his neck and his breathing stopped. "Slade, make love to me," she asked softly, as she kissed her way down his neck to his shoulder.

"I have one condition," he said without turning around.

"What?" She leaned over his shoulder to see his face.

His eyes met hers and she saw purpose there. "You'll set us *both* up an appointment with that doctor to have that therapy."

"But I don't nee—"

"You probably need it more than I do," he said cutting her off.

"Okay, I'll do that this afternoon." If that's what it took for him to agree to try EMDR, then she would do it with him too. Even if she didn't need it. The therapist would see that and let her go. "But first you're going to show me how a real man makes love to a woman. That's your end of this deal, and I'm really curious how that works, since I've never met a *real* man before," she said, forcing playfulness into her tone.

With a growl, he spun to grab her around the waist and she giggled as her back bounced on the bed and he buried his face in her stomach. She thought he'd move up toward her breasts, but he didn't. His tongue flicked out to lick down toward her hip, his body moved in that direction too and a delicious shiver rocked her.

"I think I'll start down here with lesson one," he growled as he gently spread her legs, laid between them and put her calves over her shoulders. He turned his face to the side and kissed his way up her left inner thigh to the crease and his beard stubble was like sandpaper on her tender skin. Each rough kiss ratcheted the tension inside her body tighter, sent a feathery tickling sensation zipping over her nipples up to her scalp.

Taylor squirmed, Slade looked up and his nostrils flared. "We'll save those *overly sensitive* nipples of yours for dessert. I'm about to show you that's not the only sensitive place on your beautiful body."

Hearing the sexy promise, the rough texture of his voice, feeling the vibrations of the words on her skin, made her insides quiver. She watched his dark head slowly descend between her legs, and hot lava built there. She held her breath and anticipation gathered near her navel. His wet heat scalded her excited flesh, and she whined as she threw her head back to the mattress and clutched the sheet.

He licked a slow circle around her clit, her stomach muscles undulated and her inner muscles flexed. His head dipped lower, and her body jerked with little jolts of pleasure as he nipped his way down her folds, sucked them between his lips. When he dipped his tongue inside, a long low-pitched moan gurgled in her throat, as her inner walls clenched and her body itched to feel him inside. Never had she had this desperate need to have a man inside her.

"Please just come up here, and fuck me," she begged, her voice raw.

"No, I'm not nearly done, little bit. You taste too damned good, and you haven't come for me yet," he mumbled, between hot, excited breaths, which excited her.

Suddenly his tongue flattened and he slowly dragged it up her folds toward her clit. Taylor's fists clutched the sheet, and she rolled her head to the side to bite her bottom lip and hold back the scream building there. The warmth of his lips surrounded the throbbing bud, his lips spread and then he sucked the bud between his teeth with a loud slurp.

An electric shock vibrated through her and Taylor screamed. He sucked faster, the sexy sound of the continuous slurps echoed in her skull. Her body arced off of the bed, and he slipped two of his fingers inside her body as he sucked harder. The bud became raw and sensitive, the sensations too intense. Taylor whimpered, squirmed to get away, but his mouth followed her to continue the sensual torture. Suddenly, her body seized, her bones melted and her teeth chattered, as bright white light appeared behind her lids then swirled into collage of beautiful colors as a tidal wave of an orgasm drowned her in pleasure.

A dark, rumbling laugh tickled her stomach before a kiss landed there and Slade crawled up her body. Leaning in, he kissed her softly and she tasted herself on his lips. A latent tremor rocked through her at the sensual surprise, and she sighed.

"Did you enjoy lesson one, little bit?" he asked, and she could only nod. "Good," he said dropping a kiss on her shoulder, as he laid down beside her and leaned up on his elbow. "Let's move on to lesson two now. I want to suck those beautiful breasts of yours, while I feel your body squeeze my cock when you come. You're so small, we're going to have to get creative to make that possible."

She'd always felt dirty when Mark talked dirty to her. He was always pushing the envelope with it, making it sound nasty, not sexy. Slade's dirty words and delivery made her feel beautiful, desirable. Need sparked inside her again and she wanted nothing more than to feel him stretching her when he made her come again.

She sat up on her knees and smiled. "Let's try you sitting against the headboard and I sit on you. Does that sound good?"

Slade's green eyes heated, as he crawled up the headboard and sat there. He held his arms open to her, and something inside her chest shifted. This man *was* the real deal. A real man who knew how to treat a woman. To cherish one.

I have to warn you, I don't do anything other than casual sex.

Taylor was damned curious why this man felt that way, because he sure didn't seem like a casual type of man. He had all the qualities that made for great relationships. He was kind, caring, protective and loyal. She needed to remember his policy though and not let her heart get involved here, which could easily happen. If she'd cared about Mark after all he'd done to her, she could wake up and find herself loving this man.

Slade's arms dropped to his sides and he frowned.

"You change your mind?" he asked, waking her up.

"Are you kidding?" she asked with a grin, pushing him back against the headboard. "Round two includes dessert!" Taylor straddled his legs and reached for his cock, but he grabbed her shoulders and pulled her up to his chest.

"I want more of those sweet kisses as an appetizer first. You need to see how damned good you taste," he growled, as he covered her mouth and skimmed his hands down her body to grip her ass. His cock swelled between them as he went deeper with his tongue and swirled it with hers. Her salty sweet taste excited her taste buds and she moaned.

Not that she had any experience at kissing, but she couldn't help but believe this man was a master at it. He could probably make her come from this alone, she thought, her core muscles clenching and her breath coming in small gasps.

But she wanted more—she wanted to feel him inside of her. Taylor put her hands to his muscled chest and pushed.

"I need you inside of me," Taylor growled, as she found his cock between them and positioned herself over it.

Holding his glittering eyes, Taylor pushed her hips down hard, he groaned and she hissed as the head of his cock slipped inside her body. The burning stretch was incredible and her body quivered around him. Taking all of him was going to require a little time though, she knew that now. Slade's head dipped down and she tensed when his mouth covered her breast. He didn't suck her though, he ran his tongue around her nipple in light, irritating circles and it swelled in his mouth. His thumb made a pass over her other nipple, and Taylor arched her back into his touch and closed her eyes, gasping when more of him slipped inside of her.

The burn was intense now as he stretched her, but she couldn't focus on it because of the delicious friction of his tongue on her breast. With every circle he made around her nipple, her body wilted more and she slipped lower on his shaft. His thighs tensed under her and he suddenly stopped. His mouth left her, but he rested his forehead on her breast and moaned.

"So fucking tight, so hot," he said in a hoarse whisper, dragging in agonized breaths. "I need a minute, or I'm going to come."

One, two, three seconds passed as he rested there breathing, then heaving a deep breath, he grabbed her shoulders and shoved her down onto his cock. Taylor screamed as she took all of him in that push. Her chin dropped to her chest as she took shallow breaths trying to process the most incredible pleasure pain she'd ever felt in her life. Her inner muscles make butterfly light spasms around him, because that's all the stretch she had left.

He tipped her chin up and his tortured eyes met hers. "Are you okay?"

Taylor nodded, because she couldn't find her voice.

Leaning over her, Slade slid his arm behind her, draped her over it and sucked her nipple into his mouth again. He licked a circle, but his arm tightened and he sucked hard. He made short needy little sucks and her nipple slipped between this teeth. Taylor moaned loudly feeling the tugs between her legs, feeling the sting of his teeth raking over her.

Her inner muscles tried to clamp down on him but all she could do was whimper as she vibrated around his thickness. The vibrations took over her whole body, her head was so filled with pleasure it had nowhere to go, and felt like it would explode. Suddenly Taylor shattered, her body shook violently and nonsensical words gurgled in her throat. As Slade pulled her to his chest and hugged her tight, he shook too. With a shuddering breath, and a final tremor he lifted her and she moaned as he left her body. Gently, he laid her on the bed, then collapsed beside her and pulled her into his side.

His snores began almost immediately, and Taylor smiled.

CHAPTER FIFTEEN

Fierce pounding woke him up, and at first Slade thought it was inside his head. But that couldn't be, because he felt light inside like he hadn't in a long time. His body felt energized, his head clear. The banging continued and a sleepy kitten-like moan drew his attention to his side.

Taylor stirred, rubbed her face against his chest, and her eyes fluttered open. "What time is it?" she asked groggily. "What's that banging?"

"Someone's at the door." He glanced at the clock on the nightstand and his eyes widened. "And it's nearly four o'clock!" Shoving her off of him, he sat up and waited for his brain to find its place in his skull. The banging started again, and he pushed off the bed to stagger to the bedroom door, then made his way through the living room to his front door.

He unlocked it, then opened it a crack. Caleb stood there frowning.

"What's up?" Slade asked, his voice rusty.

"Well, *bossman*. If you're finished getting your *afternoon delight*, and your nap, Dexter has the footage you wanted and thinks you should see it."

"I didn't get much sleep last night," Slade said defensively.

"For *obvious* reasons," Caleb shot back, trying to glance over his shoulder.

"Mind your own fucking business," he growled, some of the lightness inside dissipating as he narrowed his eyes and stepped to the side to block his view. "I'll be there in a minute."

Slamming the door in Caleb's face, he turned and found Taylor standing there naked and his cock hardened. He looked down and saw he needed to go to the bathroom, because he'd been so wiped out, so wrecked from his mind-blowing orgasm, he hadn't even bothered to remove the rubber.

"I'm getting in the shower," she announced, and turned to give him an amazing view of her round backside.

"Oh, no you don't," he growled, walking swiftly past her. "You used all the hot water this morning. It's my turn."

"We could conserve the hot water and shower together," she suggested, as she walked behind him. Her tone told him she had doing things together other than showering on her mind.

Slade stopped at the bathroom door, turned and grabbed her shoulders. "I don't have time right now, I have to focus. You stay here and make that call we talked about."

"I don't have clean clothes anyway," Taylor replied.

"I'll look through Logan's closet again, but I've got to go now."

"Can't I at least have a kiss?" she asked with a pout, and Slade's cock hardened more.

If he kissed her, he wouldn't be showering, and he certainly wouldn't be leaving this apartment.

The way he felt, as amazing as that sex had been, Slade knew he could spend days in here, weeks with her, and still want more. But he wasn't going to leave her without at least some kind of acknowledgement of just how fucking good it had been. She was insecure right now, and he wasn't going to do that to her.

His hand glided to her chin and he tipped her face up, her hands planted on his chest sending tingles down to his toes as she rose up, met his mouth. He felt her moan inside his chest, in his now fully erect cock as he kissed her, sucked her plump lips, but when she opened for more, he pushed her back to step inside the bathroom.

"Make that call," he growled, shutting the door in her face like he had Caleb's. It was time to focus on this case, find out who was trying to kill her and why. It was time to get down to business.

Fifteen minutes later, Slade strode into the office in full business mode, and Lola seemed to realize that as she kept close to his heels. Levi stepped out of the kitchen where he smelled something cooking, probably something southern, greasy and loaded with carbs, because that's the only thing the man from Alabama knew how to cook. But it was usually so damned good nobody complained.

"I wanted to let you know it was her cell phone they used to track her. I searched all over that car and there was no device," Levi said.

That meant a couple of things. First was it

was someone who knew her cell phone number, and secondly it meant the bad guys had their cell phone numbers now too. "Where's the phone?" Slade asked.

Levi grinned. "I drove her car and the phone out to a state park in hill country, and left it there. I thought the bad guys would probably like the view, and all that real estate should keep them occupied looking for her. Her axle and transmission are probably toast anyway."

Slade blew out a breath. Their resident grease monkey, and explosives expert was a very smart man. He'd solved the problem, at least temporarily, of Taylor being in danger. That would give Slade time to focus on other things. Like finding Zami Khalil before he was dead.

"Good thinking," Slade said, patting Levi on the shoulder as he walked toward Dexter's evil workshop down the hallway.

"I found your money," Gray shouted unhappily, as he passed his office. Slade backtracked to lean inside. "Call your mercenary, but at least try to negotiate. I think when Logan gets back we'll both get our pink slips otherwise. I sold some of his retirement stock, and took a pretty substantial hit on it."

"He's too much of a work-a-holic to ever retire anyway," Slade said with a laugh.

"I know, and that's why I did it. Just find that kid."

"Working on it," Slade replied, leaning back out to walk down the hallway. He pulled his phone out of his pocket and recalled Cade Winters number. The man must never answer his phone, Slade thought, as he left a message and hung up. He'd made exactly five steps when the phone rang back. This guy screened his calls like it was his business, and maybe it was. But it still irritated Slade. Maybe he should just let it ring, he thought, stopping outside the doorway of Dex's office. No, he needed this bastard too badly to do that.

Pushing to answer the call, he took the offensive, before Winters could. "I have a proposition for you," he said gruffly.

A deep sigh. "I told you I wasn't interested."

"Oh, I think you'll be interested now. I'm not offering you a job with Deep Six," Slade said and enjoyed the slight intake of breath on the other end of the line. Yeah, that's right asshole, with your attitude, you're not good enough for *us*.

"What do you have in mind then? Subcontract work?" Winters asked gruffly.

"No, I want to hire you as an independent contractor. You'll have no connection to Deep Six at all. You'll be a double agent guarding Prince Ahmed Khalil, and getting inside information for us. I need an answer right now, and I need you to get him to hire you today, or by Friday, his son will probably be dead."

The line went silent for almost a minute.

"Did you say Ahmed Khalil?" Winters asked, his voice dark, and the way he asked the question raised the hair on the back of his neck. Like he knew him well.

"Yeah, Prince Ahmed Khalil," Slade repeated.

"Why is Zami in danger?" And that told Slade that Winters did know Prince Khalil. Well enough to know his son's name when he *hadn't* mentioned it.

"Zami was kidnapped Sunday night or Monday morning and is being held for ransom. Do you know Ahmed?" Slade asked.

"I know of him," he said in that tone again. "And I'd be pretty damned scared of anyone who has the balls to kidnap Zami."

"Why is that?" Slade asked, doubting the man would answer him, but he did.

"He has ties to one of the largest terrorist organizations in the middle east. Some say he heads it, and funds it well. Others say that his frequent trips to the US are for reasons other than management of his oil empire. He has plenty of people here and in Saudi to handle that for him."

And that explained why Ahmed did not want security cameras on the penthouse floor he occupied. It had nothing to do with privacy for his wives, and everything to do with privacy for him and his covert activities. It also explained why he didn't want the authorities involved in the kidnapping case. Slade's whole 'Tariq is behind this situation theory' flew out the window. Now the world was his acreage to search for the kidnappers, and probably the kid.

It made sense now.

"Would Ahmed recognize you then?" Slade asked, seeing his only hope of getting someone inside disappear if that was the case.

"No, of course he wouldn't recognize me." Cade Winters laughed, and it sounded rusty, like he didn't use it much.

"Then I have a hundred thousand dollars if you can get him to hire you and you can find out what the hell is going on inside that hotel."

"That would mean he *would* recognize me after that, and it's worth more than a hundred thousand dollars to me to keep my anonymity where he's concerned."

This guy was something else, a snake who was working him without a conscience to get more money because he knew Slade's back was against a wall. If a hundred grand meant nothing to him, Slade was in the wrong arm of the security business.

But then if he chose the deadlier end of the business, providing security and private army services in the middle east and other hotspots, he'd probably be just like this man. Slade preferred to keep at least a shred of his humanity.

"Ahmed paid Deep Six extremely well to guard him, so you can probably up that to a quarter-of-a-million or so considering that he'd pay you too." The line went silent again, and tension wound like a rubber band around Slade's chest as he counted the seconds.

"I'll see what I can do, but I need the money first," Winters said shortly. "If I can't get him to hire me, I still get the money and will provide *consultant* services as needed."

Slade ground his jaw as he thought about it a minute and let the greedy bastard stew for a change while he did. "Agreed. Call Grayson, our finance guy, and give him your wire information." Slade spouted off Gray's cell phone number. "I need one other thing though."

"What's that?" Winters asked suspiciously.

"The ten-million dollar ransom has been set to deposit on Friday into two different accounts. One is an account I've been told is owned by a group with radical ties. Talk to Grayson and see if you have any information on that to help us."

"Done," Winters replied, and as Slade expected, the line went dead.

That guy was entirely too Rambo for his tastes. He claimed he was a friend of Logan's, so he had to have something to recommend him, Slade reminded himself. But Dave didn't hire him and he was starting to realize why.

With a huffed breath, he walked into Dexter's office and the geek didn't even notice or look up. As usual, his eyes were locked on a computer screen, as he played a rapid tune of clicks and clacks with his mouse and keyboard. When Slade got closer, he realized Dex was reviewing a video.

"What did you find?" he asked, as he stopped beside him to lean down and look too.

"I don't think you want to know," he replied, clicking an arrow at the bottom of the screen and the images flew by on the screen in reverse. "I keep rewinding it to see if there's something I missed, but it's just not there."

"What's not there?" Slade asked, with frustration as he stood.

Dex spun in his chair and crossed his arms over his chest. "Any other explanation for the car bomb," he said.

"*What* did you find?" Slade ground out, getting frustrated with the geek.

"The only person who was around that car from midnight until the bomb went off was Taylor Kincaid. The car didn't move either."

"Yeah, she didn't stay in the damned Hummer like I told her to when I took Lola out to scent in the parking lot," Slade grated with a huffed breath.

Dex looked confused, then his eyebrows raised. "No, I'm not talking about when she was out there with you. This was around eleven a.m. according to the timestamp on the footage. She walked by the Mercedes got into her car and drove off. She came back nine and a half minutes later and got out of the car with a large shopping bag in her hand. She stopped, ducked down between the cars for three minutes, then walked out of camera range and I assume she went back in the building."

"Is that from the restaurant footage or the hotel footage?" Slade asked.

"Hotel footage, but I checked the restaurant tape too and it just made things worse. I could actually see her kneeling down on the ground to look under the car. That bright blue business suit…" Dex waggled his eyebrows. "And that ass was hard to miss."

Slade could only stand there stunned, as his mind worked to try and find another answer. Taylor hated the prince for choosing Deep Six over her in-house security, despised the man for treating her like she was useless because she was a woman. He would just about bet she saw the writing on the wall that she was going to be fired over the kidnapping, even though she wasn't responsible for his security.

Was that enough reason for her to want to kill him? How in the hell would she have the skills necessary to both manufacture and place a bomb on a vehicle without blowing herself to smithereens in the process? She was smart, and the internet contained specific instructions these days on how to do it. Kids had done it. Or maybe she'd had help. Maybe she'd planted the device for someone else. For the kidnappers. But why would they want to kill the golden goose before they got the ransom?

Regardless of who she was working with, if the prince was the target, she'd missed. That meant, she was getting inside information from being inside Deep Six to maybe try again, or she could be feeding information she obtained here to the people behind the assassination attempt. The other scenario could be that they thought she'd double-crossed them and *sided* with Deep Six, and *that* is why they were trying to kill her.

Goddamn, his brain was fried, and the fucking buzzing was starting in his head again.

"What are you thinking?" Dexter asked.

"I'm thinking I need a fucking off-the-grid vacation like Logan's when this is over, and not with a damned woman," he growled, and Dex laughed. "I'm also thinking I need to talk to Taylor Kincaid, but if I do that, I'll clue her in that we're onto her, if she's involved." He turned toward the door, but looked back. "Keep looking for another answer. Help me figure out what the hell is going on here."

"Will do," Dexter said, turning back toward the computer. Slade walked toward the door, but stopped in his tracks to listen when Dexter mumbled. "At least I got a look at the kidnappers on the restaurant camera. It was too far and too dark for me to get a good look at them, but from their complexion when they walked under the streetlight to get in the car parked at the curb, I think they're Arab. The traffic camera got the license plate, and I'm working on running it down."

The buzzing in Slade's head got louder, the dots in his vision started and realized he'd forgotten to take his medicine that morning. He fought them as he turned back and stalked back to Dex. "Why the fuck didn't you tell me that first?!?" he demanded.

Dexter shrugged. "Since you and Taylor were killing cats in your bedroom earlier, I thought that might interest you more."

"Killing *cats*?" Slade repeated, his eyebrows crashing together. Dexter lifted brow and his meaning sank in. Blood rushed to Slade's face, and he spun toward the door again. "Just get me fucking answers, and mind your own business."

CHAPTER SIXTEEN

Slade walked down the hallway to his own office and slammed the door behind him. He needed some space and time to think about this whole situation, before he went off half-cocked and blew Taylor Kincaid's brains out like he wanted to do at the moment.

He didn't trust women to begin with, but her tortured virgin story had really tenderized the hard walls he'd built around his heart over the last five years. And he'd been a fool to let that happen. Hell, maybe she secretly liked sadism, because she was certainly masochistic. Those two mindsets typically went hand in hand.

She could've been a willing participant in what those men did to her because she was bent on self-destruction. According to her, her ex-boyfriend almost choked her to death during their potentially deadly autoerotic game, and she got scared. But she hadn't kicked him out of her house for that. No, she'd only kicked him out when she got the divorce papers and found out he was married.

That said a lot, now that he thought about it.

If she wasn't bent on self-destruction, a masochist, why else would she have planted that bomb under that car in broad daylight? She had to know she'd been seen and caught. The prince, her target, was a dignitary visiting the US. The bombing was now national news, so the FBI, ATF and all the other alphabet agencies were probably involved. They were reviewing the same video footage Dexter had reviewed, and would come to the same conclusion.

Taylor Kincaid planted that bomb under the prince's car.

The question they'd have is for whom? It was the same one he had.

Slade was not convinced she'd acted alone, or for the sole purpose of knocking off a man who insulted her though. If she'd acted alone, her partners wouldn't be trying to kill her. God, he wished now he had chased them down, then he could question them and get the answer, or turn them all over to the police with their moll, Ms. Kincaid.

The buzzing in Slade's ears grew louder, and he realized he was nearly hyperventilating, so he leaned back in his chair, closed his eyes and focused on slowing his breathing. He hadn't started having episodes again until she came into his life. They were getting worse by the day, no, by the hour, now.

That had to be her fault too.

And Dave Logan's for dumping this mess in his lap.

When this case was over, Slade really was taking a vacation. He'd leave his cell phone in a box on Dave's desk, and see how his best friend liked that. But right then, his cell phone vibrated in his pocket and Slade groaned as he sat up and pulled it out.

Excitement shot through him though when

he saw it was Jaxson Thomas calling. Slade quickly answered, hoping like hell the ex-SEAL was calling to tell him he had changed his mind about quitting. "When are you coming back?" Slade asked quickly.

Jaxson blew out a breath. "I'm not, man. I need your help though."

Slade breathed a few moments, wondering if he should just hang up the phone. He had enough problems on his hands without dealing with Jaxson's. If that's the only reason he called, he could just take a number.

"What do you need?" Slade asked, cringing when he was unable to just hang up. Jaxson had been a good Deep Six operative, and a good friend. If he needed help, Slade couldn't bring himself to turn his back.

"I've got a tail that followed me from Dallas to DC. I can't shake them, so I'm leading them to Colorado."

"Who is it?" Slade asked, sitting up in his chair.

"An Arab hit squad, I think. I saw they were middle eastern, but that's all I know. It has to be connected to the prince or the kidnapping. They probably think I know something, but I don't know shit."

"Why Colorado?" Slade asked.

"My mother lives there and I'm borrowing her van to throw them off. I'll need wheels, because I want you to keep them on my car. There's a GPS tracker on it. Make them think I'm dead, or something to buy me some room to finish the case I'm working on. We're dodging bullets too."

"Sounds dangerous. Who the hell are you working for now?" Slade asked.

"Guardian Angel Protective Services. GAPS for short. It's a new security firm opened by some of my former SEAL buddies. I'm on a close protection detail."

That he got a new job so soon after leaving Deep Six was not good news for them. Hearing he was now working with his former SEAL teammates, men he considered brothers, also cemented that he wouldn't be coming back.

"Hawk is in Houston, but I'll call him back. Levi and Caleb are available."

"Aww shit—you're gonna let Levi blow up my car aren't you?" Jaxson asked, his voice shaking. Jaxson loved that damned car, treated it like a woman. He washed it so much Slade was surprised it still had paint.

"I'm going to let them do what they need to do to get those guys off of your tail and convince them you're dead," Slade replied, but his mind started working.

If those hitmen followed Jax from Dallas, they could indeed have a connection to the prince or the kidnapping. They could even be the same guys who shot at Taylor for all he knew.

But Jax said they'd followed him to DC, so

the logistics didn't work out for that. It had to be a different crew. Even so, the Dallas connection meant those men probably had answers that would help. Levi and Caleb could kill two birds with one stone. Or keep them alive and put them in a cage until they sang.

"Don't worry, we've got your six, man. Where do you want us to meet you?" Slade asked, grabbing his pen to write down the location in Colorado that Jax spouted off. They hung up, and Slade called Levi, Caleb and Hawk then sat back in his chair to think.

"Lola's bark reminded me of something…the way she barked and acted the night she found that car bomb, was exactly the same way she reacted when she sniffed the hem of Tariq's pants in my office the day I was fired."

Damn, she was good, he thought, with anger building inside of him. The anger built to volcanic proportions as his mind replayed all of the instances of her lies in a loop. He had no idea how long he sat there steaming, until the scratching and whimpers at the door alerted him to the fact he'd locked Lola out of his office when he slammed the door.

He could definitely use her right now to calm down, Slade thought, pushing up to his feet to walk to the door. He opened it, and Lola was there, but so was Taylor Kincaid with her fist raised about to knock. He noticed that she had on one of his t-shirts and wanted to growl. She'd been in his drawers again.

"I, ah, was coming to tell you that I made our

appointments. She set us up for three and four o'clock next Tuesday."

"Fine," Slade said, pushing the door closed, but she stopped it.

"I also wanted to see if you were hungry. I can make you something…"

She wanted to fucking take care of him? This is just the reason he kept his sexual encounters casual. He fell off the wagon one time, opened himself up just a little, cared just a little, and this is what he got. A woman who lied to him and was now acting like they were married to get further under his skin.

"I don't need you to take care of me, Ms. Kincaid. Levi cooked something and I'll eat that when I get hungry. It's for all the *employees* so fix yourself a plate if you're interested."

"Ms. Kincaid?" she repeated, her voice trembling, her eyes glassy.

"That's your name isn't it?" he asked, fighting the tug in his gut when she bit her lower lip.

"Yes, but—" she started, but Slade pushed the door closed in her face, and turned backed to his desk. He sat in the chair, and the door opened and closed.

Chest heaving, shoulders near her ears, Taylor stalked to his desk. He didn't meet her eyes, but her heat and scent teased him as she leaned over him..

"If you forgot my name in the three hours since you pulled your cock out of me, it's *Taylor*," she hissed, and her short breaths bushed his jaw. "Is this another lesson on how a *real man* treats a woman? If it is, I can't say I like it."

His blood pressure skyrocketed, but Slade didn't respond. Lola shoved her way in between them with a whine to nudge his thigh with her muzzle, and he reached down to scratch between her ears.

"Slade?" a soft husky voice said from the doorway, and Taylor turned around.

Slade's eyes ticked over a tight sports bra that pushed up a pair of perky breasts, a very toned stomach and rounded hips, down a pair of very athletic legs before gliding back up to meet a pair of bright blue eyes.

"Hey, Cee Cee—come on in." Relief washed through him as he pushed up to his feet. "Ms. Kincaid was just leaving."

Taylor's angry gaze swung back to his and Slade could almost see the smoke collecting at the top of her shiny sable hair. She looked back at Cee Cee. "I wasn't quite finished with him, so if you'll give us a moment…"

"No problem," Cee Cee replied hitching a thumb over her shoulder. "I'm hungry, so I'll just run back out and grab a burger. Levi said there was food in the kitchen on his way out, but it's all gone."

Slade walked around Taylor to stand in front of her. "Let me grab my keys, and I'll take you to dinner somewhere so we can talk." Slade needed to get the hell away from this compound and Taylor

Kincaid for a little while.

"I'm hungry too," Taylor said sharply.

He looked at the ceiling, gathered his composure then turned around. She obviously didn't get he didn't want to be around her right now. Slade was about to make that perfectly clear whether it hurt her feelings or not.

"There's peanut butter and jelly or tuna in the pantry. Make yourself a sandwich. You're not invited to go out with us."

Slade walked around Taylor, grabbed his keys from his desk and moved toward the door. Suddenly, his feet flew out from under him and Cee Cee came at him full speed. He grabbed her, tried to shove her aside, but they tumbled through the doorway and landed in a heap. With a growl, he rolled off of her and sat to face Taylor who stood in the doorway grinning.

"You're pretty damned clumsy for a former Marine. You should take *karate*, I hear it helps with balance." Slade heard the rumble of laughter in her chest, but she pinched her lips to suppress it. Taylor turned away, and her parting shot had Slade grinding his teeth. "I had plans anyway. Hawk mentioned something about strip poker on the Nintendo tonight, so don't hurry back." With a finger-wave over her shoulder, she walked down the hallway and disappeared.

"Wow—does she work here too?" Cee Cee asked, her eyes swinging back to his.

"Did David hire her?"

"No, I hired her—*temporarily*. She'll probably be gone by the time he gets back." Slade arched his back to spring to his feet. *To prison most likely.*

Cee Cee executed a similar move, then brushed off her ass and laughed. "You might be saying the same when David gets back and sees me here."

"That won't happen, I'm not going to let it happen," he assured gruffly. "What would you like for dinner? It' a long drive in either direction to get something, but we can find anything you want. I'm in no hurry to get back." *Considering the woman I fucked earlier today is playing strip poker with another man tonight.*

Slade forced down the jealousy that curled in his gut. He had nothing to be jealous about. He did not ever want to have sex with Taylor Kincaid again. That was a one and done deal that never should have happened. Hawkins could have her. Hell, every man in the company could have her for all he cared, and the trouble that came with her.

"I think I'll just grab a PBJ and find somewhere to crash. I'm exhausted."

Even though Cecelia was military and probably slept in barracks with men before, Slade thought it wouldn't be a great idea for her to do that with *these* men.

"The sofa pulls out, and the blankets and pillows are in the linen closet in the bathroom. Make yourself at home until we can figure out better sleeping arrangements. The guys are in the barracks, so you shouldn't have any problem from them."

"I wouldn't have any problem with them anyway," Cee Cee said, with a wink. "I can handle them."

Slade had no doubt about that, but he wasn't taking chances with Logan's sister. "I'll see you in the morning, and we can talk about what you'll be doing."

"I'm ready," she replied with a wide, white smile. "I've been waiting seven years for this. This place will be ship shape by the time my brother gets home."

"Ship shape?" Slade couldn't help his chuckle. "You learn that in the Army?"

"Nah, I dated a sailor recently, and it rubbed off," she replied, with a waggle of her eyebrows. "I'm sure you'll be treated to the other words he taught me too in the near future."

Slade liked her. She was open and friendly, and seemed to be unflappable. They needed unflappable in this office.

"That's a relief, because if he hadn't taught you, I'm sure these guys would have educated you fast. Call me if you need anything," he said, turning toward the door.

"All I need is sleep, but if you run into *her* again, you might need a helmet."

Her—meaning Taylor. Which reminded him she needed clothes, and he needed her to have them so she would leave his t-shirts alone. Cecelia was a taller than Taylor by a few inches, and a little larger, but her clothes should fit. They'd probably be loose fitting, but that would be a damned good thing in Slade's opinion.

"I hate to ask this, but do you have some clothes that Taylor can borrow?" Slade asked turning back toward her. "Just a few things so she doesn't have to borrow my t-shirts?"

One thing for sure was the busty little hellion couldn't wear Cecelia's bras. She had a good bit of size on her there.

"Sure, she's smaller than me, but I have some workout clothes that have gotten too small since I've been working out more regularly, and a couple of pairs of BDU pants. They're in my truck if you want to follow me outside?"

Slade followed her to the door and down the steps. They walked to her truck, and he waited while she unzipped her duffle bag and dug through it.

"Where can I run around here?" she asked, as she turned around and handed him a stack of folded clothes.

"There are plenty of country roads around here, but the shoulders on the main road are soft and narrow. I'd suggest the treadmill. We have a whole workout facility behind the barracks, if you want to use it."

"I like running outside, but I'll probably take you up on that when it rains."

Slade needed to do some PT too. He hadn't

had time in two or three weeks, but that was an excuse. When someone wanted to do PT, they did PT.

"I'll go running with you if you want," he offered.

It would also mean she wouldn't be running alone. They were in a pretty remote area, but as Taylor proved this morning, that did not guarantee you were safe. Especially when you double-cross your asshole partners in crime. Anger stoked inside him again, and simmered in his stomach.

"Oh six hundred sound good to you?" she asked, a challenge in her tone. "I have to warn you I do ten miles most of the time."

"Oh six hundred it is. I'll meet you at the gate," Slade replied, turning to walk toward the barracks, the renewed anger burning brighter with every step he took.

Yeah, he could definitely use some PT to burn off steam. His therapist told him that would help with his PTSD episodes, and it had for a long time. And then came Taylor Kincaid and taking the reins at Deep Six and they reappeared.

Starting tomorrow morning, Slade was going to run that woman, and these problems right out of his head. He was going to get his shit together, and find his Zen again, so he could think straight.

CHAPTER SEVENTEEN

Taylor lay on Hawk's bunk, and angrily flipped through a military surplus magazine she found on Hawk's trunk, not even reading the pages. The top bunk in this set was empty, so he offered to take it since it was easier for him to get up there. He, Levi and Caleb were leaving before dawn on some kind of mission anyway, he said.

Right now, they were being loud and obnoxious—little boys in men's bodies, as they fought imaginary enemies and each other in a video game. Hopefully, since they had to leave early, they'd turn in soon, so she could get some rest. There probably wouldn't be any rest for her tonight though. Taylor couldn't ever remember being as mad as she was right at the minute. Not even with Mark, who she was angry at frequently. Almost every time he visited her.

Slade's intention when she walked in his office had been to hurt her, to push her away and let her know it was over. To make her feel small and worthless.

He had succeeded in spades.

Licking her thumb, Taylor slammed the magazine shut and started at the front again.

He was much more of an asshole than Mark had ever been to her. At least Mark took her out to dinner sometimes, wined and dined her occasionally, sent her flowers at work a time or two to make up for being an asshole. If Slade planted a fucking field of them for her, she wouldn't forgive him.

Not that they were a couple or anything, she had no illusions there.

He shown her with his reaction to that musclebound blonde woman who came into his office that she meant nothing to him. That he was moving on to his next piece of ass.

That made her feel dirty and used.

Taylor's vision blurred, and she sucked in a breath. She was not going to cry over that bastard. She was going to move on just like he had. Forget that they'd ever had sex, just like he had. In three fucking hours.

A tear plopped on the page as she flipped it and Taylor slammed her eyes shut, took deep breaths, and didn't open them again until she heard the barracks door open.

Her heart was not supposed to leap in her chest when she saw Slade standing there in the doorway, but it did, and she wanted to rip it out of her chest.

His eyes landed on her, glided to Hawk then back to her and she saw his biceps flex, as he gripped the doorknob tightly. Like green lasers, his eyes burned holes in her as he strode across the floor to the bunk, and tossed a stack of clothes on the end of the bed.

"Don't tear those up, and give them back to Cee Cee before you leave," he said, his voice cold and flat. He turned and walked back to the door and slammed it on his way out.

"What the fuck is in his craw?" Caleb asked, glancing at the door.

"Who the hell knows," Levi replied. "Just play dude, we have to go to bed."

Taylor didn't know what was in his craw either, or what she'd done to be the target of his anger. She wished like hell he'd just come out with it, and tell her so they could move past it. Even if they weren't sleeping together, they had to work together for now.

Until she could find another job.

That was going to be on the top of her to-do list tomorrow. Taylor had her resume in her email, and she was going to find it, polish it up and go somewhere she would be respected. If a place like that existed. She was starting to doubt she'd ever find it. Maybe she needed to apply to law school and become a lawyer. That would only take her three more years.

She needed money to support herself though. And even when she took the pre-law track in college she never had any intention of becoming a lawyer. That was boring, and tedious stuff. Taylor had wanted to do something important to help people, something honorable like her father had done. And she'd failed so badly, she had to become a security supervisor at a ritzy hotel where the only thing she supervised was the time clock.

When the door opened again, Taylor leaned up on her elbow. Buddy whined as Slade pushed him inside the door and shut it behind him. His sad and confused eyes as he looked back at the door mimicked how she felt inside. It looked like Slade wasn't only done with her, he was done with her dog as well. So much for his promise to train him.

"Here, Buddy," she said, and his head hung low as he walked over to the bed. He perked up when she scooted back and patted the mattress though. With a loud *woof!* he leaped up onto the bunk and it shook as he moved around to find his spot behind her. Taylor dropped the magazine and rolled over to hug him tight.

You're the only man I need in my life, Buddy.

He licked the side of her face and snuggled his head into her chest, and Taylor's insides finally settled. She laid there and his coat soaked up her silent tears until she fell asleep.

Buddy's whine woke her entirely too soon, and it was *that* whine that told her he needed to go out—*now*. Taylor scrambled up, scrubbed the sleep from her eyes and got out of the bed. Buddy dropped down to the floor to look up at her and whined again. She glanced at the top bunk and saw it was empty, and knew the guys were already gone.

With a wide yawn, she grabbed his collar and hunched over to walk with him to the door. Slade could at least have left her a leash, she thought, as she opened the door, and he half-dragged her across the outer room to the door. She glanced at Slade's apartment door, because she couldn't help herself, and wondered if he was in there having sex with the blonde. Kissing her like he'd kissed Taylor.

A sharp pain sliced through her chest and she rubbed it.

"I don't give a damn," she grumbled as she twisted the doorknob and led Buddy outside noticing that dawn was just breaking.

She inhaled deeply of the fresh country air and exhaled, before she led Buddy out into the yard and let go of his collar. With a loud *woof!* he took off across the yard and Taylor groaned as she ran after him, calling his name. He ran around Slade's Humvee, and headed for the gate and when Taylor rounded the vehicle, she stumbled then stopped.

Slade stood there at the gate dressed in running shorts and a t-shirt with the blonde, who was wearing bright pink shorts that looked more like underwear and a black sports bra. Buddy stopped beside Slade and his tail wagged his body. He jumped up on Slade and put his paws on his chest, and Slade's loud, "Buddy, *sitz!*" rang through the trees and inside her skull.

Emotion tightened her chest, worked up to clog her throat but Taylor swallowed it down as she made her feet work again to go get him, before they opened the gate. It seemed to her like she was walking in slow motion and it took forever for her to reach them, but in reality it was only a minute.

"Going for a run?" she asked perkily, as she jerked Buddy's collar so he'd move away from the blonde who was crouched down petting him.

"Yeah, so hold onto your damned dog so he doesn't get out when we open the gate," Slade grumbled, without looking at her.

The blonde studied him then studied Taylor, before a wide smile broke over her pretty face. She stepped toward Taylor and stuck out her hand.

"I'm Cee Cee Logan," she announced, holding Taylor's eyes. "I'm glad to see it won't be a sausage fest around here."

Her husky voice reminded Taylor of Lauren Bacall's voice. Lauren smoked a pack a day to achieve that sound, but she highly doubted this woman did considering her level of fitness. Taylor was amazed that she could like this woman and hate her at the same time.

Slade growled as she took Cee Cee's hand and Taylor's lips wiggled. "I'm Taylor Kincaid," she said louder than necessary. "It's very nice to meet you, and yeah I've pretty much been *embroiled* in a sausage fest since I got here, so I'm glad to see you too."

The woman's open and friendly smile made Taylor relax a little. She decided right then that this was a woman she could be friends with, if she wasn't sleeping with Slade. Maybe when he was done with her too, they could be friends. As fast as he worked that could be this afternoon.

Cee Cee hitched a thumb over her shoulder, and winked at her. "Don't worry, I'm gonna run the grumpy out of him, before I bring him back," she said, and Taylor did laugh.

"I don't think that's possible. I don't call him grumpy, though, I call him *Smiley*." Slade's head whipped up from the gadget he was playing with and his angry eyes speared her, and Taylor smiled.

"Oh, it's possible. I'll either run it out of him, or run him into the ground." Cee Cee gave Slade a sideways glance. "He looks pretty out of shape, so if he gets tired I'll just let him rest on the side of the road while I lap him."

"You're not going to lap anyone," Slade growled, as he slapped the heel of his hand against a red button on a box right inside the gate. It rattled open, and Taylor grabbed Buddy's collar when he lurched to follow him as he strode through the gate.

Trouble in paradise? Taylor bit back a giggle, as she watched Cee Cee walk outside the gate and begin stretching. For a man who'd gotten not one, but *two* rounds of sex yesterday, with two different women, he was awfully grumpy. That thought wiped the smile right off of her face, and the laughter from her heart.

With a huffed breath, she held Buddy until the gate closed, then turned him loose. She jogged back to the barracks herself, and Buddy ran by her side. Taylor was going to use Slade's bathroom to shower, so she didn't have to use the stalls the guys used in the bathroom in the barracks. Yesterday, during the meeting, before she left and almost gotten herself killed, Slade told her she would be working with Mac to weed through the employee lists. That is exactly what she was going to do today to keep her mind off of a grumpy, hard-hearted man-whore who wore underwear designed for children.

I wonder what underwear he has on today under those mesh running shorts.

Taylor almost tripped over her own feet as a wave of desire punched through her. Maybe she'd look through his underwear drawer and try to figure it out, she thought, as she opened the door and let Buddy in. No, she didn't care, and that was none of her business.

As a matter of fact, Taylor was going to change and leave his t-shirt on the bed too after she showered. She didn't want any reminders of him at all. She was going to work hard to help figure out who planted that car bomb to exonerate herself, keep her nose out of his business and work on finding herself another job.

The sooner she could get away from *Mr.* Slade, the better.

Her eyebrows puckered as she grabbed the doorknob at his bedroom. Nobody had just one name. Slade only used one name, and she wondered why. His name was probably as goofy as his underwear and he was embarrassed to use it.

Archibald Horatio Slade. Casper Simon Slade. Taylor giggled. No maybe it was a girly name.

Carol Regan Slade. Ashley Rowan Slade. *Adrian*, she thought with a gasp then slapped a hand over her mouth. *Adrian*. She'd bet his name was Adrian. And then one of her father's favorite songs played in her head and she giggled.

A Boy Named Sue, by Johnny Cash. It fit the cowardly bastard who didn't have the balls to break it off with her like a *real* man. And now that damned song was going to be stuck in her head for the rest of her day.

Before Taylor left here, she would know his full name because she needed a reference. Since she hadn't worked with Dave Logan, that would be him. That would give her a reason to ask Mac and Dex to see if they knew.

Maybe she'd also use it as an opening too, to see if she could find out what *was* in his craw, as Caleb said. Slade had changed directions with her so quickly, gone from scorching hot to freezing cold in a minute, either he was a cold-hearted unfeeling, *cowardly* bastard, or something had upset him.

Taylor walked into his bedroom and avoided looking at the big bed as she made her way to the bath. She'd take a long hot shower, and maybe she'd feel better. If he had no hot water when he got back, that was too bad too sad. It would be his punishment for being an insensitive asshole. He could just go to the barracks shower.

The steam was so thick in the shower she could barely see the knob to turn it off when the water went tepid. Her muscles felt loose and Taylor felt energized as she slid the door open and stepped out of the shower. Scrubbing herself with the loofa for what seemed like an hour had finally made her feel clean again. With a heavy sigh, she jerked the fluffy towel down from the hook and wrapped it around herself then tucked in the end. She went to the vanity, and pulled down another towel and wrapped it around her wet hair.

Whether Slade liked it or not, she was going to need a toothbrush soon. Finger-brushing her teeth with toothpaste only went so far. Maybe she'd just use *his* damned toothbrush, she thought, walking to the vanity where it lay. Her hand closed around it, but she heard voices in the bedroom and froze.

It was too soon for them to have run ten miles wasn't it?

Taylor crept to the door to press her ear against it and she definitely heard a man and a woman's voice. When Cee Cee laughed, she knew it was her in there. The only man she'd be in there with would be Slade. She turned and put her back against the door.

God, was she going to be trapped in here and have to listen to them have sex?

That would be the ultimate humiliation. Sickness boiled in her stomach and she put a hand there. She'd just get back in the shower and turn on the cold water so she didn't have to listen if that happened. Turning back to the door, she pressed her ear to the wet wood again.

"I told you to stretch. You should've stretched," Cee Cee said.

"Shut the hell up," Slade ground out.

"I'll go get you an ice pack and some Ben Gay, old man," she offered.

"I don't need a fucking ice pack. Just leave me alone," Slade growled, but then moaned loudly. "I'll take a shower and it'll be fine."

Taylor's heart stopped beating, and she jerked back from the door. Her eyes darted around the room for a place to hide, but the only place to hide was the shower stall. Slade would come in there and she'd be busted.

And she hadn't left him any hot water either. He was going to be pissed.

Taylor danced from foot to foot as she considered her options, and decided she had none. She leaned into the door again to see if they left and it opened, slamming into her. Bells went off in her skull as her forehead struck the door and she staggered backwards to sit on the toilet.

"What in the fuck are you doing in here?" Slade shouted, and Taylor bent over holding her hand to her forehead, feeling the knot that had been going down swell again. Goddamn, before long she was going to look like a unicorn at the rate she was going.

"Are you okay?" he asked in a softer tone, as he stopped in front of her.

"You hit my forehead again, asshole," she

replied rocking. "I'm dizzy this time, so I may need to go to the hospital." Not really, but at least that would get her out of here.

"I'm sorry! I didn't know you were behind the door." His knees bent, but he hissed a breath and stood back up to knead his left thigh. "I can't bend down to look. I pulled a quad and it hurts like a bitch. Stand up and let me look at it."

Taylor stood up, but she didn't stop to let him look at it. "I don't need you to help me. I'll be fine," she said, grabbing the door, but he grabbed her arm.

"But I need you to help me," he said, the rough timber of his voice exciting her. "I know you used all the hot water, so I can't take a shower. I need you to rub out this cramp."

The thought of putting her hands on him again caused a shiver to rock her, but Taylor was mad at him. And she had more self-respect than to do it after the way he treated her. She didn't want to help him, *or* touch him.

"Get your girlfriend to do it," she said, as she pulled the door open and walked out.

In a limping gait, Slade followed her into the bedroom, but stopped to moan. "I don't have a damned girlfriend," he snarled, as he limped to the bed and sat down to knead his thigh. "I don't do relationships remember?"

"Yeah, I remember. Get the flavor of the day to do it then." Anger rushed up to her head, and the knot throbbed, as she walked to the door, grabbed the doorknob and twisted it violently.

"Taylor, wait," he said, and the pleading tone of his voice stopped her. "*Please*—I need you to help me."

Her hand gripped the knob so tightly her fingers went numb. She wanted so damned badly to walk out on him. Treat him as coldly as he had treated her. But she was a better person than that. No, she was a damned doormat, she thought, as she spun back to face him. She let any dirty bastard who wanted to wipe his feet on her do it. Slade had only changed his attitude toward her, because he needed something from her. That was going to change, just not right at this moment. Clenching her jaw, Taylor walked to the nightstand grabbed the bottle of baby oil and pointed her finger at him.

"Take your shorts off and lay back," she commanded, and he leaned back on his elbows, hooked his thumbs in his waistband then shoved them down.

"Ow, o*wwww*," he moaned when he lifted his leg to push them past his knees.

With a huffed breath, Taylor grabbed them and yanked them down, bent and pulled them off over his running shoes. When she raised back up, red lip prints caught her gaze and she gasped. He had on the underwear she told him she liked.

He wore them for Cee Cee.

Ice water flowed through her veins as Taylor dragged her eyes up his body, trying not to take

222

inventory of every tight muscle, but she failed. Her eyes met his, and the heat she saw there sent moisture flowing south in her body.

"Why'd you do it, little bit?" he asked, and his voice sounding tortured, regretful.

What in the hell was he talking about?

"You asked me to help you, remember?" she replied, thinking maybe he hit his head too.

His eyes narrowed. "You know what I'm talking about," he said in a harsher tone. "The gig's up, Taylor. Just tell me, and we'll figure it out."

"I hit my head again, so I might be a little slow. I have no idea what the heck you're talking about, Slade, so why don't you tell me."

He sat up and huffed a breath. "Why did you plant that bomb on Ahmed Khalil's car? Who are you working with?"

Shock slammed into her taking her breath as she staggered back clutching the bottle of oil. Maybe he'd hit his head and was not coherent. That is the only explanation she could find as to why this man would think she had tried to kill Prince Khalil. That she had the wherewithal and evilness necessary to try and kill a person. With a *bomb*!

"Are you *insane*?!?" she shrieked hoarsely, trying to wrap her mind around what he thought.

"I was wondering the same about you," he replied calmly, pinning her with is eyes. Those eyes told her that is what he really believed. That he not only thought she was capable of doing it, she'd done

223

it. "Who are you working with, Taylor? Let's just end this."

"I'm trying to work with *you*, asshole, to figure out who did this. Who both the *bomber* and the kidnappers are. You *know* damned well I was with you that night, so there's no way I could've planted that bomb."

"I'm not talking about that night. I'm talking about during the day before the bombing. Dex has video footage that shows you planting the bomb."

"Well *Dex* must've manufactured it then," Taylor growled, her mind swirling with anger and disbelief as she took two steps toward the bed. Her hands shook as she uncapped the oil. "And I think the cogs in that *brilliant* investigative mind of yours must be rusty."

Taylor's hands shook as she lifted the bottle over his head and squeezed it with both hands. Slade gasped, and the bottle gurgled as a stream of oil slithered over his face into his eyes, and he fought to rub it out. When he stopped rubbing to blindly reach for her, Taylor stepped out of his reach, turned and headed for the door.

She yanked the towel from her hair and tossed it and the empty bottle to the floor, realizing as she walked out the door she only wore a towel. Her rage was so complete, Taylor didn't give a damn that all she wore was a towel. She was going to find the computer geek and choke the answers out of him, buck naked if she had to!

CHAPTER EIGHTEEN

Doubt flooded Slade, as he grabbed the edge of the sheet to wipe the oil from his face. Was there another explanation for what he'd seen with his own eyes on that tape?

Considering her violent reaction? He'd say there had to be.

The muscle in his thigh knotted up as Slade pushed up to his feet. He fought through the pain to find his shorts and put them on. He had to get over to the office, because if Taylor got to Dex, hell was going to rain down on his head like it had Slade's. He limped to the door, and gritted his teeth to lean down and jerk the towel up from the floor.

It smelled like her when he brought it to his face and he groaned into it as he wiped the rest of the oil out of his eyes. He limped through the door, and hop-walked to the front door of the barracks. It took him ten minutes to get to the front porch of the office. By the time he did, his muscle was spasming and burning like fire. Jumping under his skin like it wanted out. The pain was intense, but he climbed the steps to the front door.

When he opened the door, Lola barked, and Buddy yelped. The both must've followed Taylor out of his apartment to the office. That surprised him, because Lola usually never left his side. She didn't follow anyone except him. It looked like everyone had deserted him, he thought sourly, as he walked inside.

He limped to the hallway, and if the shouts he heard down the hall were any indication, Taylor was peeling Dexter's skin off inch by inch. Slade had to get down there and settle things down before she went in for the kill. He needed Dex alive to figure out who had put the bomb on that car. Three agonizing minutes later, he leaned on the door jamb of Dexter's office to catch his breath. He flinched when Taylor started in on a fresh round of fileting.

"You claim to be a fucking genius, but you must need stronger glasses, butthead!" she shrieked, her chest heaving as she leaned in to glare at Dexter. He stood there and took it, looking ashamed. "If Mac can spot two men sitting in a car there, it seems you should have too! But *nooo*—you jumped to fucking conclusions and dragged Slade into your conspiracy theory too!"

Mac stood beside Taylor looking uncomfortable and Cee Cee stood on her other side, wrapped in a towel too, looking as angry as Taylor was. Dexter just stood there staring at her, his shoulders slumped. When Taylor's chest heaved with another breath and her mouth dropped open to start again, Slade walked into the office.

"That's enough," he said, darkly, and Dexter's eyes flew to his.

"It's about damned time!" Dex shouted, his face turning red.

"Why are you angry with me?!?" Slade

shouted back. So much for deescalating the situation he thought, moving to stand beside Cee Cee.

"Because *you* are the one who decided not to ask her about it, dumbass. I just pointed out the issue, and I thought you'd talk to her about it, give her a chance to explain things." Dexter pushed through the women to pin Slade with his glare. "But *nooo*—" he shouted, like Taylor had a moment ago to him. He pushed Slade's chest and he stumbled back. "*You* just decided she was guilty and acted like an ass toward her!" Dexter leaned into his face. "You *are* an ass, and I don't blame her for quitting!"

Fear stretched Slade's heart to his toes, before it snapped back up to quiver in his chest. His eyes flew to Taylor, but she wouldn't look at him. He limped around Dexter and grabbed her arm. She jerked it out of his grasp, and her damned towel slipped to reveal the top of her dusky pink areolas. He reached out to pull it up, and she stepped back to adjust it.

"Come with me to my office so we can talk, please," he pleaded, as guilt flooded him.

"Ooh, so *now* you want to talk?" Taylor snarled, her eyes snapping to his.

"I think the device was remotely detonated," Mac informed, stepping up to him. "There was a car at the back of the lot with two men in it. They sat there all day, and were there when it went off, then they left. Did anyone check the tapes for the day before?" Mac frowned and shook his head. "Never mind, that bomb could've been planted a week, a month before."

"So you don't think the prince was the target?" Slade asked, his eyebrows raised. If the bomb was remotely detonated, the specific target would have been those guards, and that just didn't make sense to him.

"No, I think the guards were the targets," Mac replied gruffly. "Someone wanted them out of the way. The kidnapping may have been to get Jaxson and Deep Six out of the picture, along with the ransom. It's awfully strange that Taylor was fired that day too, don't you think? Now, the prince is completely vulnerable. I can't help but think that was the purpose."

Slade thought about that a minute, then a light bulb went off.

"So you think the car bomb was to get rid of Ahmed's protection to clear the way for them to kill him after they get the money?"

"That's exactly what I think," Mac replied, with a nod.

Mac's theory was solid, and it made a helluva lot more sense than them killing the golden goose before they got the egg from him.

"Cade Winters is trying to get in touch with you, he said he has some information," Gray said walking into the office. "He tried to get in touch with you earlier, but said you didn't answer your damned phone. His words."

"Cade Winters?" Cee Cee squeaked, and Slade looked over to see her face turn as white as the towel she had wrapped around her body.

"And Hawk called and said to tell you they're almost at the LZ, which I assume means landing zone. Looks like things are hopping at Deep Six this morning, and it's not even eight o'clock yet," Gray said, with a laugh that irritated Slade. "I got some interesting information for Cade yesterday too, so once your asshole unpuckers, come and see me."

Gray turned and walked away, and Slade's asshole was indeed puckered as he stood there staring behind him. All the information he'd just received collided in his brain in a blinding flash, as he tried to figure out which issue he needed to deal with first. This being in charge shit was for the birds. He wanted his old life back, the one where the most he had to worry about was which woman he was having a drink with that night.

"I'm going to kill Logan when he gets back," he growled as he limped out of Dex's office into the hallway. Turning back he pointed at Mac. "You get me answers on that employee list."

His eyes tracked to Cee Cee. "You go to my apartment and get me some clothes so I can take a fucking shower and get this oil off of me. Find my phone, it's somewhere in the bedroom. And get me an ice pack, my damned leg is killing me."

His eyes swung to Dexter, who was standing there glaring at him with his arms folded over his chest. "You get me that information on the license plates. Find out who the fuck those men were in that vehicle—you have an hour."

Slade huffed a breath, his stomach muscles clenched and he forced his eye's to meet Taylor's accusing stare. "And *you* get in my office. I need to talk to you," he said, his tone deflated, because he had zero hope that she'd come to his office or that she would let him apologize.

He was with Dexter now. He would not blame Taylor Kincaid if she walked right out of that front gate and never looked back. It felt like a knife stabbed into his thigh with every hop step he made toward his office, but he deserved that pain and more. As much as he'd dealt to Taylor Kincaid. He opened his door and shut it behind him, then leaned on it to think.

A moment later, the door shoved into his back, he fell forward, stepped down on his left leg to catch himself and fire shot up his leg, through his groan and he howled as he caught himself on the edge of the desk.

A sharp laugh speared through his brain, as the door shut. "I'm almost tempted to go back out and do that again," Taylor said, as she walked up beside him. "You have about thirty seconds to apologize, or you're going to be hurting in places you never knew existed."

Anger was good—at least she came to talk to him, Slade thought, as he fought through the pain to turn around and lean on the desk. She crowded him, and glared up at him. "Talk asshole, your time is ticking away."

"I'm sorry," he said quickly.

"Yes you are," she agreed, the tension in her mouth easing a bit.

"A sorry asshole," he elaborated, feeling like he was on a roll now and wanting to see that beautiful face totally relaxed again. To see the anger fade and forgiveness shine in her eyes. But that was probably too much to hope for right now.

"Go on," she said, leaning away to cross her arms over her breasts.

"An arrogant, assuming asshole who can't tell you how sorry he is," Slade said, and her eyebrows lifted, her eyes softening the slightest degree. He leaned up and took her shoulders in his hands and they stiffened. "An arrogant, assuming asshole who is the sorriest man on earth, little bit."

"Don't call me that," she hissed, her eyes sparking again and he swallowed hard.

"Okay. The sorriest man on earth, *Taylor*. Please forgive me."

"Try Ms. Kincaid. Isn't that what you called me last night?" she asked angrily, and Slade's heart took a nosedive in his chest. His hands fell away, and he sighed as defeat filled him.

"I'm so damned sorry, Taylor." He couldn't keep his eyes on hers, they focused on the purple knot at the center of her forehead, and her hand flew up to cover it.

"That's your damned fault too," she hissed.

"I know, and I'm sorry for that too." He didn't even try to argue the point that she'd been in *his* bathroom when it happened, he had too many strikes against him.

"Why do you think they're trying to kill me?" Taylor asked suddenly, surprising him.

"I don't know. They're evidently after Jaxson Thomas too," he replied. "That's one of the rea—" he started, but stopped. If he told her that was one of the reasons he believed she'd planted that bomb, he knew he'd lose any ground he'd gained with her. There was no excuse for the assumptions he'd made without being damned sure he was right.

"One of the reasons *what?*" she filled in, her eyes narrowing.

"One of the reasons we need to figure this out," he improvised, only breathing again when her shoulders relaxed. God, he felt like he was back in Afghanistan walking through a minefield again. He definitely had to watch his step, and Lola wasn't going to help him here.

"Okay, so what's your grand plan here to figure it out?" she asked.

"I don't have one. I need more pieces to this thousand piece puzzle to come up with one," he admitted. "Like you said, investigation is not my strong suit."

Her eyes glided down his chest then flew back

up. "No, you'd be the muscle in this organization not the brains, you beefhead."

"I am a beefhead," Slade agreed, and was pleased when the anger in her eyes dissipated, and her arms dropped to her sides.

He was more pleased when he noticed the towel had slipped down again, a little lower even than before. She evidently noticed where his eyes were and yanked it back up.

"Eyes are up here, Smiley." Slade's eyes locked on hers, and he forced them to stay there. "I want you to apologize to Buddy too," she said.

His eyebrows shot up in disbelief. "You want me to apologize to Buddy?" he repeated, and couldn't stop his laugh.

Her eyebrows crashed together. "Yes, you hurt his feelings last night too. He loves you, and you shoved him out of your room like he was garbage."

The tone of her voice, her eyes, told him she wasn't just talking about Buddy. That thought sent pain knifing through him, but it wasn't in his thigh. It also caused sickness to curl in his gut, because he didn't want her love. But he didn't want her to leave either.

"Okay, I'll apologize to the dog too." Slade took her shoulders again, and when they didn't stiffen, he took it as a good sign. "I'd get down on my knees and beg you to forgive me, little bit, but I can't right now."

"I told you not to call me that," she said, but

her tone was weak and she moved a little closer.

"What can I say? I'm a beefhead who forgets things." He pulled her a little closer, wrapped his arms loosely around her back, and his insides finally unclenched when she didn't pull away. "Will you stay and help me finish this case?"

"It looks like I don't have much choice. After seeing that tape, the police probably think I'm guilty as hell too. A jury would believe that too, if they arrested me. They would never guess that I dropped my keys under the car parked beside the Mercedes on my way back from picking up lunch."

Anger mixed with surprise and Slade shoved her back. "You give them a damned pass, but not me?" he growled, his fingers digging into her shoulders. "They can think you're guilty after looking at that tape, but I have to grovel?"

"No, *you* have to grovel, because you had the opportunity to *talk* to me about it, but chose to *assume* I was guilty and be an asshole to me. Next time use your *words* and ask me, *beefhead*."

"Yes, ma'am," Slade replied, pulling her to him again, hugging her to his chest, and dammit, kissing the top of her hair. His door opened and his eyes flew there.

"*Oh*, should I come back?" Cee Cee asked, her tone sparkly with something.

"No, he definitely needs a shower," Taylor said, pulling away to rub the back of her hand across her face, before wiping it on the towel. "He smells like he had a run-in with a skunk, and looks like he tried to fix that by swimming in a vat of oil."

"Yeah, he does look kind of greasy. How'd that happen?" Cee Cee asked, wrinkling her pert nose.

"He's a clumsy beefhead, I guess," Taylor replied with a giggle.

"I guess since I'm the new grunt around here, he'll expect me to clean the oil slick out of the shower when he's done in there," Cee Cee said, shooting him a glare.

He knew right then exactly why Dave Logan didn't hire women. His friend must know that they traveled in packs and attacked like wild hyenas when they smelled blood.

"Just give me my damned clothes so I can get cleaned up and talk to Gray."

CHAPTER NINETEEN

"Logan just called," Gray said casually, as Slade walked into his office thirty minutes later.

"G*rrr*—why didn't you hold him on the phone, until I got here?" Slade ground out as he sat in the chair across from Gray's desk. He wondered why in the hell Logan hadn't called *him* since he's the one he left in the hot seat. Probably because he knew Slade had more than a few choice words for him.

"Well, he was whispering, so I guess he had to sneak to call in." Gray shrugged then finally looked up from his computer. "He hung up all of a sudden, so Susan must've caught him."

"Did he say where they were?" If Slade had any idea where they'd gone, he would track him down. This shit had gotten out of control.

"I had him for about two minutes. We barely had a chance to say hello, but he said he'd call back later, if he could." From the way Gray said it, he knew just as well as Slade did that Logan was not going to be calling back anytime soon.

"Okay, my asshole is unpuckered. A little." Slade heaved a breath. "What did Winters tell you? He didn't answer when I called him a few minutes ago."

And that was going to stop. If he paid that man a hundred grand, he was going to answer the fucking phone when he called.

"The group associated with the Saudi account

is not a radical group. It's an *anti*-radical group, and Tariq Khalil is one of the leaders."

Slade sat up straighter in his chair, glad to have his question answered about whether Winters managed to get inside. "That doesn't make a helluva lot of sense. But nothing in this case has so far. What do you think that means?"

"It means, at a minimum, Tariq Khalil knows about the kidnapping, but there's more."

Shoving a hand through his hair, Slade groaned, not sure he could take hearing more.

"What else?" he asked anyway.

"He hates his brother and thinks he's not fit to be the leader of their family, or their sheikdom, because he's so hardline. I don't know how he found out, but Winters also said six of the members of Tariq's faction used their passports over the last few months to enter the US." Gray leaned back in his chair to tent his fingers over his chest. "They're visiting Texas."

"You're not done yet though, are you?" He saw it in Gray's eyes.

"Nope," he replied, popping the p.

"What else?" Slade asked, his chest tightening, as he added all these pieces to the spaghetti bowl of information he already had.

"He overheard Tariq talking on the phone and he thinks there's a sleeper terrorist cell here that may have been, or may be, activated by Ahmed. Supposedly, those men are here to help him stop his brother."

"As in pull off a coup? Maybe assassinate him on American soil?" Slade asked, his heart shooting up to his throat.

That would explain who the car bombers were and what their purpose was. Were they also the ones trying to kill Taylor? She didn't seem to be any threat to them, because she didn't know any more than Slade did.

"Where better than the good old USA where he has diplomatic immunity? If Tariq is successful, he assumes control of the sheikdom and he wouldn't waive immunity for himself, since he'll the head of state there then. The Saudi government might step in, but it's highly doubtful. He says there's been a lot of chatter about something coming down, but nothing specific. Winters thinks you should call Homeland Security. He says he's not in a position to do that at the moment."

Slade shot up to his feet and groaned as his thigh muscle jerked. Rubbing it, he sat on the corner of the desk. "That bastard sure is long-winded with you, when I couldn't get a word out of him." *And I paid him a hundred thousand dollars.* Frustration burned his gut.

This operation had just moved beyond his attempt to clear Deep Six's name. It went beyond saving the contract or even the kidnapping. Yeah, he'd like to save the kid, but now it sounded like the whole damned state, or even the nation, could be in jeopardy.

"I'm the man who wired a hundred thousand dollars into his Swiss bank account, so I guess that had something to do with it. But odd thing…he knew my old boss at the NSA, actually mentioned him. Was this guy a former Spook or something?"

"Not that I'm aware," Slade replied shortly.

Winters had freaked out badly enough on him for *reading* his resume. Slade couldn't imagine how he'd react to him sharing that information. He was not about to mention Winters was Delta Force, not CIA. Just about the same damned thing. Only meaner and more skilled in killing someone without a soul knowing, even the target.

"Huh, he sure sounded like a Spook," Gray commented, pursing his lips.

Slade thought over the details of what he'd just learned, added in what he already knew to come to one conclusion. "I can't call Homeland Security."

Gray frowned. "Why not?"

"Because they'd want to talk to me in person, and would probably recognize me from that parking lot video. I know they'd recognize Taylor. I'd just about bet they're already involved in that investigation."

"So call them anonymously," Gray suggested, and Slade thought about it.

If he did that, they'd be working on the case too, and he wouldn't know where they were. If somehow their efforts overlapped, both he and

Taylor could end up in jail. But how could he not call them if this state, or hell, the whole country was at risk?

If something came down and he didn't call, he'd be just as guilty as the terrorists for the bloodshed from whatever nastiness those terrorists were cooking up.

"You said you heard from Hawk?" Slade asked.

"Just that last call. I haven't heard back from him since they landed."

Slade eased off the desk. "Let me know if you hear from him, I'm going to get a burner phone from Dex, and I'll be out for a while."

He needed to get away from the compound if he was going to make that call so the pings wouldn't be on the only nearby cell tower. The feds were sneaky bastards and that's the first thing they'd check. They'd be on Deep Six, and in turn Taylor's doorstep, within hours.

"Oh and don't call me on the burner, they can trace that back here. I'm not taking my phone either. I'll just get with you when I get back." God, he had so damned much to think about, to remember.

"Good luck," Gray said, looking back down at his computer as if he didn't have a care in the world. That irritated Slade, because right now? Slade felt like the weight of the world rested on his shoulders and he didn't like it one bit.

He would feel a helluva lot better once Dex

ran down those license plates and figured out who the car bombers were. At least then, he could turn that over to the feds and prove Taylor wasn't responsible. That didn't answer the question of who was trying to kill her though, and why. Or who was trying to kill Jaxson, wherever the hell he was, and why. Maybe if Levi and Caleb captured the guys chasing Jaxon, he could find the answers to both questions.

Slade huffed a breath, as he left Gray's office to find Dexter.

***

Taylor finally caught up with Slade at the front door of the office. She was damned worried about him, because to her he looked a lot like he had the night of the explosion when he had that major PTSD episode.

"Slade wait!" she yelled, and he stopped.

"I want to go with you wherever you're going," she said, but he shook his head.

"I'll be back in a little while. You just stay put."

He opened the door, and she noticed he had a box in his other hand that contained one of those disposable-type cellphones. She followed him onto the porch, and Buddy and Lola bounded out behind her.

"Did you lose your cell phone?" she asked, grabbing his arm. "I thought I saw it in your office earlier when I went in there looking for you."

He glanced over his shoulder at her and the

241

sun glinted off of the beads of sweat gathering on his forehead. "I know where it's at. I have something to do, so just go back inside."

Taylor let go of his arm to put her hands on her hips. "I'm supposed to be a member of this team, but you won't tell me anything. Didn't you learn anything from what happened this morning?" she asked hotly.

This man was so damned frustrating sometimes, she didn't know why she bothered.

Because for some damned reason you care about him and don't want him to go off and have an episode and maybe get himself killed.

Taylor would be damned glad when Tuesday came and they could see the EMDR therapist. She was excited to see if it worked as well as the testimonials she'd read on the internet. Those she trusted, even though she didn't trust Mark's claims when he tried to get her back.

"I learned plenty, but you need to stay here," he said gruffly, as he started toward his Humvee again. Taylor followed, and leaned against the door so he couldn't open it. He glared down at her, but she didn't move.

"Why can't I go with you?" she asked stubbornly.

"Because you're not safe yet." Slade sighed. "Those guys who tried to shoot you could still be lying in wait for another try. You're safe here."

"You're not safe driving in the condition

you're in right now, as stressed out as you are, but you're going anyway," she countered.

"*You* are stressing me out," he growled and his eyes narrowed. She folded her arms over her chest, and he huffed a breath. "I promise I won't be gone long. Now, *move!*"

Taylor stared at him a moment more, and saw that he wasn't going to change his mind.

"Fine, go get yourself killed then," she ground out, emotion tightening her chest as she bent to grab Buddy's collar. "We'll just be here making your funeral plans." Her lower lip quivered and she bit it as she stood and dragged Buddy a couple of feet.

"Taylor?" Slade said, and she stopped.

"Yeah?" She turned around hoping he'd changed his mind.

"I promise I won't get myself killed." His fingers tightened on the top of the door and his jaw worked. "But, come give me a kiss just in case, if that will make you feel better."

Taylor released Buddy's collar and walked back to the vehicle. Slade grabbed her and pulled her behind the cover of the door, and she slid her hands up his chest to circle his neck. He held her eyes for a second, before his head lowered and his mouth covered hers.

Taylor leaned into his chest and his hands found her ass to lift her against him. They dug in, and Taylor moaned into his mouth. His tongue found hers and her insides went liquid as their souls connected, and she sighed. He lowered her to the ground, came in for one more sweet pass, then pushed her away and got behind the wheel.

"Take care of Lola for me, if I get myself killed," he said with a smile, after rolling down the window. "She'll want her pillow moved to the cemetery."

"Don't kid about that," Taylor growled, feeling sick.

"Don't be so melodramatic, little bit, and I won't." He winked at her, then cranked the engine and looked over his shoulder to reverse. Taylor grabbed Buddy's collar when he lunged after the vehicle. The gate opened, Taylor watched him leave and she couldn't fight the gnawing feeling in her gut that something bad was about to happen.

She turned back toward the office, and saw Dexter step onto the porch. She walked that way and Buddy and Lola followed her.

"Where the heck are you going?" Taylor asked, hoping they weren't all deserting her.

The only ones left inside were Cee Cee and Gray. Slade said she was safe here, but she wasn't so sure anymore. Taylor noticed that the woman carried a pistol in a belly band holster under her clothes, and that gave her a level of comfort, but the men in the office weren't armed.

Gray wouldn't be much help if shit hit the fan, because he wouldn't want to get his five-hundred-dollar suit dirty. The most Dex could do would probably be throw a keyboard at any bad buys who decided to pay them a visit.

But there was safety in numbers, and Taylor would feel better if he wasn't leaving. She was starting to realize the severity of this situation, and didn't know why she didn't before.

For some reason it hit her hard when Slade left.

If she had a damned pistol she could protect herself. She needed a pistol and Cee Cee might just be the one to ask, since Slade didn't think her having one was a priority.

"I'm going to pick up the prisoners," Dexter said with excitement.

"Prisoners?" she repeated, her heart skidding to a stop. That's good…bring the bad guys right into the compound and feed them supper before they kill us.

"Yeah, Hawk's about to land at the pad. They don't have room to bring them back. Want to come with?" he asked.

"No, I think I'll stay here, but thanks for asking." Taylor would probably feel better if she had something to do to occupy herself, so she didn't worry herself sick before Slade got back and this feeling went away. "Is there anything I can do to help you while you're gone?"

She'd offered to help Mac earlier with the employee list, but he said he had it under control. Control being the operative part of that statement.

The man was a control freak evidently.

"No, I have a report running, and it will stop when it's finished." He looked at the sky when a faint whooshing sound echoed through the compound. "Oh, there's Hawk. I've got to go, they'll be at the pad in five, and Hawk gets kind of testy if he has to wait."

Taylor looked up, as the noise got louder, and shaded her eyes to look at the afternoon sky. Her eyes zoned in on a black dot which grew larger, and larger and realized it was a black helicopter then slid to Dexter who got into a Humvee much like Slade's to drive across the compound. He disappeared after he rounded the barracks and she wondered where exactly this *pad* was located.

The helicopter passed directly over the compound but it didn't touch down. After hovering high above for a moment, it shot forward over the woods and disappeared. Taylor heard Buddy bark, but it sounded very distant. She wouldn't doubt if she was deaf from the loud engine noise that still rang inside her skull. Glancing toward the gate, Taylor saw Fletch's truck pull through, but she didn't see Buddy.

Suddenly a flash of golden fur darted from behind and Buddy appeared hot on the heels of a squirrel. The little animal streaked through the gate and Buddy followed right before it closed shut. Taylor took off running, and Fletcher honked the horn and waved, but she didn't stop.

The gate was almost closed when she got

there, but she squeezed through. Dragging in breaths, Taylor looked up and down the road for Buddy, and finally saw him trotting along the shoulder of the road in the distance.

She took off running, a pain sliced through her side, but she held it and still ran. Her chest burned badly telling her just how out of shape she'd become in the last year, and she would do something about that soon. As soon as this was over, she'd go back to the dojo where she hadn't gone in six months, since Mark left.

But right now she had a dog to catch, and she was losing ground on him.

"Buddy, *sitz!*" she shouted, hoping he would obey the command.

He didn't and Taylor tried to pick up her pace and gain ground as she passed the end of the tall fence surrounding the compound. The sun suddenly disappeared as tall woods appeared to occlude it, sweat streaked down her neck, slid down her spine to her yoga pants, her legs went numb, but she didn't stop running.

When she passed a wide dirt trail leading into the woods, she heard an engine rev loudly, but she didn't dare take her eyes off of Buddy, who had now moved down in the ditch at the side of the road to sniff something there. Taylor was thankful, because she was about out of gas. She could barely breathe as she slid down the steep embankment and walked toward him.

Tires squealed back down the roadway, but she was too tired to look back. She was going to drag Buddy back to the compound then she was taking another shower. Taylor stopped to swipe her arm over her forehead, then wiped it on her pants. A pop preceded what felt like a stinging mosquito bite on her arm, and she slapped her arm.

She moved her hand she saw blood on her fingers—too much for a mosquito bite. Her stomach rolled as she looked back over her shoulder just as a black SUV pulled to a stop about fifty yards from her. The doors of the truck flew open, two men piled out and Taylor screamed as she started running.

CHAPTER TWENTY

Adrenaline shot through her and Taylor screamed again, as she ran down the ditch. She needed to get into those woods for cover, she thought, clawing her way up the back of the embankment. Another shot ricocheted off of a tree very close to her ear as she entered the woods, and adrenaline shot through her making her heart pound.

The men behind her shouted in a foreign language, and it echoed in the woods to ring inside of her skull. Buddy barked loudly and Taylor prayed they didn't shoot him. She prayed harder they didn't get a good shot on her, as she weaved and dodged through the trees blindly. She couldn't run forever, she thought barely dragging in breaths her chest was so tight, in fact she couldn't run much longer at all.

Think. Anticipate. Prepare.

She drew on her martial arts training and it calmed her, as she scanned the area in front of her for a place to set up as she ran. Do what they don't expect you to do because you're small—go on the offensive. Hide and take them off guard.

But where? Taylor finally stopped when she couldn't run another step and looked around the woods for a place to hide. Trees and more trees. Since she was small, she could hide behind one, but that wasn't enough cover. Her feet started moving again, but at a walk as she continued to scan the area for some kind of cover. The men made a lot of noise in the woods behind her as they searched for her, so she knew exactly how far back they were.

She needed somewhere with space to fight, but she also needed a place to hide so she had surprise on her side. A large boulder caught her eye, and Taylor stopped to make sure she couldn't be penned in there. It was a clearing in that the trees were farther apart, so she had room, and that rock would surely be better protection from bullets than a tree.

Taylor jogged over there and crouched behind it to wait. She meditated, focused on controlling breathing, and harnessing her energy.

The men's heavy footsteps drew nearer, Taylor's muscles tensed, and she bit back a whimper. To get ready, she inhaled deeply and exhaled, and forced her muscles to loosen and to relax. She shook out her arms and stretched her legs to rotate her ankles.

Buddy's playful bark, like he thought finding her was a game, made her blood run cold with fear. It was a game—of life or death, and if he outed her she lost more than the game, she lost her life. But the puppy couldn't know that, as he continued yapping as he bounded through the woods breaking sticks and rustling leaves.

When his playful noises told her he was within ten feet of the rock, Taylor stopped breathing. Buddy took two more rustling steps toward her, then barked and she knew he'd found her. She had a decision to make, or those men would too.

Stand and fight here or run?

The men's gait picked up, and they shouted excitedly. Taylor shot to her feet, rounded the rock deciding to run, but she knew she'd waited too long when her eyes met a pair of cold, flat eyes and the business end of a Glock pointed directly at the center of her chest.

The man was at the perfect distance to shoot her, and she was too far away to stop him.

Think. Anticipate. Prepare.

Taylor raised her hands high, flashed her eyes and forced her mouth into a smile that she hoped was sexy. She took a step toward him exaggerating her walk, sticking out her chest.

Eight more feet.

His eyes left hers to skim down her body then snagged on her breasts on the way back up and stayed there. He licked his lips and his face flushed.

Five more feet.

A man would be dead by now, but she had her body to use as a weapon. And her size. Because she was small this big brute probably thought she was harmless. And she was, unless she could get close enough to him.

Taylor kept walking toward him, slowly and carefully. She kept her eyes steady, but watched the arm holding the gun drift lower.

Three more feet. Almost there.

Suddenly, the man's body jerked as if he woke

up and the gun pointed directly at her heart again. Now or never, she thought.

"Hi*yaaaah*!" she shouted, and it echoed through the woods as she brought her forearm against his to push the weapon aside. Her right hand rolled behind it and she jerked the pistol out of his grasp by the barrel.

With no time to reverse it, she tossed it aside and brought the heel of her hand up under his chin. His head rocked back and when it snapped down she landed a second punch to his nose. Bones crunched as it shifted to the left and blood spurted out to drip down his chin. A fierce growl rumbled in his throat, then fire lit his eyes as he charged her. Taylor feinted to land a hard blow to his sternum as he lumbered by, and he grunted.

He spun, flailed his arms to grab for her, but Taylor sidestepped him and brought her heel up in a hard strike right above his kneecap. It made a sickening crunch as his knee popped out of joint, and he screamed loudly as he staggered back and fell to the ground. Pressing her advantage, Taylor went in for the kill shot, a kick to his temple, but he held up his hands to whimper as he scooted back from her using his good leg.

Turning, her heart pounded as she searched for the gun, but she didn't see it. Buddy barked again, and she spun. He appeared in the clearing, and behind him stood another man with a pistol who had it aimed right between her eyes. Twelve feet or so

252

separated them, and this man's look said he wasn't falling for her games.

When the man on the ground spoke rapidly to him in whatever language they spoke, his face turned red, his eyes swung back to her, and he raised his arm. Taylor squeezed her eyes closed, because she didn't want to see the bullet that killed her. A shot rang out and her body went cold. A floaty feeling washed through her that felt very peaceful, surreal. Her hair felt light and her ears buzzed.

Was this it? Was this how it felt to be dead?

She hadn't had any pain, so that's a good thing. But where the hell was the bright white light that everyone who'd died and come back talked about?

Taylor wondered if this was how her father felt when he took his last breath. If so, it wasn't all that bad really. Excitement even buzzed through her. She'd get to see him soon. He could hug her again and tell her it was going to be fine. They would be fine. He'd probably ask about her mother. Oh God—how would she tell him that she was remarried?

No, her father wouldn't care. He'd want her mother to be happy. He knew when he joined the service that he might die. They both knew that. Too bad Taylor hadn't realized it, because then maybe she wouldn't have been so damned torn apart when it happened.

"Taylor, *breathe!*" someone shouted, then her

right cheek stung, before her left caught on fire and her eyes popped open. Fletch stood in front of her, but he wasn't wearing white.

They'd sent him to carry her to the pearly gates?

Taylor fought the hysterical laughter that bubbled in her chest. It had to be some cosmic joke. But he released her shoulder and stepped back to stuff a pistol in his waistband of his cargo pants and she didn't float off. Her breath whooshed out of her lungs and they burned.

"I'm not dead?" she asked, her voice a squeak.

"No, but that Arab over there probably wishes you were." Fletcher hitched his thumb, and glanced toward the injured man who sat against a tree glaring at her. "Remind me never to piss you off again, okay?" he said with a laugh.

Taylor glanced around Fletch and saw the other guy lying face down in the leaves not moving. A bloodstain covered his back, and Taylor saw a bullet hole in his white shirt near his left shoulder. "Is he—"

"No, he just passed out, I think." Fletch shrugged as if he shot men every day. Who knows, maybe he did. These Deep Six guys were a strange bunch. "I'll call Hawk to haul his ass to the hospital." Fletcher's eyes got deadly serious. She'd never seen the snarky man that way before. "The other one goes back to the compound with us though. I'm sure Slade will be very interested to find out why he was shooting at you."

"I'd be interested in knowing that too," Taylor replied.

Fletch pulled out his cell phone and dialed. "Two tangos down. One GSW needs transport to the hospital…" He laughed, then his eyes slid to her. "The other tangled with a little keg of dynamite and got his ass kicked, but he's mobile…roger—we'll wait."

Buddy walked up to her and licked her hand. It was obvious he was scared. As scared as Taylor should have been during the ordeal. She knelt down and stroked her hand over his head, then started shaking. Not a normal shake. Her whole body shook so hard her teeth rattled and her brain vibrated in her skull as she sat back on her ass. Sweat streaked through her hair to slide down her temples. Her ears rang loudly and suddenly her throat closed off. Reaching up her hand she clawed at it as she fought to draw breath.

Black dots danced in her line of sight and panic seized her. Taylor couldn't speak, but looked up at Fletch, and he suddenly realized she had a problem. Kneeling down beside her he grabbed her shoulders, but it was too late. Everything went black, and Taylor absolutely could not believe she'd survived all that just to die.

Taylor's eyes fluttered open and a loud whooshing noise deafened her. That was nothing compared to the vibrations under her back though.

She felt them in her teeth. Her eyes darted around as she tried to figure out exactly where she was. Her eyes flew out the window then slammed shut, against the blindingly bright sunlight that reflected off of puffy white clouds to pierce her brain.

Was she in heaven?

Those clouds looked awfully close.

Her heart sped up and her chest tightened, then she realized she wouldn't have a heartbeat if she were dead. She opened her eyes again and tried to sit up, but a hand dropped on her shoulder to push her back down.

"She's awake, radio Slade," Levi said into a small wire by his mouth as his eyes met hers. "We'll be at the hospital in a few. Just relax."

Taylor took inventory of every bone and muscle in her body. Other than feeling like she was wrung out inside and her head stuffed with cotton, she didn't hurt anywhere. Shaking off Levi's hand, she sat up.

"I don't *want* to go to the hospital!" she shouted, because with his headphones on and the noise, she didn't think he'd hear her otherwise.

"You *need* to go," he yelled back.

"*No*, I'm fine!" Taylor shouted.

The helicopter dipped, the man lying on the floor beside her, the Arab thug that Fletch had shot, moaned and Taylor's stomach lurched. She might not be okay though, if she didn't get herself into a seat and put on a seatbelt.

256

Scooting on her butt, she moved around Levi and across the floor toward the row of three seats at the back of the helicopter. The helicopter dipped again to the right this time, and she whimpered as she dragged herself up into a seat. Her hands shook as she grabbed the ends of the belt and yanked them across her lap to snap them.

Taylor did not like to fly, she'd only done it twice in her life, and now she was doing it in an aircraft that was a lot less stable than a jumbo jet.

Levi's eyes slid over her body, then moved back to meet hers. "Hawk, radio Slade and tell him to abort. She says she's fine."

Taylor's shoulders relaxed, and she huffed a breath. She knew she'd been unconscious, but had no idea why. All she remembered was what happened in those woods, those men chasing her and her taking one down, and Fletch shooting the other man. The one who was moaning on the floor of the helicopter, which meant he wasn't dead either, but the fact that his white shirt was now almost red said that *he* needed to be at a hospital or he might be soon.

During the landing Hawk made on the big X on the rooftop of the hospital, Taylor kept her eyes squeezed shut, and her fingers firmly dug into the cushioned armrests of her seat. Somehow she managed not to throw up, but it had been a close call. When he took off again shortly after, she held her breath. Takeoff had been a little smoother, but she still didn't dare look out the window.

A hand patted hers and she opened her eyes. Levi sat beside her, and a smile kicked up the left corner of his mouth, as he leaned closer to her ear.

"Slade says to tell you Caleb brought Buddy back to the compound and he's fine. He also says to tell you he's going to kick your ass when we get back. I told him to save me a seat up front." Leaning away, he threw his head back and laughed. That meant Slade was back at the compound safely too.

Slade was back at the compound safely.

Her breath came easier as she laid her head against the back of the seat and closed her eyes. The whir of the helicopter rotors suddenly became soothing to her, and she drifted off to sleep remembering their kiss before he left.

CHAPTER TWENTY-ONE

Slade didn't know how much more he could take. He was a man living on the edge, and the drop when he tumbled over looked to be farther and farther by the minute. Thirty minutes were added to that drop, while he stood and watched, held his breath beside the Humvee, as Hawk descended toward the pad.

Taylor Kincaid could have been killed today and it would've been his fault, because he was responsible for keeping her safe. For keeping all of the Deep Six employees safe, while Logan was away. She'd not only endangered *her* life with her stupidity today, she could've gotten three of his men killed too.

What in the fuck possessed her to leave the compound, when he'd specifically told her to say put before he left?

As it was, because of her, Fletcher would be no help to them for a while, since he was down at the police station being questioned about the shooting and would probably be there at least until morning. But Slade was so damned thankful that Fletch had gone after her when he heard the gunshots.

If not, she would be dead right now.

His insides quivered and his heart jerked, as he squinted against the dust thrown up to swirl around his head when the skids finally touched down on the pavement. Ducking, he ran for the door, but it opened as he reached the edge of the pad. Caleb hopped out and tried to stop him, but Slade only wanted to see one person, and she was still inside unbuckling her seat belt.

She looked up with a gasp when he stuck his head inside the door. Slade just held her eyes, drank in her beautiful, but pale face and ground his teeth as he tried to decide whether he wanted to kill her or kiss the hell out of her.

The blades finally stopped and the engine noise wound down, but it still echoed in his head as she dragged her hands down to her lap and finished releasing the belt. She eased out of the seat to stand, but her knees buckled and she caught herself on the armrest.

"Do you need help?" he ground out, putting his knee in the door opening.

"No, I'm fine," she replied, before making her way to the door. Slade didn't move, and she put her hands on his shoulders. "Move, so I can get out."

Emotion and so much relief shot up to his head, it made him dizzy as Slade put his hands at her waist to drag her out of the door. He didn't set her down, he clamped his arms around her waist and ground his mouth into hers. It wasn't a soft and easy touching of mouths, Slade put all the frustration, the worry, that he'd felt in the last two hours into the punishing kiss.

Taylor moaned, and her fingers clutched his shirt when he finally sat her down in front of him. Their eyes met and just held as they both dragged in breaths. Slade tried to force words past his lips, but they were trapped in his throat. He couldn't talk to her right now or he would come off wrong, he thought, grabbing her wrist to drag her toward the Humvee.

Slade had too much on his mind right now to add in an argument with her. Later, once he had some answers as to who the men he held hostage now worked for, he would be calmer, more able to have a conversation without yelling at her. To get those answers though, he needed fucking Cade Winters to call him back. That man was the only one Slade knew who claimed to be fluent in Farsi, but again he was having to chase the bastard to get his help.

He opened the door and helped Taylor up inside, then slammed it and skirted the front to get inside. His phone vibrated in his pocket as he grabbed the door handle. Stopping, Slade pulled it out, hoping it was Winters calling him back. But it was Gray, probably calling to relay information from Winters, since that seemed to be the only way he would communicate with Slade. And it was starting to piss him off badly.

"Yeah?" Slade growled.

"Cade will be here shortly. He said he could get away as soon as Ahmed leaves for a meeting in an hour, since he's not invited to go along." Gray's loud laugh grated on Slade's nerves. "Ahmed hired two new Arab guards, so he's kind of cut Cade from the circle of trust."

"Good to know," he grumped, as he got behind the wheel and slammed the door.

With Gray being the chosen intermediary between himself and Winters, Slade felt sort of like Winters did with those guards around. He thought maybe Winters *wanted* him to feel that way.

"I have Taylor and she's fine," Slade said, cranking the engine. "Levi and Hawk should be there in a minute, and we'll talk when I get there."

"Okay, but Dex found some information too," Gray said, before Slade hung up. "I think those prisoners may be able to help us with it."

"The license plate info?" Slade asked quickly, his heart rising a notch in his chest.

"Just get back here and let Dex explain it," Gray replied, with a laugh. "I'm an accountant, not a computer whiz, and he speaks a tongue I don't understand, as much as those prisoners."

With a growl, Slade disconnected and pocketed the phone. He wished his nerves were as calm as the accountant's seemed to be, but his insides practically hummed with frenetic energy as he put the Hummer into drive. Slade knew that hum and fought it by clenching his abs. He couldn't fall apart yet. He had too many answers to get, and too little time to get them, because at nine o'clock Friday morning, the banks would open and that ransom would be paid.

Parking by the tree in front of the office, Slade was out of the vehicle and running for the porch before Taylor opened her door. Lola barked when he walked inside, but he didn't stop to pet her. She followed behind him to Dexter's office.

"What in the hell did you find?" Slade grated, as he walked inside and the computer nerd jumped before looking at him.

"Hello to you too," he said, looking back at his screen.

"Talk to me Dexter, or someone is going to get hurt. I've been waiting to hear this entirely too long."

"I got the names this morning, but I've been trying to run down the connection."

"You've had the names *all day*?!?" Slade shouted, and Dex jumped again.

He looked up and his eyebrows crashed together. "Don't fucking yell at me, man. The names don't mean shit without the connection, and if you haven't noticed I've been kind of busy!"

"I'm sorry," Slade said in a calmer tone.

Biting the hand that was giving him information right now was a bad idea. He'd wait to kick Dex's ass when this was over, just like he was waiting to do the same to Taylor, who stopped beside him right then. But the way he felt, he wanted to kick everyone's ass right now including his own for not walking out of this place when he found those phones on his desk.

Dex jerked a piece of paper from beside his computer and shoved it out to him. "These are the

names attached to the rental cars. The names are
common middle eastern so I was searching in Saudi,
but it's been like looking for a needle in a haystack.
You might find out quicker by asking those prisoners
in the conference room."

"If I spoke Farsi, I would," Slade said, taking
it from him to scan it. He heard Taylor make a funny
sound, and his eyes flew to her. "What's wrong?" he
asked.

"I ah, think I need to go lay down," she
replied, biting her lower lip drawing his eyes there.

"Fine, just go in my room," he offered,
because he damned sure wasn't letting her sleep on
Hawk's bunk again. Last night had been nearly
sleepless for him, until he snuck in there and saw
Hawkins on the top bunk.

Her eyes slid to Dexter then back to him, and
she put her hand on his arm. The need in her eyes
was so intense, the pleading so strong, Slade had to
drag his away.

"I don't know when, or if I'll be done
tonight." Slade wasn't going to rest, or anything else,
until he heard everything those prisoners had to say.
They were out of time.

Taylor's face fell, but she nodded then turned
and walked out. Dexter whistled, and Slade spun
around. "You work fast, buddy. Looks like you've
got one on the hook. You'll need a bigger stringer
soon." He winked, and Slade frowned.

"Mind your own damned business," he

growled as he strode out of the room, instead of punching the grin off of Dexter's face, but Cee Cee stopped him in the hallway.

"Gray asked me to tell you that Cade is here," she said, her voice tense. "I'm heading to the gym, and then out for a while if that's okay?"

"That's fine," Slade said, and strode past her.

He walked to the conference room, and pushed open the door. A tall, rocked up man in a tight t-shirt and camo pants, who had to be Winters, stopped talking to turn and scowl at him, and the three prisoners looked at him too.

"Rule *one*. Do *not* interrupt me while I'm talking to prisoners. Who the fuck are you?"

Slade took a couple of quick breaths to get a handle on his anger, before he stormed over there and introduced himself with his fist. Instead he clenched them at his sides and the paper in his hand crumpled.

"Your worst fucking nightmare, if you don't show a little respect *real fast*, asshole," Slade growled, and Lola stopped beside his leg to growl too. Winters' eyes slid to Lola, then back to him. "The money I paid you says I'm your boss, so I need a minute of your time—*now*."

"I can't leave them alone," Winters replied gruffly. "They are on opposite sides of the Khalil fence and I don't want them exchanging notes or blows."

"*Caleb!*" Slade shouted, and the sound

bounced off of the paneled walls. He'd seen him and Levi in the kitchen when he passed it a few minutes ago.

Hasty footsteps sounded in the hallway, then Caleb stood in the doorway holding a sandwich with a big bite gone in his hand.

"What do you need, bossman?" he asked around the bite that was in his cheek.

Slade's eyes held Winters' as he pulled his pistol from his waistband and racked a shell into the chamber then handed it to Caleb. He pointed at the table.

"Sit down at the table and finish your sandwich, but I want you to guard these prisoners. If any one of them opens their mouth, I want you to shoot them in the fucking kneecap." Caleb choked on his sandwich, but the corner of Winters' mouth ticked, as grudging respect entered his eyes. "They have two chances before they get it in the balls."

Winters turned and spoke rapidly to each man, and they nodded. The one in the corner with his swollen leg propped on a chair flinched as he grabbed his knee. It would serve these bastards right if they all three got shot before they returned. He'd like to do it himself for what they tried to do to Taylor, but he needed them alive, thus the non-lethal locations he selected.

Slade walked out of the conference room, and surprisingly Winters followed him to his office. They went inside, and Winters closed the door then leaned on it.

"Sit down," he said, glaring at Winters, because that seemed to be the only thing the man understood.

"I'd rather stand," he said coolly. "I have work to do tonight, so if you have something to say, just say it so I can get it done."

The cold and calculating demeanor of this man reminded Slade of some of the guys in Afghanistan who had one tour too many under their belts. The ones who *wanted* to take tours, signed up for them, because there was something at home they wanted to avoid. Usually a woman, or a mountain of bills. While they were in the sandbox they got combat pay and some of those bills were suspended, or paid by Uncle Sam.

Slade laid the wad of crumpled paper on the desk and smoothed it out then held it out to him. "I need you to find out who these men are and what their connection is to the prince and his brother." Winters took the paper from him and studied it. "I told you Zami was kidnapped. Well, one of those men is the kidnapper and the other is responsible for the car bombing that killed the guards."

"Who is Taylor Kincaid," Winters asked, his clear eyes seeming to bore into Slade's skull.

"Why?" Slade asked, his core muscles tightening.

"One of the prisoners mentioned her name, and I connected it with the car bombing."

"Well you can *unconnect* her," Slade grated, vowing to keep Taylor as far away from this man as he could. "She had nothing to do with it, and that is all a mistake. I need you to find out who did it, so I can clear her name."

"*Ooh*—hit a nerve, huh?" he said, and a travesty of a smile creased his face. It didn't reach his eyes though. "The feds disagree and want to find her for questioning. And a German man with a dog, a dog that looks a whole lot like yours. Did you train her in German?"

Slamming his hands on his desk, Slade stood and glared at him. "I'm not the one you're here to interrogate. Get the fuck out of my office and do your job."

Winters snapped off a salute, and Slade didn't miss the middle finger that lingered up as it reached his chest. He turned and jerked open the door, but eased it closed behind him, then Slade heard rusty laughter echo down the hall.

The bastard was messing with him.

CHAPTER TWENTY-TWO

Slade was so tired, he almost had to tie a rope to his ass and have someone drag him to his bedroom by the time Winters finished his interrogation of the prisoners at five am on Friday morning. He had exactly two hours to sleep, before he had to get up again. That's what they'd agreed upon before they broke up the meeting after Winters finished.

He found out after Winters took the first prisoner into the room Dex was supposed to use for storage and locked the door, why the man requested a private room. The sounds that came out of that empty, uninsulated room at times told him that Winters did not feel bound by the Geneva Convention rules or any rules on prisoner interrogation for that matter.

Slade didn't have a problem with that.

Caleb, Levi and Slade sat in the conference room with the prisoners and all of them heard those sounds but no one interfered. When Winters brought one of them back sobbing with new red welts and bruises, lumps and bumps, they didn't comment. From the gagging noises the guy with the broken nose and leg made in the room during his last round with Winters, Slade felt sure they'd need a bucket of bleach and mop tomorrow.

But he didn't care—they would deal with that tomorrow.

The man might be brutal, cruel and probably heartless, but his methods worked. Cade Winters had gotten them all of the answers they needed, and then some.

Because of that man and his brutality, they were meeting again in the conference room at zero seven hundred to hand out assignments. Those assignments would include delivering the prisoners to the Office of Homeland Security, providing the information to them that cleared Taylor in the car bombing, and rescuing Zami Khalil from the hotel where he was being held by the men his uncle paid to kidnap him.

The Haji with the broken leg told Winters the most. Evidently, he was one of Tariq's right-hand men. The man sang like a canary though about how Tariq had sent them to kill Taylor so she would be blamed for the bombing and the feds would stop investigating. How Tariq had hired two different teams, one to kidnap Zami who was being held at a local hotel somewhere, and another who planned to take out Ahmed as soon as the ransom was wired tomorrow.

The two men Caleb and Levi captured in Colorado could only tell him that they were professional hitmen hired by Ahmed Khalil, but had no idea why Ahmed wanted Jaxson dead. If that's what those men told Winters during his interrogation, Slade had every reason to believe it was the truth.

Dexter, Mackenzie and Cee Cee were still

working though. They would sleep tomorrow, after the assignments were given. It was up to them to find out tonight where Zami Khalil was being held, so he could be rescued in the morning, hopefully before the wire transfer. Mac thought he had a lead and left a few hours ago to check it out. It seemed to him that Winters was a machine, because he said he had to check some things out, then he was going back to the hotel to be in position tomorrow morning.

Slade stopped at his bedroom door and thought about sleeping on the sofa, so he could actually sleep. Lola took her pillow beside the kennel where Buddy was snoring. He hoped Taylor was snoring too, so he could quietly crawl into bed without her waking up. She'd want to talk, hear what happened or worse most likely. Worse might be worth losing sleep over, but the other stuff he definitely didn't want. His eyes were as stiff as his freaking leg when he looked over at the small sofa. His muscle strain felt better after the ice pack and half a bottle of ibuprofen, but he was due to take more of them, and the bottle was in the kitchen at the office.

If he slept on that sofa, he knew he wouldn't be getting any sleep either, so with a huffed breath, he twisted the knob and walked inside the darkened bedroom. Quietly, he untied his boots and slid them off, then reached for the button on his jeans.

"Is that you?" Taylor asked in that sleepy, sexy kitten tone of hers, and Slade bit back a groan for more than one reason.

271

"It's me," he replied, shoving his jeans off, and pulling his shirt over his head.

"What underwear do you have on now?" she asked.

Slade went rock hard under the Superman underwear that Cee Cee had probably just jerked out of his underwear drawer when she was gathering clothes to bring to him. He hoped that was the case anyway, because he'd hate to think she'd catalogued them like Taylor had.

"Sponge Bob," he replied, shoving them down to his ankles.

"Liar," she growled. "You don't have any Sponge Bob. I know I'd have seen those."

"Okay, you're right." He laughed taking two steps toward the bed. He had two hours, who the hell needed sleep? He was buzzing with adrenaline anyway from his excitement at possibly having this darned situation resolved tomorrow. "It's those ones with the elephant face on them."

She gasped and he smiled. Those had been a gag gift from Logan one year for Christmas. He knew about Slade's underwear fetish, because he'd pulled several pair out of the washer one day to wash his own.

"I like those even better than the lips," she said, surprising him.

"Really?" he asked, stopping beside the bed. It was his turn to gasp when she reached out and closed her hand around his cock and heat sizzled through his body.

"Yeah, I like the trunk, but I'm not sure this trunk would fit in it." Her throaty giggle danced through his insides. Smoothing her hand up his shaft to the head, she stopped there to rub her thumb over the top, and he trembled, before he took a step back and her hand dropped.

"You sure do know how to disappoint a girl," she said, her voice coming from where he'd been standing. He reached out and touched the top of her head which hung out over the side of the bed, and another tremor shook him. If he'd have just stood still a moment longer, she would have—*no* he needed sleep.

"I'm afraid I would disappoint you, because I'm exhausted and only have two hours before I have to get up, little bit."

"You could always just lay there and think of England." She giggled again, and sounded wide awake now. And horny. God he'd bet she was wet, and he could slip right between those amazing thighs of hers and—*no* he had to sleep.

"I'd do the work," she added, with a whoosh of breath as her head left his hand and he heard the covers rustle.

Slade laughed as he knelt on the bed, but groaned when his thigh muscle pulled. He felt for his pillow and rolled to lay down. Maybe if he gave her an update she'd be appeased. At least it would only take five minutes. She'd probably like that better than five minute sex in his opinion, which is about four minutes longer than he'd last tonight.

"I have some good news for you," he said, and her body tensed beside him.

"I could use some good news," she said, her voice losing its playful sparkle.

"It looks like you're off the hook for the car bomb as soon as we deliver the prisoners to Homeland Security tomorrow."

"Oh, thank God."

"Thank Him, but also thank the asshole who interrogated them within an inch of their lives. Tomorrow is going to be a very busy day for us." Slade was sure thankful to him, but he wasn't *about* to tell him that. Because he really was an asshole.

"Will it be over then?" she asked, and the bed dipped. Her hand landed on his abs and they contracted as her breath brushed his shoulder.

"I sure hope so."

"Does that mean you won't need me anymore?" She asked, and her voice trembled. "That you're going to fire me?"

"*Hell no!*" Slade shouted, pulling her across his chest, knowing that was a mistake when her rough puckered nipples raked his chest and his cock hardened more. She laid her head there and he stroked her hair. "I'm not going to fire you. We'll just have other cases to work on."

"I didn't do much work on this one. I just got in the way, and caused trouble mostly."

274

"You kicked ass today, and I'm proud of you. If we hadn't caught those guys in the woods, we wouldn't have the answers we need," he said, and it was the honest truth.

She giggled and it vibrated in his chest. "I did kick ass didn't I? If I'd have had a pistol, I'd have killed them."

"And you'd be in jail because you'd have had to talk to the police, and they'd realize you are the woman Homeland Security has been looking for. We wouldn't have the answers that will end this case tomorrow if that had happened. You did exactly the right thing out there, so stop second guessing yourself and replaying it."

"Thank you for helping to clear me," she murmured, then kissed his chest. "Slade?"

"Yeah?" he replied, hoping the slur he heard in her voice was sleepiness.

"I'm glad you're not firing me and that we're doing the EMDR therapy together on Tuesday. I think you're right and I do need it."

Slade's body tensed, as worry shot through him. "Is that what happened out there in the woods today? You had an event?"

"I thought it was a panic attack at first, but I've never had one before. I think it was something else. It happened after everything was over." His arms wrapped around her and he hugged her.

"Tell the therapist about it on Tuesday and ask her opinion. I'm glad we're doing it together too." Slade hadn't been on board with the idea at first, but he was now. Because he needed to make sure she got over this shit. He was not about to let her go through what he'd been through for five years.

"Sleep deprivation is a trigger, so relax and let's get some sleep." Taylor moved off of him to snuggle into his side. Slade pulled her into his side and it felt so damned good, so right he was asleep within thirty seconds.

What felt like thirty seconds later banging started at the outer door of his apartment, and Slade scrambled out of bed to drag on his jeans and stagger to the door. He opened it and Dexter stood there looking white.

"Foreign accounts, time difference, transferred early," Dex said, in between gasping breaths, and Slade's blood ran cold. He looked at the clock on the wall and saw it was six forty-five. The money wasn't supposed to transfer for another two hours and fifteen minutes.

"The money transferred already?" Slade asked, his voice rusty with sleep as he wondered if this was a bad dream.

Dexter nodded. "Cade said Ahmed's dead too. Hurry." He waved as he jogged back toward the front door of the barracks.

Slade spun around and ran for the bedroom ignoring that his thigh muscle protested. He flipped on the bedroom light, and Taylor sat straight up in the bed looking dazed. "Get up, and get dressed—

hurry," he said, slipping on his boots and snapping the closures. "We've got a Charlie Foxtrot." He grabbed his shirt off of the floor and pulled it over his head.

"A Charlie *what?*" Taylor asked rubbing her eyes.

"A *clusterfuck!* I can't wait for you." He jogged to the table by the door, grabbed his pistol and shoved it into his waistband then took off for the office.

When he got to the office, Gray was waiting for him in the lobby looking grim. "It went at one this morning. I'm sorry man, I should've thought about the time difference."

"Did Mac and Dexter find the hotel?" he asked, but didn't stop to wait for the answer. Gray followed behind him down the hallway. "Yes, Mac and Cee Cee are there now. They say they're still in the hotel, and haven't moved. But Ahmed is dead," Gray said, sounding sick. It was about damned time the accountant lost his cool, but it was too damned late. "Cade wants you to call him right away."

"Tell them to hold tight, we're on the way." Well wasn't that ironic, Slade thought as he walked into Dexter's office. Now, Winters expected him to call him right away when every time Slade needed him, he took his damned sweet time getting back to him? He could just cool his heels this time. Ahmed was dead, and that's all he needed to know.

"Did you hear me when I said Ahmed is *dead?*" Gray shrieked.

"I heard you," Slade replied calmly. "Where are Levi and Caleb? Hawk? We need them, and anyone else you can round up. If they're not in the barracks, get on the horn, Gray. The time is the same in Grand Cayman as here, so we still have time to save the kid."

At first Slade thought Tariq's plan might be to just kill Ahmed and take him back to Saudi with him. But this morning it hit him. There was no way he'd leave that boy alive. He was Ahmed's heir, he would inherit the sheikdom and title—and most importantly, the money. Tariq's plan was to kill him if they didn't get him out of there.

They were just waiting on the money to transfer to The Caymans.

CHAPTER TWENTY-THREE

Slade crouched at the corner of the first floor of the seedy motel building and waited. He glanced around to see if everyone was in position, and saw Caleb was still working his way up to the roof of the building on the other side of the parking lot with his rifle. He hoped he didn't fall through it. Mac had taken a position at the other end of the building. Taylor was in the Hummer, on standby to call the motel manager and the police if there was a firefight. She would also call the FBI as soon as Zami was rescued.

Levi was crouched beside what they believed was the kidnappers vehicle. He'd let the air out of the tires on the right side of the car, so there would be no getaway. Fletch was right above the target room on the second story.

Considering the hotel where Tariq and Ahmed had stayed was five star luxury, the contrast was stark between that and this flamingo pink pit where Tariq put up his nephew and the kidnappers. Because he planned to kill him, and didn't want to spend the extra money to make him comfortable. Or it could be the hostage-takers didn't want to spend the money. The other possibility is they could've chosen this place because it was such a dump. They thought nobody would ever consider looking here for a royal.

Well, they were wrong. Mackenzie had.

Because he had the best damned detective mind in the state, and Deep Six was very lucky to have him. He heard rusty wheels squeaking and raised his pistol, but lowered it when a laundry cart pushed past the corner out of a corridor and turned toward him. Cee Cee looked absolutely ridiculous in the ratty pink maid costume, and he grinned.

There'd almost been a fight between her and Taylor as to which of them would handle this for the team. Slade settled it, but not to Taylor's satisfaction. She was pretty pissed when he told her it was dangerous, and she'd just had an event. He didn't want to chance her having another.

What he didn't tell her was he was also concerned that if there was a gunfight, she could be caught in the crossfire. He knew she'd have had an *event* then. On him most likely.

Lola nudged his hip, he glanced down at her and she made a sharp whimper.

"Almost party time, my love," he whispered and felt her fur quiver.

Slade felt a similar quiver inside himself when he said the words he'd used when they did bomb detection together in the sandbox. But they weren't dealing with a bomb this time thank goodness. This should be pretty cut and dry, and quick hopefully.

Surprise the tangos, take them out, and get the kid out of there quickly. Cee Cee rapped her knuckles on the door, and Slade tensed.

"Housekeeping," she said in lazy drawl, her

tense posture anything but lazy. The fact that she had her pistol right there within reach made him feel better. But the tangos didn't open the door, she knocked again harder. "Housekeeping!"

Her hand drifted to the doorknob where a *Do Not Disturb* sign hung. She twisted, but it was evidently locked. Looking at him, she shrugged, then her eyes slid to the window and her face went pale.

"Oh *shiiiit*," she hissed, shoving the cart aside to run down the walkway toward him. Slade shot to his feet and pulled her around the corner.

"*What*?!?" he demanded, his heart pounding in his chest.

"Zami is in there, but…" She sucked in a few quick breaths. "Something's not right though. He moved the curtain and he looked scared. Awfully heavy for a seven-year-old too. He had on a black tactical vest and the pockets were stuffed."

"You think he's wired with an explosive?" Slade asked with sickness curling in his gut. These bastards were all about explosives evidently. Just like their countrymen had been in the sandbox. It was a cowardly approach, and they were good at it.

"Yeah, he may be. I don't know much about them, but his eyes and that vest…"

"Levi, make your way down here, buddy," Slade said into the mic near his mouth. He was their explosives expert. Slade and Lola could find them but dismantling and deactivating them or setting them was Levi's expertise.

"Did you see anyone else in the room with him?" Slade asked.

Cee Cee shook her head. "Would they let him look out the window?" she asked, and her point was good. No, they wouldn't have.

The fact that these men were connected to the ones who remotely detonated the device at the hotel, gave him pause. If they were using explosives, the kidnappers could very well be the car bombers too. Maybe Tariq had hired them for both tasks, since the prince hadn't been the target in the car bombing. He'd hired an assassin for that, and the mission had been accomplished.

He knew now why they chose this *disposable* motel.

Sweat beaded on Slade's forehead and his breathing became shallow as he scanned the complex for occupied vehicles. He relaxed when he didn't notice any, and glanced at his watch to see they had twenty five minutes until the transfer. *This* bomb was probably a timed device, not set for remote detonation, he thought. The only specific target they had this time was strapped with the device in that hotel room.

They were probably watching nearby for both the explosion and the transfer. Once it happened they'd get on a plane back to Saudi.

Not if Slade could help it.

He knew their names, and since the team wasn't going to be able to take them into custody here like he thought they would, he was going to make sure someone did. Surely their documents were the same ones they used to rent the car. If TSA and Homeland Security knew their names, they could catch them at the airport.

But first, they had to sort out this problem. Slade watched Levi duck-walk around vehicles until he crouched behind the tan sedan parked at the curb across from Slade's position. He looked around then darted across the walkway.

"Levi that kid is wired, a tactical vest probably with C-4, on a timer most likely."

"Did you see the timer?" he asked, putting his hands on his hips.

"No, but I'd just about bet it's set for zero nine hundred," he replied, and Levi glanced at his watch and groaned. "Yeah, and the door is locked." Slade held the mic closer to his mouth. "Fletch, I need you to get into that room fast."

"Roger that," he replied, and Slade heard his footsteps as he ran for the stairway.

"Cee Cee, I need you to get to the Hummer and have Taylor call Homeland Security and TSA. Give them those names, and tell them they're terrorists trying to leave the country."

Slade didn't give a shit at this point if the feds tracked the cell phone numbers here. They weren't quick enough to be there immediately, but he could use the backup when this was over. They could take Zami into custody and figure out what to do with him. Mac, Dexter and Gray, who insisted on going with them, should be on their doorstep in just a few minutes when the office opened with the prisoners and the information to clear Taylor, and at least arrest Tariq.

Slade's phone vibrated in his pocket and he ground his teeth. Cade Winters was persistent, he had to give that to him. But he didn't have the time at the moment to talk about Ahmed's assassination. All he needed to know was that the man was dead, and that prong of the situation resolved. Not the way he wanted it to be, but resolved.

Fletch appeared out of the same corridor that Cee Cee had near the center of the row of rooms and crept along the wall to the room. Since this motel was so decrepit, they still used key locks thank God. Putting his pistol under his arm, Fletch reached into his pocket and pulled out a small black case to unzip it. He pulled out a tool, then put the case between this teeth and grabbed the knob. Concentrating, he worked the tool in the lock for a minute then all of a sudden he dropped the tool to grab his pistol and back away from the room. Slade saw the door was open a crack and breathed again.

"Okay, we go on three," Slade said, and started counting, but the door creaked inward, and Zami appeared on the walkway in only his underwear and that damned vest. Several wires led to the stuffed pockets and Slade saw the red LED counter near the child's hip. "It is on a timer, and you have ten minutes, Levi."

Levi stepped around him to study the kid a second, before he searched his pockets and pulled them inside out. "Easy peasy, but I don't have my wire cutters with me. I didn't expect to be dismantling a bomb here," he said, and Slade's heart stopped, as he ran through what he had in the Humvee.

"I have nail clippers in my purse. Will that work?" Taylor asked, and Slade wanted to kiss her right then. Levi was already, weaving his way to the Humvee.

"That's perfect, little bit," he said, then his eyes shot back to Zami who looked terrified. He'd love to tell him everything was going to be okay, but he didn't speak Farsi and he had a feeling the kid didn't speak English.

Levi jogged toward the door, and grabbed Zami's arm. He screamed and pulled away to run down the sidewalk toward Slade. Levi ran after him, and Slade moved out to catch him. The door beside the room opened and a red-eyed man with a long unkempt gray beard stuck his head out the door to frown at them. From the tattoos and black spiked band on his wrist, Slade connected him to the badass chopper motorcycle parked in front of the room. A black haired woman, ducked under his arm to look too and her eyes narrowed. They moved back into the room and the door slammed.

Lola barked, and quivered, then laid flat. Not

only was there a bomb here, she'd found the scent he'd put her in the hotel parking lot, Zami's scent.

Slade swept Zami up and pulled him around the corner. Levi stopped beside them and immediately crouched to run his hands over the wires on the device, but Zami jerked away and dodged both of their attempts to grab him.

God, Slade wished he spoke Farsi. That would make things a helluva lot easier here.

He quickly pulled out his cellphone and hit redial. Cade Winters immediately answered and started blasting him, but Slade cut him off. "I need your help. Zami Khalil is strapped with a bomb and it's going off in..." Slade's eyes danced as they tried to find the timer as the kid dodged Levi. "Eight minutes, if we don't calm Zami down so Levi can disarm it. Talk to him."

Slade held the phone out to Zami trying to indicate he needed to take it. The child finally stopped, looked uncertain but walked to him to take it. Evidently whatever Winters was telling him calmed him down, because his shoulders slumped and he nodded. Levi had already knelt beside him and was fiddling with the wires.

Sirens whined in the distance, and Slade knew Taylor wouldn't need to call the police now. The biker evidently wasn't a Hell's Angel or on the run from the law, because he'd called them first, and they would be in the middle of this very shortly.

"Hurry up, Levi," Slade said, glancing to see

the timer was down to four minutes.

"Hurrying," he replied, flinching as he snipped a black wire. The timer still ticked, and the sirens got closer. The fact that Levi was flinching, sweating now, didn't give Slade comfort at all. Time was running out and he needed to get the rest of the team clear of the area.

"Fletch—Taylor—y'all clear out."

"Clear out?" Taylor repeated, her voice concerned.

"Yeah, three minutes now, and Levi's working on it, but I don't want you here if it goes off. Call Lola would you?"

"I'm not going anywhere," she replied, her voice trembling.

"Get your asses out of here—all of you!" Slade growled into the mic.

Taylor yelled for Lola and Slade turned to her to point at the Hummer. "Lola, *pass auf!*"

Yes, baby—take care of her if this doesn't work out right.

It was looking less and less likely that it would by the second as Levi cursed and jerked the clippers away from a wire he was about to snip. They were down to ninety seconds when he heard the Humvee crank, and Slade breathed when he saw Cee Cee behind the wheel taking them out of the parking lot.

Taylor watched in the rearview as Cee Cee drove out of the parking lot and Lola watched over the backseat through the back window. She finally breathed again when Slade's voice came over her headset just as dozens of police cars with screaming sirens whizzed into the parking lot of the motel from every direction.

"We're clear," he said, sounding relieved but frustrated too. "Y'all head back to base because we're going to be tied up a while."

Relief made her weak and she slumped in her seat as emotion shot to her head to throb at her temples. "Slade, I—" *love you.*

No—that wouldn't work with him. And it shouldn't work for her either.

They hadn't known each other long enough to justify it. Both of them had been hurt in the most unimaginable ways possible by people who claimed to love them. It wasn't logical at all, but for her it had been love at first kiss. And considering all they'd been through together in the last week though, logic flew out the window as did the rules.

They knew things about each other that nobody else in the world knew, or would care about even if they did. Slade freaking cared—too much sometimes. About her, about his team, about everyone on this planet. He even cared about her undisciplined, troublesome dog, as much as he cared for Lola. That right there said he was a good man.

Slade had a hero's heart, just like her father.

She loved him, but she wasn't going to push it on him. It would be devastating if she found out he didn't, or couldn't ever, feel the same way about her, but if that was the case she'd deal with it. Taylor couldn't stop the tears that clouded her vision as she sent up thanks that he hadn't been blown up, so she had a chance to find out.

"You okay?" Cee Cee asked as she stopped at the intersection where they'd probably be sitting for a while, because it was blocked by a police cruiser as a uniformed officer waved more vehicles with flashing lights through.

"As soon as Slade gets back to the compound, I will be."

"What's going on with you two?" Cee Cee asked, and Taylor glanced at her.

"I don't know, but I want the chance to find out." Taylor huffed a breath, as she picked up the company cell phone that Dexter had given her before they left the compound. She pressed the first number she needed to call—Homeland Security, and held the phone to her ear.

"Next to my daddy, he's just about the best damned man I've ever met in my life. But he's also the most—uh, yes ma'am. I need to speak to the person with the most authority there, please. It's an emergency—I need to report terrorist activity."

By the time they reached the outskirts of Dallas, Taylor had finished with the call and was exhausted from the mountain of questions she had to answer for the agent they connected her with. The same agent that Mac had turned over the prisoners to an hour prior.

Taylor laid her head against the seat and closed her eyes. A wet tongue stroked across her cheek, and she reached back to scratch Lola's muzzle, which earned her another lick.

"He's okay, LoLo," she assured. Lola's hot breath tickled her ear as she sniffed there. "Because of your daddy, we're all okay." Taylor giggled as she leaned away from another swipe from her tongue and pushed her into the backseat. A minute later the drone of the tires dragged her into her subconscious.

"What in the hell is Cade doing here again?" Cee Cee grumbled, waking Taylor up as she stopped the Humvee in the same spot Slade normally parked it. "I pray to God that Slade didn't hire him."

"What's with you and him?" Taylor asked, being as nosy as Cee Cee had been with her about Slade. It was obvious from her violent reactions to him, which Taylor couldn't miss, that they had a history of some sort. "How do you know him?"

"He almost lived at my house when I was a teenager, because his father was an asshole. We dated until I decided to join the Army after college, and he decided that I wasn't joining. The showdown was not pretty, with him, or my brother."

"Typical men," Taylor said, as she opened her door. She slid out then opened the back door to let Lola out.

"If Cade Winters is a typical man, I don't need one," Cee Cee scoffed as she walked around the front of the Humvee. "None of the men I've dated since him have been like that, so I think he's more *atypical*. The last one was a Navy SEAL, and he was definitely a real man." Cee Cee waggled her eyebrows and Taylor giggled. "I just couldn't handle not seeing him any more than I did."

They turned toward the porch, and stopped, because Cade Winters blocked the steps, his heavily muscled arms folded over his equally beefy chest as he pinned Cee Cee with a cold stare. Taylor watched the staredown between them go on for a full minute as his jaw worked, but he didn't say anything. Finally, he unfolded his arms, walked down the steps and passed them without a word to go to his huge pickup truck.

Taylor caught Cee Cee following him with her eyes, and realized this woman wasn't as over *that* man as she pretended, her reactions to him said so.

They walked to the steps, but the front door opened and Dexter leaned out, and his eyes skimmed over them to look around the yard.

"I got it, Cade!" he shouted, before ducking back inside and Taylor groaned. She hoped like hell his excitement didn't mean there was more drama was going on at Deep Six. She honest-to-God didn't know how much more she could take.

Cade Winters shoved Cee Cee to the side on the steps and elbowed Taylor in his haste to get back inside the office. Whatever it was, that man's pants were on fire to find out what Dexter had broken.

Actually, even as tired as she was, Taylor's curiosity was piqued as well.

"I'd take a nap, but I don't want to pull out the sofa while *he's* here or strip down to my skivvies. That man will *never* see my skivvies again," Cee Cee said grumpily, as she walked inside behind Taylor and shut the door. She knew Cee Cee had to be as tired as she was, probably more. Taylor had planned to go take a nap herself in Slade's apartment, but now she would feel guilty.

"I'd say go to the barracks, but I saw the other Humvee there so the guys are back too. They might be sleeping, but I doubt it."

Dave Logan was going to have to figure out something on the sleeping arrangements at this compound. Especially since he now had women working here.

"*Yes!* You are fucking *brilliant*, man! You saved me so much damned time!" someone shouted in a gravelly, but booming baritone and Taylor and Cee Cee looked at each other.

"It's about damned time someone around here realized that," Dexter replied, his voice echoing down the hallway.

Now, Taylor definitely had to go find out what those two were up to. "Just lay down on the sofa in your clothes. I'm going to find out what the heck they're doing in there," she said, as she walked down the hallway.

She walked inside Dexter's office and saw a

folding table had been set up, and three disassembled cell phones lay on top. "What are you doing? Sounded like you were watching a football game or something."

"None of your business," Cade replied gruffly, stepping in front of the table.

"She's going to know anyway, because Slade will tell her," Dexter said, with a sigh, and Cade glared at him over his shoulder.

"I don't trust him as far as I can throw him. He has a big mouth, and not a scrap of sense when it comes to OPSEC," Cade grated.

"This is not a secure facility, man. We don't usually handle classified ops," Dexter said, and grunted a couple of times as he worked on whatever he was doing behind Cade. "We trust each other and the place is small so there are no secrets here."

"Sounds too damned loosey goosey to me," Cade grumbled.

"We get the job done, even though Logan is a hardass sometimes." Dexter laughed.

"I knew there was a reason we're friends." Cade replied, the two men continuing to talk like they didn't even realize she was in the room.

Well, what they also didn't realize was she was not leaving until she found out what he and Dexter were working on. It may not concern her at the moment, but it could later. Taylor did not like to be blindsided.

"That may change," Dex said and Cade

moved slightly right so she could see that Dexter held up something that looked like a small computer chip. "You haven't met his new wife yet."

Cade's eyes slid to her and he frowned, tried to look fierce, but she smiled. "I'm not going anywhere," she said, crossing her arms over her chest.

"Who is she? What's she like?" he asked his eyes boring into Taylor.

"A lot like that one, only meaner." He laughed, then grunted again. "Former FBI SAIC—and just about the smartest woman I've ever met," Dexter said, with respect in his tone.

"Not smart enough to stay out of a man's world, evidently. Just like those women who are trying to get into spec ops these days," Cade replied, with a snort.

A man's world? Anger forced up her throat to burn inside her skull as she unfolded her arms and walked up to him. She poked him in the sternum, and he scowled down at her, way down, but he didn't scare her.

"Listen here, Mister *Man*. It's no damned wonder Cee Cee has no use for you. We don't need to stay out of *your* world. *You* need to learn to live in this *new* and *improved* woman's world. *If* you've got enough gray matter to survive, *which* I highly doubt, because you're not evolved enough." A tool clattered on the table as Dexter choked out a laugh.

"See?" he said, in a strangled voice, as he stood. "I think I have it man. I just need to put them in the reader and run the algorithm."

"Don't forget the GPS locations, and if you can speed things up I'd appreciate it. My contact is on standby with his team," he said, his eyes boring into hers in a stare down similar to the one he had with Cee Cee in the yard.

"I'm still not leaving," she said, folding her arms across her chest again.

Dexter fiddled with some kind of contraption beside his laptop. The thing looked like it wasn't even functional, with wires hanging out and parts visible on top. She saw three little pieces shoved into the front of it, and he typed something into his computer then turned around.

"Should be an hour or so," Dex said, and Cade Winters nodded.

Taylor unfolded her arms, walked around the table and stood in front of the laptop. The first thing she saw was the header. *A. Khalil Terrorist Cell.*

She didn't need to see more. Spinning around to Dexter, she demanded. "You got his three cell phones didn't you? How'd you get them?"

"He didn't get them," Winters replied, gruffly, and his eyes glittered like hard blue crystals in the fluorescent lighting. "I got them after Ahmed was assassinated."

From his tone of voice and attitude, Taylor wouldn't doubt that Cade Winters had been the assassin. He had just that kind of air about him. Cold and lethal.

"You killed him? she asked, fear putting a little squeak in her voice. This man's eyes said he was a killer, and she had just challenged him like she was ten-foot tall and bulletproof.

"Who's missing gray matter now?" Winters asked cockily with a raised brow. "Your boyfriend obviously *doesn't* tell you everything. Let's just say the prince trusted the wrong guards." His nonchalant shrug told her he didn't much care that Khalil had been killed.

"He's *not* my boyfriend, I work here," Taylor corrected. This man didn't need to know her business. And Slade *wasn't* her boyfriend technically. Dexter's laugh contradicted her though.

"Funny you knew just who I was talking about, isn't it?" Cade said smugly.

Grrrr—this man had to be the most arrogant and frustrating bastard she'd ever come across. He must have noticed her frustration, because the corner of his hard mouth ticked up.

She lifted her chin and turned toward the door. "I have the answer I needed, so I'm leaving now."

Dexter's laughter bounced off the walls as she walked down the hallway. She saw that Cee Cee had indeed laid down and gone to sleep on the sofa, so even though it was the middle of the day, she was going to Slade's apartment and do the same.

Let the bastard think what he wanted.

CHAPTER TWENTY-FOUR

Slade was bone tired as he and Levi pulled up in front of the barracks and stopped at nearly zero three hundred, but his insides felt like he had grabbed hold of an electric wire and was still hanging on. His brain felt like alphabet soup as he opened the door and slid to the ground. It should, he had been grilled and flambéed by the head honcho in charge of terrorism at every alphabet agency in the United States government.

And then the locals got what was left of him, so they could file their reports.

But at the end of a very long day, he felt like this goat fuck might actually be finished. Zami was taken by Child Protective Services until they could figure out who to release him to. It would most likely be his mother, and the other widows of Ahmed Khalil, who would take him back to Saudi when they figured out how to get home.

Tariq had been arrested and questioned, but it was a futile effort. The man basically admitted guilt to his interrogators with a smile. But when he got tired of being grilled, he stood and walked out and not a one of them could stop him. He was going back to Saudi in the morning, leaving the men who got caught doing his dirty work to face the music alone.

Just as Slade suspected it would end.

The only thing hanging was the suspected

terrorist cell in Dallas, and whether Ahmed had activated them before he was killed. That's what Cade Winters had been calling him about. He needed Dexter's help to extract the information from the SIM cards in the phones he'd found on Ahmed's body after he took out the guards who assassinated Ahmed. Ahmed paid the ultimate price for not thoroughly checking references before he hired those men, because they were the assassins hired by Tariq.

With a huffed breath, Slade entered his apartment and shut the door wondering if Taylor was in bed waiting for him like she had last night. He knew he was getting entirely too comfortable having her there, but he couldn't help hoping she would be. Tomorrow he'd start figuring out how to gently remove her from his bed, and his life. Especially since they were going to work together. The need to protect her at every turn, to defend her, told him he was also getting entirely too attached to her. Because he'd broken his own hard and fast rule since he bid Jeannie goodbye. He'd let a woman sleep in his bed overnight. But tonight he needed her there.

The adrenaline that had puckered his ass while Levi dismantled that bomb, and the subsequent boost from being interrogated was still pumping through his veins. He was so high on it, he was hallucinating, because he actually thought he saw Taylor laying on his bed bathed in candlelight when he passed the bedroom door.

The buzz inside his body was so loud, Slade

knew when he crashed it would be a very bad one, unless he could burn some of it off somehow. If Taylor was up, that would be sex. If she was asleep, he'd take a shower and deal with it himself.

"You did good today, baby girl," he praised, as he bent down to hug Lola's neck. She barked and he patted her head as he stood. Buddy whined at him from inside his kennel beside her pillow.

"Did I do good too?" Taylor asked, and he spun to find her standing in the doorway of his bedroom naked. His cock went rock solid and his eyes slid down to her proud breasts, tipped by the most amazing nipples he'd ever seen.

"You did fantastic, little bit," he said walking toward her. She fell into his arms and lifted her face for a kiss. It was brief, but fire sizzled down his body to his cock, before he pulled back.

"I need you," he growled, and she smiled as her hand slid down his arm to take his and he shivered. Taylor led him into the bedroom, and he saw that he hadn't been hallucinating. She had two candles on either side of the bed burning. She led him to the bed and crawled into it.

"Lay down and let me give you a massage to relax you a little," she said, and Slade quickly shucked his clothes, laid his pistol on the nightstand and got into bed. Feeling her small hands work his muscles again would probably help tremendously. He laid face down on the pillow, and she straddled him then reached for the oil he saw on the nightstand. She was ready, had set this whole scene up and he couldn't say he didn't like the result. He heard her squeeze the oil in her hands, then sighed when her fingers dug into his flesh.

"I know you're exhausted, but don't you go to sleep on me this time. I want to get to option two," she said with a giggle, kneading his shoulders, building the tension inside of him instead of reliving it. "We have all day to sleep tomorrow, all day Sunday too."

Slade was going to make sure she was out of his bedroom, and had a bunk or something by Sunday. Monday they'd start over on different terms. Resisting her when his body craved her would be tough. But Slade knew a clean break was best for both of them. He had a bad feeling she was getting too attached to him too.

Taylor slid her body down his, massaging out the knots in his muscles until she reached his feet. She squirted more oil in her palm, and worked his ankles. When she hit that secret spot she'd found with her mouth the other night, Slade's cock went rock solid and he groaned loudly.

"I know your secrets," she whispered, her voice heavy with desire. He was just as heavy with desire, and he needed her right now. Twisting, he rolled over, and sat up to grab her hips. She squealed when he reversed their position, and pinned her to the bed.

Before she could react, he covered her mouth

with his, taking advantage of her surprised gasp by invading her mouth with his tongue. Taylor wiggled under him, mumbled protests in his mouth, then her throaty moan vibrated through his tongue as the squirming slowed to needy thrusts against his upper thigh and her tongue finally embraced his.

Her body wilted and her calf wrapped around him, as she shoved her fingers into the hair at his nape, pulling him closer, opening wider for his assault. For endless minutes, he kissed her, soaked up the sweetness of her mouth, absorbed her excited moans and mewls until breathing hard, his heart pounding in his ears, Slade pulled back to kiss her jaw, lick his way down her long neck to her collarbone where he circled his tongue in the indentation. A shiver racked her and she whimpered. He lifted his head to meet her eyes.

"I fucking love those sounds you make," he growled, his dick harder than it had ever been in his life. He wanted to bury himself in her right then, feel the tight fist of her passage close around his aching cock, but there was so much more of her body to explore first. This was not going to be a quickie, because he wanted her to store up good memories to replace the traumatic ones she had from her ex-boyfriend. But she seemed to like a little domination in the bedroom. He was going to give it to her, but in the way it should've been given in the first place. Before he was done with her, she would be begging him to fuck her.

Pushing up to his knees, Slade bowed his head to the task at hand and kissed and licked his way down to her breasts, savoring the heady salty-sweet flavor of her skin which worked every taste bud he had into a frenzy. At her breasts, he stopped to admire them and her nipples puckered tightly in invitation, her back arched and her eyes begged as she looked down at him.

Easing down on top of her, he rested on his elbows and waited. With a frustrated little mewl, her back arched higher pushing her breasts closer to his mouth. Slade lowered his head toward her right breast, her breathing stopped and he smiled as he just hovered there and breathed. His tongue tingled to taste her, his body craved it, but he waited, building her frustration along with his own.

After a minute, her body vibrated with her need, it was like electricity between them. With a series of small grumpy sounds that echoed inside his head, Taylor wriggled under him to spread her legs wider, press her heat, her oily wetness against his hip before she lifted her right shoulder off of the bed cupped her breast and brought her nipple to his lips, but he didn't take it.

"Suck me," she commanded in a raspy whisper.

"*Please* suck me, Slade" he corrected roughly, meeting her eyes as his tongue shot out to quickly flick her nipple.

A tremor rocked her followed by two quick

secondary jolts before a rumble vibrated in her chest. "We don't have all night—just *do* it!" she hissed.

"We have as long as it takes for you to ask nicely for what you want, little bit," he said, and she plopped back on the bed to glare up at him. He skimmed his hand up her side to pinch her nipple and she moaned. "Rephrase that and I'll give you want you want."

When she pursed her lips rebelliously, he rolled her nipple between his fingers. With each twist her breath hitched and her back inched up toward him again. Finally, she whimpered, threw her head back and begged, "Arrrgh—p*leeease*, suck me, Slade!"

Shoving his hands under her body, Slade lifted her to his mouth and sucked her greedily inside. Her taste engulfed him, as he flicked the rigid tip with his tongue. He nipped it with his teeth, worried it and Taylor screamed. The sound zipped through him like lightning to sizzle at the head of his cock. He sucked harder, rasped the flat of his tongue over her nipple and swallowed her desperate mewls.

Her calf rubbed frantically against his thigh, her hips gyrated faster and faster against him. Slade wedged his hand between them to find her core, and she was soaking wet. She was more than ready for him, and he had to get inside of her right then.

Releasing her nipple with a wet pop, Slade leaned over to grab the condom he saw on the nightstand and quickly sheathed himself. He knelt above her, shoved her legs apart and moved between them. He lifted her hips high until only her shoulders were left on the mattress then positioned himself at her pulsating opening.

Grinding his teeth, he dug his fingers into the back of her thighs as he fought back the driving need to thrust inside of her. Slade wanted to see her eyes, know that she was okay with what was going on. She was small, and the last thing he wanted to do was hurt her.

"Look at me, Taylor," he croaked, and her heavy-lidded eyes fluttered open. "Tell me if I hurt you, and I'll slow down, or stop, or we can try another position." Slade waited for her nod before thrusting his hips forward. He watched her eyes widen, heard her pained hiss as the head of his cock slipped past the tight band at her opening.

Her muscles went rigid, her hot walls closed around him and his balls tightened but he held still. Slade had no idea how this worked the other night. She was just too damned small, too tight for him to fit. He pulled back, but she clamped her calves around his waist, and he slid a little further inside her body.

"N*oooo* don't stop!" Taylor shrieked, squirming to try and take more of him inside her body, but Slade's fingers dug into her hips to stop her, and she let out a frustrated growl. "Give me *more* dammit!"

A shiver racked him at the desperation he heard in her words. It matched his own which clawed at his insides, but he didn't move. "Is that how you ask for what you want from me, little bit? Am I hurting you?" he demanded.

The words gurgled in her throat before becoming coherent. "No, I just need more, *pleeeeease.*" A tired sob slipped past her lips and Slade's fingers loosened on her hips as guilt washed through him.

He needed to remember it had been a long and harrowing day for both of them. He was tired, she was tired, and it was up to him to either finish this or call it off. One more push would tell him where this was going.

His fingers curled into her flesh and he pulled her toward him as he jabbed his hips forward planting two more inches of his cock inside her throbbing portal. Taylor rolled her face to the side, moaned as she fisted her hands in the sheet and her body twitched spasmodically around him.

"Mmm...so good, so damned good," she moaned heaving short uneven breaths. "Please— *please,* Slade, give me more."

The sound of his name on her lips, the sweet, sensual agony in her voice snapped the leash on his control. Holding her tightly, he pulled her toward him as he slammed his hips forward and Taylor screamed. Suddenly he found himself buried balls-deep inside a silk-lined vise that squeezed him so tightly, he wasn't sure he would ever be able to pull out again. That he'd ever want to. Endorphins and adrenaline marinated his brain, making him lightheaded as he fought for breath in short erratic gasps.

"You okay?" he asked, barely hearing his voice over the pounding in his ears. *Please say yes.*

"Yes, *please*—I just need you to move!" Her body tremored and her inner muscles thrummed around him, and he knew she was very close to an orgasm, and he was going to help her find it, because he knew one thrust and he'd probably come too.

He found the engorged bud between her legs with his thumb, applied pressure there and her body jerked violently. Making tight circles around the swollen nub, he quickly had her panting. He added quick juts of his hips, forcing his cock to strike a spot inside her body he knew would get her there fast.

The incredible friction heated his cock, her breathing became labored, a low-pitched moan rumbled in her chest before moving up to her throat where it became a growl. Suddenly her body tensed and she howled as her inner muscles clamped down around him and she shook uncontrollably. Like hot lava, her body drew come to the end of his dick as Slade lowered her, lengthened his strokes to go deeper, pounded into her faster. With every stroke her sheath became slicker, got hotter. His cock was surrounded by her slick walls, tingling and on fire as her body quivered around him as she continued to orgasm. Fireworks suddenly exploded behind his closed lids, and a rush of pleasure drowned him and he roared as his body seized and he poured into her wet warmth.

Taylor still shook as he pulled out of her to collapse beside her. He rolled her into his side and held her tightly until the tremors faded. Her breath came out in a whoosh when her body finally stilled and he kissed her hair. Giving her one final squeeze, he took a deep, heady lungful of her floral scent which was made more exotic now by the smell of their lovemaking, by his scent imprinted on her skin.

With a deep sigh, he pushed her away and forced himself to get out of the bed.

"Where are you going?" she asked weakly, sounding a little hurt and a lot insecure.

Slade hardened his heart and plastered over the rawness in his gut with determination as he walked toward the bathroom. "I have to get rid of this condom, then I'm going to sleep on the sofa," he replied as he walked inside.

He'd broken a lot of rules with this woman, and was paying for it now. The desire to stay in that bed and cuddle with her right now, to wake up with her in the morning suctioned to his chest wanting him again, was almost as burning as his need to fuck her had been tonight. He wasn't going to wait until Sunday, Slade had to start weaning himself off of her tonight, building a buffer between them. Because by Sunday, he might be too addicted to her keep his resolve. He had never felt this crazy need for a woman before, the craving to be with her twenty-four hours a day, even Jeannie, and it scared the hell out of him.

This had moved beyond a physical need now to an emotional one, and that could spell disaster to his peace of mind, hell to his sanity, if he didn't break it off now.

While he waited those ninety seconds he had left to live at that hotel, Taylor Kincaid had been what he thought about, what he regretted—what he fucking worried about.

Not his mother, not Lola and not Jeannie.

CHAPTER TWENTY-FIVE

Taylor would give John Cash Slade, she found out his full name from the forms he filled out at the therapist office during their first visit and got a good laugh at the irony, one final chance to get his shit together. If after today things didn't change, she would hit enter to send the email that would take her to the small Texas town near the Panhandle where she'd become assistant police chief.

The job she'd been offered could be the position that set her up to assume a similar position in a larger town later. It was exactly the break she needed to jumpstart her career, but she'd had it on draft in her email for a week.

Thank goodness Levi had recovered her car from wherever he'd taken it, or had it towed, after he pulled it from the ditch. Both the axle and transmission had been broken, but he fixed them and didn't charge her a dime. And she'd taken two days drive up to the Panhandle for her interview with the *female* chief who offered her the job the following day.

The only draw to remain at the job, which she'd had now for three weeks, had been treating her with cold politeness. Since the night after they rescued Zami Khalil from that motel and he'd come back to his apartment to fuck her senseless then gone to sleep on the sofa, he'd been polite but detached. It was almost like he'd cut her from his life because he'd gotten his fill of her that night, because the next morning he had been a man on a mission to get Dexter's empty storage room converted into a woman's barracks for her and Cee Cee to share.

I have to warn you, I don't do anything other than casual sex.

Taylor should have taken him at his word, because it looked to her like he hadn't lied about that. But he at least owed her an explanation as to why he operated that way. Something had to happen to cause him to adopt that stance.

Today was Slade's final EMDR session, and he said the therapist would release him. That totally surprised Taylor, because the therapist told *her* she needed at least two more sessions to address all of her issues which she wasn't even aware she had. Most of them were caused by men, her father, Matt and then Mark, so maybe she should adopt the casual sex rule too, or avoid them altogether.

If Cade Winters is a typical man, I don't need one. Insert John Cash Slade there, and Cee Cee's words fit her situation too.

Slade thanked her for introducing him to EMDR and said he had weaned off of his meds now, and felt like a million bucks without them. After her two sessions herself, Taylor felt like a tarnished penny. Her self-worth and self-confidence was in the toilet because of him. No, that was her own fault. For believing he might change his mind, because she was convinced he felt the connection between them too.

"You ready?" Slade asked, jerking her from her thoughts.

Taylor pushed up from the sofa in the living room of the office, and smoothed out the jean skirt that Cee Cee had loaned her. She still hadn't made the trip to her house to pick up her own clothes. It's a good thing, because then she'd have two places to pack up when she moved.

"You finish your phone call?" she asked as she followed Slade to the front door.

"Yeah, sorry that was Logan, and I had to take it. He and Susan will be back at the end of the week." The relief in his voice was obvious.

They walked to the Humvee, and he went to the driver's side and got in. Taylor moved more slowly getting into her seat, as she thought over how she would open up the conversation she was determined to have with him before they got to the therapist's office.

"You okay?" he asked as he cranked the engine. "You're awfully quiet today and that scares me." His laugh excited every nerve in her body, but also irritated them too.

"I have a lot on my mind," she replied fastening her belt.

"Where'd you go the two days you took off? Somewhere fun?" he asked conversationally as he backed up, but Taylor thought she heard tension in his tone.

"It was nice yeah, and productive." She'd

wait until they got on the road. They were already going to be late, because he'd taken that call.

Slade stopped to hit the release button for the gate, then glanced at her. "Probably a lot more productive than we've been around here. Once Logan gets back things will pick up. He's a genius at finding things to keep us busy, or creating them."

He pulled through the gate, and she watched in the sideview mirror as it closed behind them. She had exactly thirty-two minutes to finish this conversation.

"I was offered another job, so I'm sorry to say I might not be here to meet him," Taylor said adopting the same business-like tone he'd used with her.

In her peripheral vision, she saw his hands tighten on the wheel, his body tense which was a good sign wasn't it? "Did you take it?" he asked gruffly.

"I'm thinking about it, yeah. It's a good opportunity, and probably a better fit for me."

"What's the job? Doing what? Where?" he fired off the questions, and Taylor was glad to hear his tone wasn't quite as placid as it had been.

"Assistant chief at a small police department in the Panhandle," Taylor replied vaguely.

He didn't need to know where she was going if she decided to leave. She was going to break from him as cleanly as he had broken from her if that happened—she had to.

"Where in the Panhandle?" he pressed, shooting her a hot glance. His jaw worked, and his hands tightened on the wheel. "I haven't gotten a call for a reference."

"Because I asked her not to call since I still work for Deep Six. She hired me based on my qualifications. Mr. Baker was fired from the hotel, so she spoke to his replacement, my former second-in-command, who gave me a glowing recommendation."

"You fucking went job hunting without telling me?" he asked, his foot pressing harder on the gas evidently, because they sped up.

"Slade, this isn't any different than any other job search," she replied coolly. "I didn't do anything wrong." Taylor was secretly enjoying his agitation. At least he wasn't being cold to her right now. Angry yes, but not cold.

"It *is* different dammit!" he shouted, swerving a little then correcting.

"How do you figure?" she asked. His eyes pinned her to the seat, his jaw worked, but he didn't respond. "Tell me, Slade—why do you think I owe you more considering the way you've been treating me?"

"I treated you like any other employee," he growled.

"And I treated you like any other boss. That's what you wanted isn't it?" Taylor shot back, not able to keep the anger and frustration from her tone.

They drove for ten full minutes in complete

silence, but the air in the cab of the Humvee sizzled with tension. She kind of felt like she did that day at the motel while she waited on pins and needles for the bomb to explode and turn them all to confetti.

"You did it to hurt me, didn't you?" he grated, as he moved up the ramp to get on the interstate and she could see him grinding his teeth.

"Why would it hurt you?" she asked, her own teeth clenched. "You got your casual sex, had your fill of me and we're done. I accept that."

Taylor was surprised, and her heart raced as Slade whipped the Humvee down the next exit ramp. She had to grab the door handle to keep from flying across the cab when he roared through the intersection at the bottom and made a sharp right. He drove for a minute, then swerved into what looked to be a children's park and killed the engine.

The bomb had evidently exploded. He turned into the seat to face her, his clean-shaven cheeks ruddy, his eyes livid. "You. Did. This. To. *Hurt*. Me. *Admit* it, Taylor!" he ground out.

"No, but someone in the past evidently hurt you, so you expect it from every woman on earth now. Why don't you tell me about her?" she replied calmly.

He blew out a breath, turned to face the wheel again and propped his arms on the wheel to lean over it. His back heaved as he breathed, and Taylor waited. If he talked to her, they'd work it out. If he decided to clam up and crank the engine, she would send that email when they got back to the compound.

"My goddamn face was almost blown off in that explosion and I had a tube in my head to control the swelling in my brain. I was in the hospital in Germany for three months, and it was touch and go," Slade said, his voice tight. "They sent me back here when I was stable enough for the reconstructive surgery and my girlfriend visited me in the hospital on the day I got home."

"She walked out on you?" Taylor filled in, with sickness curling in her gut and her heart shattering for him at how devastated he must've been.

"Took one look at me and almost vomited, before she ran out," Slade confirmed with a harsh, humorless laugh.

The rawness in his voice sliced up Taylor's insides like a razor blade and she wanted to vomit too. To serve his country like a hero, then to come home injured and be treated like that by a woman he obviously loved had to be a worse blow than the explosion. She felt his pain deep inside of her and she understood now.

"I also found out later she'd been dating one of my friends while I was deployed."

A moan slipped from her mouth, and he looked at her. God, the pain in his eyes was too much and hers filled with hot tears. "I'm sorry for making you relive this and I'm sorry if what I did hurt you, Slade." Her lip trembled as she fought to contain the shit storm of emotion swirling through her. "I promise that wasn't my intention."

He studied her a moment, seemed to look straight into her soul. What she saw in his eyes caused a sharp pain to slice through her. This man might look whole, and he was getting a handle on the ramifications from the explosion, but he hadn't even addressed the secondary blow dealt him when he got home by his girlfriend.. Until he dealt with those feelings too, that devastation, he would never be able to have a relationship with *any* woman again.

"Have you told the therapist about this?" she asked quickly.

"We kind of had bigger fish to fry," he said gruffly, dragging his eyes away.

Taylor leaned over and put her hand on his forearm and he tensed. "I think this is a bigger fish than you think, Slade. Will you promise to tell her?" It took a second, but he nodded and Taylor moved back to her seat with a sprout of hope growing inside her heart.

"We need to go, or we'll be late," he said gruffly, as he cranked the Hummer.

***

"On a scale of one to seven, how strong do you feel now, Slade?" Dr. Soren's asked lowering her hand to her lap.

I am strong.

"Ten?" he replied, with a relieved laugh, and she smiled.

He felt lighter inside than he had in five years,

free of the stress and guilt related to the memories of that night in Afghanistan. It was a fucking miracle in his opinion. This woman had performed something five years of regular therapy and medication couldn't, in three one-hour sessions using two freaking fingers, and taps on the backs of his hands.

"Congratulations then, I think this is your last session," she said with a broad smile.

Slade put his hands on the sofa to stand, opened his mouth to thank her, but hesitated.

Will you promise to tell her?

"Unless there's something else we need to deal with?" Dr. Soren asked, studying him intently.

"There is…" He sat back on the sofa and rested his forearms on his knees. "When I was transferred back stateside after my injury, my ah, girlfriend, came to see me at the hospital." Tension ratcheted up inside his chest, constricting his breath as the memory of the horrified look on her face flashed into his mind. "She took one look at me and left. I found out later she'd been dating one of my friends."

"How did that make you feel?" she asked.

"How do you think it made me feel?" he repeated with a harsh laugh.

"Double traumatized?" she guessed.

"Yes, ma'am. I was pretty devastated, especially since I didn't know how I'd look, what kind of functions I'd have when the surgery and physical therapy were over." Slade's breathing increased as the tension inside him grew. "I had no idea what kind of life I'd have."

"And were you committed to this woman?" she asked.

"We dated three years, and she said she loved me. I was going to ask her to marry me when I got home from Afghanistan."

The doctor cleared her throat. "Focus on that memory and watch my fingers," she said lifting her fingers. Slade followed them with his eyes with Jeannie's horrified face in his mind and pain sliced through him, grief and fear, despair so deep he thought he'd throw up himself. He watched those fingers continue to move and suddenly her face morphed into Taylor's face and the tension eased, lightness filled him and he felt like he was floating.

Her fingers stopped, and Slade relaxed. "You are good enough," she said, and held her fingers up again. She moved them rapidly and he followed them for long minutes until they dropped to her lap and he relaxed again.

"On a scale of one to seven how good do you feel about yourself now?" she asked, and he blew out a breath.

"You're a magician," he accused with a laugh.

"No, but this therapy is amazing isn't it?" she replied smiling. "Let's do another round with hand taps, just in case."

Slade felt almost drunk with happiness by the time he bid Dr. Soren goodbye with a warm hug, because he was too choked up to say the words. He walked into the waiting room, and Taylor looked up at him. Something clicked in his brain, and she was so damned beautiful to him at that moment, his heart so full, his eyes burned.

"Your turn, little bit," he said, and her eyebrows raised as he walked over to pull her up from the chair and into his chest. She looked up at him with questions in her eyes. "Let me give you a kiss for luck, just in case." Slade swallowed her surprised gasp in his mouth, tingles, heat and something else washed through and he got that light floaty feeling again. It felt so damned good, she tasted so good, he didn't want to let it or her go, wouldn't have, but she pushed him away.

"Hold that thought, Smiley," Taylor said with a pat to his chest, and a giggle that tickled his insides. His eyes fixed on the sway of her ass as she walked to Dr. Soren's office and a shudder wracked him.

Time had a way of fixing things, but divine intervention fixed them faster. Taylor Kincaid coming into his life had to be proof it existed. If she hadn't shown up in his life he wouldn't have known about this therapy. Without this therapy, he would have continued to live his life in the dark hole where he'd resided since coming home from Afghanistan.

She'd shined light into that dark place and he felt better than he had in five years. Slade felt ready now to live again, really live, and to love again—real love, not just sex.

His heart was open now and he wanted Taylor to fill it, because he wasn't afraid anymore. Dr. Soren had done that with the wave of her fingers, but it would take time for them to explore the possibilities. To have that time, Slade would have to convince her to stay.

That he wouldn't be able to convince her to stay, because he'd pushed her so far away, was the only thing that scared him now.

Maybe there was some grand plan at work here. When Susan called at the end of last week to tell him they'd be gone another two weeks, Slade had been pissed. He wanted Dex to trace that call, so he could go drag Logan home.

Now, he wasn't sure if the week he had left would be enough time.

CHAPTER TWENTY-SIX

"Hey did you see the newspaper?" Dexter asked, walking into Slade's office to throw a folded newspaper on his desk.

"No, what's going on?" Slade picked up the paper and unfolded it, then scanned the front page. *Dallas Terror Event Averted* was the headline on the front page, and he scanned the article, his eyes snagging on Deep Six Security, then he backtracked to see Dexter's real name specifically mentioned. He looked up at him with a grin. "Congrats, man, you're a hero!"

"They arrested *seventeen* people! Ten more arrests are in the works," he said proudly and shrugged. "It's only a one sentence mention, and they misspelled my name but the company got a big plug. I hope it helps business, because I'm bored. Strange thing though, Winters name wasn't mentioned."

It wouldn't be. Mr. Covert Operator would not allow it.

Slade folded the paper, and handed it back to him. "Well, you won't be bored for long. Logan and Susan are coming back this afternoon, so put on your seatbelt. There are a ton of inquires in his email, and you know he'll take every case."

"We need every case, because I found new gadgets we need," Dexter said, his eyes excited.

"You're always finding new gadgets, *especially* when you're bored. Since I spent a hundred grand to get Winters to help us though, I doubt Logan will approve them. He may even cut my salary to make ends meet."

Slade was a little worried about that. He knew Logan was going to blow a gasket on him at the very least when he found out. Hopefully, he could get out of here before that happened. If Gray kept his mouth shut until he was gone, Logan would have two weeks to cool off, before he got back. He'd asked him to, but Slade knew after a *month* away, the first thing Logan would request when he walked in the door were the financial reports.

Maybe he should just leave his cell phone on the desk, like Logan had done, and get out of here now.

But he wanted Susan to meet Taylor, before they left.

His heart did a funny little leap in his chest, and he sighed. Yesterday, when Taylor finally accepted his apology and let him watch while she deleted that email she had been ready to send to take that job, Slade had almost had a breakdown. The two-week vacation to Padre Island he planned for them to get to know each other better had convinced her he was serious about wanting to see where things went with them. He knew where things were going and he couldn't wait to get there.

"Damn, you've got that look…" Dexter said, with a sigh.

Slade's eyes shot up to his, and ran his fingers over his face. It felt normal, he felt normal. Better than normal—he felt fucking wonderful.

"What look?" he asked.

"*That* look," Dexter replied, clarifying nothing. But before Slade could force him to expand, he walked out, mumbling something about buying bottled water, because he wasn't drinking from the tap here anymore.

Taylor appeared in his doorway wearing cutoff shorts and a top that left her midsection bare, but his eyes zoned in on her rigid nipples and his dick went rock solid.

"Eyes are up here, Smiley," she said wiggling her finger to draw his eyes up to hers as she walked in to stand beside his chair. She smiled and the sun came out inside of him spreading warmth throughout his body.

"You are so damned beautiful today, it hurts my eyes to look at you." The words popped out of his mouth, shocking him.

"Thank you, but I look the same today that I did yesterday," she said breathily, as she leaned down to press her mouth to his.

Yes, she did. And she'd look the same tomorrow. But the looks were a bonus with this woman. He wanted the whole damned package with her. Because of her, he was almost whole again, something he thought he'd never be again.

Slade spun his chair, pulled her down into his lap and kissed her harder. Taylor sighed and he took the opportunity to deepen the kiss. With a moan, she slid her hand to his neck then she shoved it into his hair. Slade grabbed her hip to hold her tighter against his throbbing erection. He'd just had her this morning, and he wanted her again.

Right now—here in his office—on his desk. A shiver rocked him and he blindly swiped his arm across his desk to clear it sending things clattering to the floor.

"Don't even think about it," Logan growled, and Slade froze.

Taylor whimpered, as she scrambled off his lap and Slade lunged up to his feet.

"Welcome back," he said, clearing his throat. Taylor just stood beside him, her face flaming and her body tense.

"I hear we have some new women at Deep Six," Susan said, shoving Dave to the side so she could grin at Slade. "I'd say it's about time we end this sausage fest."

Logan shot Slade a look that curdled his blood.

"Yeah, we saw Cee Cee when we came in," he grated, and his tone told Slade there would be hell to pay.

Susan walked to Taylor and stuck out her hand. "I'm Susan Whit—"she cut her eyes back at Dave and laughed. "Susan Logan."

"Taylor Kincaid," she replied taking her hand.

If Dave's eyes were laser beams, Slade would be sliced to shreds right now. It was time for them to get the hell out of here. Slade dropped his arm over Taylor's shoulders and guided her away from Susan. "Yeah, we were just waiting for y'all to come in. It's our turn for a two-week vacation, buddy."

Dave blocked the doorway. "I need to get a SITREP from you before you leave."

"Like the one you gave me when you left?" he shot back angrily.

Susan stepped between them and put her hand in the center of Dave's chest to shove him out of the doorway. "You walk into this office and you're whole attitude changes. Take a chill, we just had our fun. Let them go have theirs. I'm sure the sky didn't fall while we were gone, terrorists didn't attack Dallas, and we're not bankrupt."

"I'm sure you're right, but I want to know what the hell happened while I was gone," Dave protested.

Holy hell, Susan had come much too close to hitting the nail on the head for him. Slade wasn't sticking around for the fireworks when they found that out. Turning Taylor, he hustled her to the door, refusing to let her stop to talk to Cee Cee.

"My cell phone is in my desk drawer, if you need it."

With a quick wave, he slammed the door, and grabbed Taylor's hand. They ran for the Humvee as he called for Lola and Buddy who were playing in the yard.

EPILOGUE

"I guess this means I'm stuck with you forever," Lola yapped, casting a sideways stare at Buddy before she threw her muzzle up haughtily.

She was definitely a diva who thought she was smarter than the average dog. And Buddy had to admit she was right. She had been to war and on exciting adventures with her master and sniffed bombs to keep the soldiers she protected safe. Lola was a hero like her master, she even had a medal and Buddy loved her. He just wished she was nicer to him sometimes.

But she is only trying to keep you out of the kennel, Buddy reminded himself.

"You mean I'm stuck with *you* for life now," he woofed back, even though that sounded like the best thing that had ever happened to him. Well, besides that mean man leaving him with his mommy. "You're boring and only want to work…and you talk funny."

If she could be mean, he could too. But it hurt his heart to be mean, because he loved Lola so much. She was beautiful, and brave and smart like his mommy. He wished she loved him like his mommy loved her master.

"That's because I was born in Germany, you stupid mutt."

"I'm not a *mutt*—I'm a laba-ba-ra-*dor*," he growled fiercely.

Maybe he was stupid though. Goofy at the very least, he thought, and his chin dropped. He wished Lola loved him like her master loved his mommy. But nobody loved him, because all he did was cause trouble.

He really tried to be good, but those squirrels teased him, so he had to chase them. One day he was going to catch one of them too, and he'd show them what for. And when he got bored, he chewed stuff up because he couldn't help himself.

Chewing up his mommy's new shoes had been a big mistake though. He'd spent the day in his kennel for that, so he wouldn't be doing that again. It didn't taste that good anyway, and made his stomach hurt.

Since Lola's master came into their lives though, Buddy rarely got bored. He liked to teach him stuff, and play ball with him. That made Lola jealous sometimes.

Maybe that's why she didn't love him.

Lola nudged him with her muzzle.

"What's wrong mutt?" she asked, and his fur bristled, because Buddy *hated* when she called him that. "I'm the one who should be dog-faced, since my master doesn't need me anymore." Lola sighed as she looked at the man standing in the fancy black suit next to his mommy. "He hasn't in a long time now."

"He needs you because he *loves* you," Buddy woofed, swallowing hard because he did too.

"I know he still loves me, but he doesn't *need*

me." Lola sucked in a deep breath, and dropped her muzzle before lifting it quickly. "But this is a happy day! Our humans are getting married." Lola looked back at her master and his mommy as they licked each other. "Look how happy they are…"

They were, and looked nice in their new clothes too. That white dress his mommy had on was so white it hurt his eyes to look at it though, so he looked at Lola instead. She wore white too Their humans had gotten her a white vest to carry something down the aisle to them. He'd just got to watch. Because he wasn't as smart as Lola.

"That new white vest looks pretty on you," Buddy yapped, then snapped his jaw shut, not believing he'd actually said it. He was only supposed to think things like that, or she might figure out he loved her and make fun of him.

"S*hhh*!" Lola growled, and Buddy sat down beside her again.

He was going to be good today, because Lola was right. This was a special day for their humans, and he was not going to get in trouble in front of all these people on the beach.

They were on the beach! The sand felt funny to his pads, but the air was amazing. He took a deep breath, and froze. His mouth watered and his insides quivered because he smelled a hot dog somewhere. A craving to have that hotdog in his mouth punched him in the gut, and Buddy frantically searched the beach to find it.

A young boy had it and he was getting away. Buddy's hotdog was getting away. With a loud *woof,* he crouched then shot off down the beach after his hot dog.

"No, Buddy, *sitz!*" Lola's master yelled loudly and Buddy dropped his butt to the ground. Sometimes it was no fun being trained, he thought sourly, as his head dipped.

Lola walked up to him and licked the side of his face and Buddy's fur quivered.

"You should've kept going and you could've shared it with me," she whispered by his ear then glanced back at her master. "Don't get too well-trained, mutt, because I love a bad boy, almost as much as I love hotdogs."

Thank you so much for purchasing and reading **TWISTED HONOR.** If you enjoyed it, I would very much appreciate you leaving a **review** for me and checking out my other books.

DEEP SIX SECURITY SERIES:
Till Death (#1, Deep Six Security), Dave Logan and Susan Whitmore's story

Dave Logan, the owner of Deep Six Security, is stunned when Dallas FBI head, Susan Whitmore, darkens his doorstep accusing him of being the cause of her losing her job, and demanding he hire her. Even as his brain says no way, the Barracuda is a woman nobody can work with, his white-knight complex forces him to offer her a job as his very overqualified temporary secretary.

A wealthy couple who ordered a designer baby, which hasn't been delivered contacts Dave for help. To get answers for them, Dave has to get inside an overly-fortified fertility clinic going undercover with Susan as his temporary wife. The situation inside is worse than they imagined, and soon their pretend 'til death do us part' could become very real unless the two alpha personalities learn to work together to stay alive.

SEALed Fate (A Deep Six Security/Hot SEALs Kindle World Crossover Novella), **Jaxson Thomas and Fallon Sharpe's Story**

Former Navy SEAL Jaxson Thomas left the teams in disgrace to save his squad from being dragged through the mud with a JAG investigation. He never thought he'd have to leave the civilian job he got after the teams in the same way, but that's exactly what happened. To keep his friends at Deep Six Security from losing their biggest contract, he takes the blame for an assignment gone bad. The SEAL mentality drilled into him for years won't let Jaxson give up though, so he goes to work for Guardian Angel Protective Services, a new security firm started by his former SEAL teammates, hoping yesterday would be his last bad day.

His first GAPS assignment tells him more bad days are coming however, when he is charged with protecting the woman directly responsible for his exit from the teams. Frumpy Fallon Sharpe is now a federal judge, and the big-mouthed redhead has taken on an East Coast mafia family who wants her dead. She will only accept a SEAL to protect her and his new boss insists that he's the man for the job, but Jaxson isn't so sure since he'd been dreaming of killing her himself for five years.

He takes the job, because he has no choice, but the last thing Jax expects to feel for Fallon Sharpe when he sees her again is attraction. Even though her waspish mouth is the same, the thick glasses and frizzy red hair are gone and those damned spindly legs that reminded him of a flamingo before have toned up and end somewhere near her ears now.

Dealing with his old hatred and this new attraction while trying to protect her was going to make the assignment the perfect storm that could lead to a Charlie Foxtrot of epic proportions if Jax wasn't careful. Maybe the last one of his life.

Coming in October/November 2015!
HELL BENT (#3, Deep Six Security)
Cade Winters and Cee Cee Logan's story.

Cade Winters has been running from his

overbearing father for fifteen years. Even he admits his method of escape was extreme though. Joining the military, eventually being recruited into the elite Delta Force and then taking a job with a black ops firm kept him busy at the far ends of the earth, which was almost far enough away from his family and the woman he left who seemed hell bent on getting herself killed.

Suddenly, it seems like all the women in his life have a death wish though, when his sister Ronnie, a Texas judge, decides to support a non-profit group that promotes re-training trafficked women before they are deported. Taking on that hot button issue has gotten her in hot water with a homegrown terrorist group who is threatening her life.

Cade goes back to Dallas to help her, but knows he has to support himself somehow, so he takes a job with his friend Logan's security company, Deep Six Security, which seems to be the only action in town. He never expects to see Logan's sister at the front desk. Evidently Cee Cee Logan hadn't gotten herself killed in the Army, and her hardheaded determination had paid off. Too bad she hadn't focused that determination on loving him, or they might be in a totally different place.

Could he work with the woman he'd loved for four years, and hated for twice as many? Especially when she seemed to blame him for their split? It looked like Cade would have to when he finds out she may be the only one who can help him save his sister.

If you love hot cowboys, I have plenty of those too:
TEXAS TROUBLE SERIES by Becky McGraw:

Manufactured by Amazon.ca
Bolton, ON

11469745R00199